FORBIDDEN MAGIC

"A yummy hot fudge sundae of a book!"
—MaryJanice Davidson, *New York Times*
bestselling author on *Forbidden Magic*

"*Charmed* meets Kim Harrison's witch series, but with a heavy
dose of erotica on top!"
—Lynsay Sands, *New York Times*
bestselling author

"Wildly erotic and dangerously sensual, this explosive paranormal thriller sizzles. McCray erupts on the scene with one of
the sexiest stories of the year. Her darkly dramatic world is
one readers won't mind visiting again . . . McCray knows how
to make a reader sweat—either from spine-tingling suspense
or soul-singeing sex . . . McCray cleverly combines present-
day reality with mythological fantasy to create a world where
beings of lore exist—and visit the earthly realm."
—*Romantic Times BOOKreviews*

"McCray's paranormal masterpiece is not for the fainthearted.
The battle between good and evil is brought to the reader in
vivid and riveting detail to the point where the reader is drawn
into the pages of this bewitching and seductive fantasy that
delivers plenty of action-packed sequences and arousing love
scenes."
—*Rendezvous*

MORE . . .

"Cheyenne McCray has written a sexy adventure spiced with adventurous sex."

—Charlaine Harris, *New York Times* bestselling author

"McCray does a remarkable job of blending the familiar and the fantastical, creating a rich paranormal world with sexy and engaging characters."

—Kelley Armstrong, *New York Times* bestselling author

"Erotic with a great big capital E. Cheyenne McCray is my new favorite author!"

—Bertrice Small, *New York Times* bestselling author

"*Forbidden Magic* is a fabulous faery tale. The writing is sharp; the story hot!"

—Virginia Henley, *New York Times* bestselling author

"Cheyenne McCray had crafted a novel that takes the imagination on an exciting flight. Full of fantasy, with a touch of darkness, a great read for anyone who loves to get lost in a book that stretches the boundaries!"

—Heather Graham, *New York Times* bestselling author

"McCray's magical tale will thrill and entrance you!"

—Sabrina Jeffries, *New York Times* bestselling author

"Explosive, erotic, and un-put-downable. Cheyenne McCray more than delivers!"

—L.A. Banks, bestselling author of
the Vampire Huntress Legends series

Chosen
PREY

CHEYENNE
McCRAY

St. Martin's Paperbacks

This is a work of fiction. All of the characters, organizations, and events portrayed in this novel are either products of the author's imagination or are used fictitiously.

CHOSEN PREY

Copyright © 2007 by Cheyenne McCray.
Excerpt from *Wicked Magic* copyright © 2007 by Cheyenne McCray.

Cover photo of couple © Shirley Green

ISBN: 0-312-93762-8
EAN: 978-0-312-93762-1

Printed in the United States of America

St. Martin's Paperbacks edition / March 2007

St. Martin's Paperbacks are published by St. Martin's Press, 175 Fifth Avenue, New York, NY 10010.

10 9 8 7 6 5 4 3 2 1

*To my critique partners
who helped make this book happen——Annie Windsor,
Mackenzie McKade, Patrice Michelle, and Tara Donn.
This one's for you!*

ACKNOWLEDGMENTS

Once again, I can't thank my editor enough. Monique Patterson is the goddess of editing.

Thank you to each and every one of St. Martin's Press's staff for everything you do—none of this would be possible without you. Olga Grlic, you are fabulous. Thank you for the most incredible cover! A special thanks to Monique's assistant, Emily Drum, who's right on top of everything.

Thanks to Patti Duplantis and Maryam Salim, who read *Chosen Prey* to give it a fresh pair of eyes.

A very important thank-you to my readers. You are all special to me and I hope you enjoy *Chosen Prey*.

Chosen Prey starts out in my hometown of Bisbee, Arizona, before it moves through other towns in Cochise County and then on to Sandy, Oregon. My thanks to Mom and Dad, who still live on a ranch outside of Bisbee, for helping me remember some of the details. Much of my descriptions of the town and the surrounding areas is accurate; however, I've taken some artistic license in several cases.

Once called Little San Francisco, Historic Bisbee is a fascinating place rich with history from its heyday as a prosperous copper-mining town. It's now a thriving artists' community and the town partially survives on tourism. Bisbee is just twenty or so miles from Tombstone, so if you visit that Wild West town be sure to take a little tour of Bisbee while you're in the area.

Many thanks to Marna D. Gatlin for assisting me in finding the perfect location for the Temple of Light, outside the beautiful town of Sandy, Oregon, near the foot of Mount Hood.

Any mistakes and inaccuracies are mine and mine alone. I used artistic license with this locale, too. It's part of the fun of being an author!

CHAPTER *ONE*

They'd found her. After all these years they'd found her.

Lyra gripped the plastic grocery bag tight in one fist and swallowed hard as she stood in her doorway and slowly turned to face the tall man on her porch. She hadn't even heard him following her until she'd opened her front door.

He'd called her by her real name. Only The People knew her real name.

"Lyra Collins?" the man repeated in a bass rumble that made her skin tingle. His eyes were shadowed by a Stetson pulled low over his forehead.

Her heart pounded as she took a step backward into her home. Adrenaline surged through her body and she fought a wild urge to run.

And run fast.

The man was frighteningly large, with broad shoulders and a tapered waist leading to lean hips. A black western shirt was tucked into black Wranglers molded to powerful thighs.

She ground her teeth at the thought of the bad guy from the Wild West, dressed all in black, coming to gun her down. Any other day, in any other situation, the whole scene might have been funny. Lyra saw no humor in it now. This handsome bastard was probably a Wild West bad guy, modern-religious style, and he might just have a six-gun hidden somewhere she couldn't see.

The People were relentless.

She moved her free hand to the door frame. She clenched it so tight her nails dug into the splintered wood. Over the stranger's shoulder, she saw neighborhood children playing in the July sunshine-bright street, their laughter and chatter a stark contrast to the fear coursing through her body. Behind the children was the side of the hill where a steep set of concrete steps led down to Main Street. If she had a chance she could make a run for it. Head someplace she could disappear again.

The man frowned. "Are you all right, ma'am?"

Lyra raised her chin. She did her best to gather her composure, battling her fear and more tingles from the rich, deep sound of his voice. She cleared her throat, dismissing his almost hypnotic effect on her. "Who are you?"

"Dare Lancaster." He touched the brim of his hat in a gentlemanly gesture that surprised her—but didn't fool her. "One of your relatives has been trying to get ahold of you, and I thought I'd let you know. A man named Ryan came to my office and said a Neal Barker is trying to find you."

Neal? Oh, my God. So I'm not being foolish or paranoid. I should have known this couldn't last forever!

Blood drained from Lyra's face. She could feel it

seeping down her throat and trickling from her body to the stained carpet beneath her feet.

Neal. The Prophet of the Temple of Light.

Her hand crept from the door frame to the canister she kept bracketed there.

"I—I haven't the slightest idea what you're talking about." She started to push the door shut, but the man stuck his booted foot between the door and the jamb.

Terror ripped through Lyra like an ice-cold wind. She dropped the grocery bag and vaguely heard glass shatter and the thump of the bag of dry cat food hitting the carpet. In a movement so fast she surprised herself, Lyra yanked the can of pepper spray out of the holster beside the door and aimed it at the man.

She pressed down on the release as hard as she could and a fine mist sprayed him full in the face.

"Ah, hell." Instead of dropping and writhing on the porch like she'd expected him to, the man merely pinched the bridge of his nose and moved his boot out of the doorway. "A simple *no* would've been better."

Lyra slammed the door, locked and bolted it, and slid the chain lock into place. Her body trembled so badly she could hardly stand. Her own eyes stung from a bit of the pepper spray that had floated back to her on the light breeze.

Blinking away hot tears, she peeked out the peephole and watched the intimidating man shake his head, pause, then stride to a large black truck parked across the street.

Odd. The People didn't often travel alone, and they didn't give up so easily. They *never* gave up, in fact. And the men always wore their hair in a long fishtail braid and had goatees. This cowboy must be a hired gun, so to speak.

She stared as the man gave his head one more shake and rubbed his eyes. He grabbed the door frame to climb into his truck. She could see the perfect lines of his powerful form and the graceful, decisive way he moved. No distractions for that cowboy. He seemed too sure of himself to belong to the Temple of Light. Too . . . in control.

She blew out a ragged breath, coughing against the pepper spray. Just before hauling himself up and into his truck, the man turned and studied her home for a moment and her heart nearly stopped beating. The way his eyes narrowed and focused made her feel like the door wasn't there at all. That he was looking straight into her soul.

Her heart began pounding and her stomach churned, acid rising up in her throat.

But the man just climbed into his truck and slammed its door shut.

Lyra turned and sagged against the door and dropped the can of spray. She slid down the wood to land on her ass next to the ruined groceries.

The truth struck her full force again, erasing the remnants of gooseflesh with clammy waves of dread.

They'd found her.

D are's eyes burned like shit as he sat in his truck. If it weren't for his police academy training years ago, he wouldn't have been able to walk straight after a direct hit.

"Well, hell." That hadn't gone exactly as planned. Obviously the woman was scared to death of this Neal Barker. Looked like he'd just have to contact Ryan Holstead and let him know that Neal Barker's "cousin" didn't want to be contacted—if in fact she was the man's relative.

In most situations Dare didn't contact—hell, in all previous cases he hadn't contacted—the client's relative or friend, just left that up to the client. But this time something in Dare's gut had told him to check out Lyra Collins for himself. Something in the sound of the client's voice had nagged at him.

Apparently his gut had been right.

Just who was Barker, and why did his name scare the woman enough for her to shoot Dare with pepper spray?

The laughter of the children playing in the street would have made him smile if his eyes weren't hurting so damn bad. The two girls and two boys scampered away and into the house next door, then the street was quiet.

Dare turned his attention back to the little house that wasn't much more than a hole in the wall along a street that wound around the mountainside. He figured Lyra Collins was watching him and no doubt she'd be calling the cops if he didn't get his ass out of there.

And he was in no mood to talk to cops. The memory of the reason he'd left the force in Tucson was always like a punch to the gut. He rubbed his right shoulder, remembering the incident from seven years ago when he'd let his partner down.

When his partner had died.

Dare had been a private investigator since and only dealt with the police when he had to.

He brought his attention back to Lyra Collins and blinked again from the burn in his eyes. His PI partner, Nick, would have a heyday—Dare would never live down taking a full-in-the-face from a scared mark.

He ground his teeth and grabbed a couple of the tissues from his glove compartment that his housekeeper always insisted he keep on hand. He rubbed the spray the best he could from the corners of his now-watery eyes. If it didn't normally make the sting worse, he'd stop at Manny's Restaurant and wash the crap out of his eyes.

After tossing the tissues aside, he turned the ignition, put the truck in gear, and glanced into his rearview mirror.

Dare frowned. A light brown van rolled up and parked on the canyon side of the street, two car lengths behind him. He recognized the van. It had been behind him as he'd driven up the canyon but had passed him once he'd stopped in front of the woman's house.

There weren't but so many roads up this particular canyon, and the type of vehicle wasn't unusual to the area, so he hadn't thought much else about it.

But now the hair at the nape of his neck told him something was off. He turned off the ignition and watched the van in his rearview mirror. A pair of men in the front seat of the van stared at his truck. Every now and then one of the men would turn and look into the back of the van as if checking something out or speaking to someone.

Dare glanced at his watch. Back at the van. Back to

his watch. For a good fifteen minutes, nothing happened and Dare tried to shake off the feeling of wrongness at the same time he puzzled over the woman's reaction. Maybe she was a cheating wife. No—the fear in her eyes had been very real. Could she be an abused wife? Could the man who contacted Dare have been a stalker? *Shit.* What if she was in the Witness Security Program?

Nothing happened in the van behind him. Maybe he was overreacting. He brought his hand up to the keys still dangling from the ignition and started the truck. After he pulled out, he guided the vehicle down the winding hill.

When he reached Main Street, his skin prickled again. *Goddamn.* He had to go back and check out that van. Something wasn't right.

After a quick turn, he drove his truck up the street just in time to see men spill out of the van. His experienced gaze raked in their appearances. *What the hell?* All sported goatees and had long braids that hung straight down their backs. All were in jeans and light brown shirts.

Immediately his cop brain sized up their build, their manner and intent, and the organized, military way they deployed.

His muscles tensed and all his instincts went on full alert. The woman was in trouble—trouble he'd brought to her door.

The men crept toward Lyra Collins's home.

Five of the men broke away and eased down the street, skirting the side yards of the houses, until they reached the alley at the end. They slipped into the back alley.

The other two opened the front gate and started down the short path to Lyra Collins's house.

L yra's hands shook as she started to clean up the spilled broken glass from the bottle of salad dressing. Mrs. Yosko's dry cat food had scattered across the floor like a mammoth jigsaw puzzle. The bananas and lettuce would surely go bad in no time, as hard as Lyra had dropped them.

What am I thinking? I have to get out of here!

She wouldn't let them take her back to the commune in Oregon. She wouldn't!

Tears came hot and unwelcome as she rushed to clean up the glass, but she couldn't stop them. She'd felt safe for so long now, happy in the small world she'd built for herself in this sleepy artists' community. Now she would have to go on the run again, establish a new identity and a new life.

What about the few friends she'd made? And what about Mrs. Y?

With quick, angry jerks of her arm, Lyra brushed tears from her eyes with the back of her hand. No self-pity. She didn't have room for that or time for it. It didn't matter that this place had become home to her. She'd grab the pack she always kept ready and find a new town to live in. She'd move across the states to some place like Florida. There were definitely places easier to get lost in. Maybe she'd head up the coast to New York City.

She'd have to leave right away, before the man came back, perhaps with more of the cult's members. But first she *had* to finish cleaning up the broken bottle of salad dressing so the elderly woman who lived with her wouldn't step on any of the glass. Lyra's heart hurt at the thought she'd have to tell Mrs. Yosko goodbye. She'd have to find someone to check in on her.

What about Mrs. Y's medication? Lyra always picked it up for her at the drugstore when she ran out. She even cooked for Mrs. Y. *Damn, damn, damn!*

The thoughts raced through Lyra's mind as she rushed as fast as she could while she picked up every piece of broken glass and stuffed it into the grocery bag. It took her a few precious moments to do that and run to the kitchen to dispose of it in the garbage can beneath the sink. Her hands shook as she washed them, then rinsed the small amount of pepper spray out of her eyes before quickly rubbing a kitchen towel over her face.

What if the man was sending The People to her home now? She hated how her heart pounded and her head ached from fear. Any moment *they* would be ready to snatch her and take her back to the Temple of Light.

Lyra hurried upstairs to Mrs. Y's room. She had to say goodbye.

She knocked on the elderly woman's closed door. "It's Linda," Lyra said, raising her voice and using the name people knew her by in Bisbee.

She heard shuffling and the white-haired lady opened the door, her bright red muumuu unbuttoned at the top, showing her yellowed slip. "Did you get the cat food?"

"Dixie's favorite—it's in the kitchen." Lyra felt like she was going to hyperventilate as she did her best to keep her voice calm. "I have to go out of town for a while."

Tears ached at the back of Lyra's eyes again. She'd really grown to love the old lady. Damn, but she'd miss her.

I have to hurry!

Just as Lyra turned to leave, Mrs. Y said in a calm voice, "Don't let them chase you off. You have to stop running."

Shock rippled through Lyra as she met the elderly woman's watery brown eyes. Mrs. Yosko didn't know about Lyra's past. She couldn't. No one in Bisbee did.

"I—I've got to go." Lyra backed out the door, turned, pounded down the stairs and then to the hall toward her room. She passed her worktable, filled with creations she had made from strips of metal cut from old lunch boxes, aluminum cans, and other metal objects.

Her mind spun from what Mrs. Yosko had said to her need to get out of the house as soon as possible. A lump grew in her throat. She would miss her quiet life, but she refused to be caged again, ever, in any way.

And what Neal would do to her . . . her stomach roiled and she felt like she was going to puke. Something she'd done many times because of him.

In her room she stuffed her cell phone into a side pocket of the worn army-issue canvas bag that contained a couple of changes of clothing and several tools of her craft. She snatched up a little yellow teddy bear from her bed and a small, flat tin from her bottom dresser drawer. Her hands were shaking even more as she jammed them in the bag before slipping her arms through both straps. She had plenty of cash in her pack—where she kept her stash. She always paid cash or used money orders for everything.

In seconds she was out of her bedroom and running down the hallway toward the living room. What had it been since the cowboy arrived on her doorstep—fifteen minutes, maybe more?

Too long!

A knock at the front door brought her to a full halt.

Her heart pounded and blood rushed in her ears.

Knocking again. Louder this time.

Lyra started to back up.

Her mind raced and she grabbed the metal bat she kept by the couch. She'd head out the back door to the alley, then swing around and get to the concrete steps leading down the side of the canyon.

Something rammed into the door so hard the old wooden door frame broke with a loud crack and the slide bolt and chain lock tore away from the frame.

No, this can't be happening.

Another slam against the door. Lyra screamed as it was ripped off its hinges and flung against the wall with a loud crash. A piece of her artwork toppled off the wall and tumbled across the floor.

Two men stood in the doorway.

These two she recognized, traveling in a pair like she expected. Like she had seen in her nightmares a hundred times.

Mark and Adam. In her house.

"Lyra." Adam held out his hand and gave an enigmatic smile, as if he hadn't just ripped the front door off its hinges. His light blue eyes were filled with obvious pleasure at having found her. "It's time you returned to the flock. The Prophecy has to be fulfilled."

She stepped back, swallowed hard, and clenched the bat tighter. "I'm not going with you. I'm not the freaking one you want from your stupid Prophecy. Just leave me alone."

Oh, God, I hope Mrs. Yosko stays in her room! She could get hurt!

The two cult members approached Lyra. They wore faded jeans and had on tan shirts. The shirts were made of the same coarse cloth the women were forced to wear for robes.

The cult's members all looked the same. Dressed the same.

"The Prophet is never wrong." Adam's looks became harder, more intense, as he took a larger step toward her and was a mere couple of feet away. "This is your destiny."

"Tell Neal Barker he can stuff *this* up his destiny." Lyra grasped the bat in both hands and swung as hard as she could at Adam's gut. His hand snapped up, the sound of metal smacking his palm loud in the quiet house before he ripped the bat out of her grip. She stumbled back and her legs hit the arm of the couch as she shouted, "Get it through your freaking heads, I'm not going!"

Adam lost the gentle smile and Mark's eyes glittered steel gray in the artificial lighting.

They dived for her.

Lyra dropped and rolled, the items inside her pack digging into her back with the movement. She reacted so quickly that she came to a stop between them and the front door.

She had to get away, and she had to get them out of Mrs. Yosko's home.

Mark was fast, though. He grabbed her wrist and jerked her to her feet.

Fear mixed with fury rocked her and she could barely see or breathe.

With her free hand she swung her fist straight at Mark's eye. Her knuckles made contact with flesh and bone, and sharp pain shot through her hand. He shouted and grabbed her arms so that he had a grip on both her wrists and she was facing away from him. Lyra kicked Mark's shins at the same time she brought her elbows back into his chest. He shouted again and she jerked free.

Adam reached for her as she whirled and dodged him—and she smacked right into the cowboy who had come to her door earlier.

Lyra couldn't hold back another scream. She tried to duck around him. He grabbed her arm and jerked her hard against his solid frame.

"No! I won't go back!" She kicked his shins, punched his chest, raked her fingernails across his cheek, fighting like a wildcat. She couldn't get away from his powerful grasp. Tears of anger and frustration flooded her cheeks and she fought even harder and kicked him again.

Through her fury she heard Mark's falsely calm tone. "Release Lyra," he said. "She's coming with us."

She went still and her gaze shot up to the cowboy's.

Welts and blood slashed his face from her nails, but he wasn't looking at her. His hard gaze rested on the men behind her.

"Only if she wants to go," the cowboy said in a deep and deadly voice that sent chills straight through her. "If she doesn't, then you'd better get out of here."

"We *are* taking her home," Mark said.

"Get lost," Lyra said as she tried to back away from Adam and Mark and the man who held her arm. But the cowboy still had a tight grip.

Mark lifted Lyra's bat with a two-fisted stance, as if he planned to swing and slam it into the cowboy's head. "Lyra's mentally disturbed. She needs to come back to our facilities to get proper care."

"You bastard!" At that moment Lyra would have clawed out Mark's eyeballs, but the damned cowboy wouldn't release her.

Mark held out one hand, reaching for her. "You don't want to get hurt again, do you, Lyra? Come home, where you belong. Where we can help you."

A metal click went off near her ear and everyone froze. From her side vision she saw the cowboy had drawn a gun. A sick feeling weighted her belly.

"This is all the help Lyra needs right now," the man drawled, gesturing with the gun. "Get your asses out of here before I shoot holes in your Goddamn knees."

Adam blanched and Mark's face turned so dark his skin was almost purple. He clenched the bat with both hands again, a dangerous look in his eyes.

"With the grace of the Prophet Jericho." Adam's voice squeaked as he grabbed Mark's arm. "You've got to understand she's a danger to herself and others."

The gun washed away her fear and left only anger. "I'll danger your ass," Lyra said as she tried again to jerk away from the cowboy. She was so pissed her entire body vibrated.

"Don't push it," the man said in that deadly calm voice, and he pointed his weapon at Mark's left knee.

Adam gave a bow from his shoulders. "In the name of Jericho and the Light."

The stranger pulled Lyra to the side and gestured toward the door with his gun.

Mark kept his hold on the bat and followed Adam onto the porch, then into the sunshine.

Lyra stared after the men who disappeared from view. Suddenly it became too quiet, and she was intensely aware of the man standing beside her, his callused hand firmly grasping her arm. Heat seemed to travel back and forth between them. The place where he was touching her felt like pure fire.

From her side vision she saw the cowboy still had a grip on his gun. She swallowed. She was so damned confused. She didn't know what to do, what to think. But one thing was obvious—the stranger wasn't with the Temple of Light.

He didn't release her. Instead he pulled her around to look directly at him. "There are more of them in the back."

A loud crashing sound came from the kitchen, and fear surged through Lyra. Her voice broke. "They won't ever give up."

"I won't let them get you, honey," the man said, a grim look on his face.

"I've got to get out of here!" Lyra jerked away from

his hold. "Mrs. Yosko—she could come down any minute and get caught in the middle. They can chase me. Just get them out of her house!"

"Stay," Dare ordered, his body tense and in fighting mode.

But Lyra spun and headed toward a window on the south side of the house.

He cursed and ducked and kept himself hidden to one side of the door leading from the kitchen to the living room, his weapon ready. His eyes still burned like hell, but the adrenaline surge more than compensated for the pain.

Wood scraped wood as Lyra raised the window at the same time he positioned himself beside the entrance to the living room.

The entryway was so narrow, only one man could come through at a time. When the first came through the doorway, Dare slammed the butt of his gun against the back of the man's head, dropping him in an instant. The second man Dare caught with a knee to the groin, but not before the bastard punched him in the nose. Blood poured down Dare's face as he rammed his boot into the third man's kneecap and heard a sickening pop as the man screamed in pain.

The fourth man's fist closed in on Dare's eye, but Dare ducked just in time. He slammed his fist into the man's jaw, knocking him back on his ass. With a side kick, Dare drove his boot into number five's gut. The man toppled sideways and crashed onto a table filled with artwork that Dare had noticed earlier.

After taking the men down, Dare wiped blood from his face with his sleeve as he bolted for the open front door. He reached the doorway just in time to see the top of Lyra's head disappearing down the hillside, the first two men following her. With one sweep of his gaze, he saw the tires of his truck had been slashed.

Shit! They'll pay for that.

He heard shouts behind him as his boot steps echoed on the stairs and then the walkway. He swung himself up and over the gate before running across the street and making it to the narrow concrete staircase that shot straight down the side of the steep hill to Main Street.

Lyra was fast, but she stumbled. Her feet slid out from under her and she landed on her ass. Just as she started to slide down the hard concrete stairs, the cult member closest to her caught her by her backpack, jerking her to a stop.

Dare lunged at the first man and grabbed the man's braid. The cult member shouted, lost his balance, and fell sideways. Dare lost his grip. The man flipped over the rail but caught the handrail. He barely clung to the metal, keeping himself from falling down the long drop of the hillside.

Dare's breathing came hard as he reached the second man, who had clamped his fingers around Lyra's wrist. The man looked behind him just in time for Dare to slam his fist into the man's nose, dropping him to the concrete steps.

After stepping over the man, Dare grabbed Lyra's upper arm, and yanked her to her feet.

Ahead of them was Main Street. The stairs ended between Manny's Restaurant and a bed-and-breakfast. Their shoes thundered on the stairs as they hurried down, Dare leading the way. At the end of the staircase, Lyra tripped and stumbled into him. He barely caught her and kept them both from falling. This time he pulled her close to keep his balance. When he looked over his shoulder he saw three cult members following them.

Dare gripped Lyra's hand and dragged her into the back entrance of Manny's Restaurant. Smells of re-fried beans and tortillas greeted his senses as they ran through the kitchen, past Manny's wife, to come up short behind the bar, face-to-face with Manny.

Lyra was breathing heavily when they came to a stop, almost running into the large bartender. Her face was bright red, her green eyes wide with fear.

Dare spared her only a glance before he turned to one of his friends and informants and said, "Manny, car keys."

The heavyset dark-haired man raised one eyebrow as he shoved his hand into his pocket, pulled out a set of keys, and tossed them to Dare. "One dent and your ass is grass, Lancaster."

Without responding Dare yanked Lyra behind him as they rounded the bar and headed through the maze of tables filled with people and out the front door. He spotted Manny's cherried-out neon blue El Dorado, hurried to unlock the passenger side, and shoved Lyra onto the seat. His breathing was heavy, his blood pounding in his temples, as he made it to the driver's side and unlocked it. He tossed his Stetson on the seat and ducked into the vehicle. He started the engine, threw it into gear, and slid into the light traffic heading down Main Street.

Lyra glanced behind them to see if they were being followed, and it felt like her heart leaped into her throat when she saw two cult members bound from the staircase onto the sidewalk. But they were on foot and had no way to catch up.

We'll be okay. We've got to be okay. Her gaze whipped around to look at the stranger who had just saved her. "Are they following us?"

The man's jaw tightened. "I'm keeping an eye out."

She struggled to catch her breath and turned her gaze back to the road. Her cheeks were hot, sweat plastered her hair to her face. Her heart pounded in time with the throb in her head, and the metallic taste of blood filled her mouth. Her ass ached from that last fall, and she had scraped the heels of her palms raw when she tried to stop herself from sliding down the concrete staircase.

"Goddamnit," the cowboy said as he glanced into the rearview mirror.

Lyra jerked her head to look through the back window of the El Dorado. Terror rode her hard as she saw the van speeding behind them.

CHAPTER *TWO*

Neal Barker's body grew taut, and he barely kept his voice from trembling with rage. "You lost her?"

Adam faltered at the other end of the cell phone. "The PI—he showed up again. He shattered Jim's kneecap, gave Joe and Steve each a concussion, and probably broke Henry's jaw. Not to mention he got Ken in the groin and I think my ribs are bruised."

Neal spoke slowly and clearly, his barely controlled fury reverberating throughout every muscle. "Seven of you couldn't handle one cowboy?"

"We—"

"Find her." Neal lowered his voice, forcing himself to calm down. Jericho had told him Lyra would bear the new Messiah, and his faith had never wavered. He was above failure of any kind. "Do what you have to and bring her to me."

"Whatever it takes, Prophet," Adam replied with conviction in his tone. "We live only to serve you and the Light."

"If you want to be my second, Adam," Neal said, "I expect you to help me fulfill the Prophecy."

"I won't fail you," Adam was saying as Neal flipped the phone shut, ending the conversation.

"So close," he growled.

Bitch. He had other matters to handle, like dealing with the leaders of his satellite compounds around the United States. If Lyra would just come back to the Temple where she belonged, he wouldn't have to screw around trying to find her.

And Ryan, that fucking asshole, was going to pay.

Neal clenched his teeth and his fists so tight that pain shot through his jaw, and his knuckles ached. Ryan Holstead had been entrusted with starting the new satellite compound of the Temple of Light near Fort Huachuca in Arizona.

Just one day ago, Ryan had spotted Lyra's signature artwork at a woman's home in Sierra Vista. The woman had purchased the piece in what had to be a shithole of a town called Bisbee.

Instead of using The People's own resources to track down Lyra through the artwork, Ryan had contacted a PI.

A fucking PI.

Not to mention the incompetent asshole had used Neal's name. *His name.*

Last night Mark and Adam had flown to Sierra Vista Airport and made it to the compound in order to clean up Ryan's mess. Today they'd gone to Bisbee to track down the PI, but before they could get to him and make sure he would forget Neal Barker's name, the PI had left his office. Neal's men had followed the man, who actually led them to Lyra Collins. Mark and Adam had recognized her at once.

But now she was on the run with that damned PI.

They would find her. Now that The People knew where she was, they *would* find her.

Mark and Adam better catch her before she disappears again.

While the men recovered Lyra and dealt with the PI, Ryan would be returned to the compound and used as an example before all Neal's men. Before all the males of the Temple of Light.

Neal's thoughts turned to Lyra Collins. He hadn't seen her since she'd left the fold five years ago. She'd been a beauty when she was a young teenager and even more so when she matured. Despite his anger, he savored the thought of the full, tempting woman she'd become.

The mental image of her was more satisfying now that he knew where she was. He could scarcely imagine what the real thing would be like once he had her back home with him, where she would fulfill her ordained destiny.

Neal moved to the mirror at one end of his opulent room that was within the Temple itself. His blue eyes looked back at him as he withdrew a band from his pocket and pulled his long black hair into a ponytail that accented his high cheekbones. The Light had blessed him with an appearance that drew women to him. He was handsome, stunning even, and he used it to his advantage.

He had never doubted he would find Lyra again, even though searching for her over the past five years had proved fruitless. The considerable funds from their "outside activities" had helped them to dig up nothing—until now.

Jericho had brought them to Lyra as promised.

As soon as Neal had learned they were close, Jericho, the original Prophet, had visited Neal as usual during his meditations. Jericho told Neal that Lyra would soon be back in the fold. She was confused. Nothing more. Confused, alone, and probably very frightened. They had to help her. Only an unstable woman would reject the destiny decreed by Jericho, Lord of the Prophets.

Lyra would, of course, be the new First Wife, share his bed, and fulfill the Prophecy. She was to bear the new Messiah. In his meditations, Jericho had informed Neal of this fact. It had been immediately following the time he'd met Sara and her daughter, Lyra, in Portland at one of his programs about the Light. At the time Lyra had been almost fifteen, and he knew he had to find some way to draw mother and daughter into the fold.

And then it had been done.

According to the Prophecy, Lyra was to be at least eighteen for it to be fulfilled. When she was of age, Neal had prepared to join with her, but she had vanished.

At the thought he fought to keep from flinging the mirror across the room. He took a deep breath, but his muscles remained tense. With a gold cigarette lighter he lit a joint he'd rolled earlier and brought it to his lips. He moistened the end of it with his saliva, and the bittersweet taste rolled over his tongue and burned his lungs as he inhaled. He closed his eyes and held the hit as long as he could. Slowly he released the smoke from his lungs and blew it out through his lips.

Neal had kept the Prophecy a secret from all but a few of his most trusted men and Sara, Lyra's mother. Jason, Neal's son—his eldest and the pride of his life—didn't even know that one day he would serve the new Messiah.

It took two more drags before Neal's muscles relaxed and he put out the joint in what he used for an ashtray. He smiled as he caressed the side of the metal. It was one of Lyra's creations, a small bowl she'd made before being brought into the Temple of Light with her mother. Of course, all of Sara's and Lyra's worldly possessions had been taken away from them so they could better serve the Light.

Neal's dick hardened at the thoughts of Lyra and he rubbed it through his robe until it ached with the need to come. He parted his clothing and slid his palm from balls to tip and closed his eyes. An image of Lyra on her knees in a position of submission expanded in his mind. On her knees with his dick in her mouth. He stroked himself harder and faster until he was gritting his teeth. On the verge of orgasm. This time he could do it. This time he could make himself come.

Lyra. Lyra. Lyra!

But he remained at that peak, unable to topple over, unable to reach climax, without the stimulation of a woman's tight hole.

With a growl his eyes shot open and he adjusted his robe to cover his erection. He knew how to relieve the frustration of the incompetence in Arizona, along with the ache in his dick.

He slipped a flogger from his closet into one of the pockets of his robes. He withdrew his cell phone from his other pocket and put it on vibrate so that it wouldn't ring out loud when he was among The People. Most had no idea of the extent of technology and communication devices Neal and his highest followers used.

After dropping the cell back into his pocket, he left his rich quarters in the Temple, headed down the stairs and to the immense sea of stained white tents spotted by several fir and cedar trees. Few of The People had ever been in the Temple, and only the people who cleaned his room had viewed what Jericho had decreed appropriate quarters for a Prophet.

Neal moved among his flock. Smoke from the campfire met his nose, along with smells of beef stew and cornbread. July sunshine warmed his face as he strode through the center of one of the circles of tents. He walked toward his wives and the other women of the commune and the older teenage girls, who all worked in harmony. Some of the women prepared the evening meal while others stitched new robes for his future wife and clothes for the babe. Others created exquisite tapestries for the Temple, depicting The Coming.

Lyra's mother, Sara, sat quietly to the side, making the blanket that would be wrapped around the child Lyra would have, along with cloth diapers and clothing to protect him when winter's chill gripped Mount Hood. The cult's compound was tucked away near its base.

Behind the campgrounds, men and older teenage boys erected a larger Temple and prepared Neal and Lyra's residence. Sounds of hammers and saws rang through the air, along with voices as The People toiled without hitch or conflict. As it should be. As it would always be for the Light's chosen.

The younger teenagers were hard at work, the boys tending to the sheep, cattle, pigs, and chickens, cleaning their pens, feeding them, and brushing them down. The girls attended to the gardens and took care of the laundry. Children gathered wood. The older ones picked up larger pieces while the younger ones collected kindling.

The People always worked within the confines of the encampment. Twelve-foot-high chain-link fences—one fence enclosed by the other—rimmed with rolls of razor wire, surrounded the compound, protecting his people from intruders. The gates and each fence were well managed by armed guards who constantly patrolled the perimeter. He had no concerns that any of The People might stray into danger if they became confused and thought about leaving. Nor did he have concerns that anyone could enter without welcome from the fold.

Only he above all others had the right to be The People's Prophet.

Right now what Neal wanted was to lessen his wrath and to relieve his tension.

He signaled to Carrie, the wife who reminded him somewhat of Lyra. Perhaps it was her full curves or her blond hair.

Carrie set aside the spoon she'd been using to stir the pot of stew and touched Maggie's shoulder to let her know she was leaving. Maggie spared Neal a glance, then lowered her eyes.

Carrie slowly walked toward Neal, her gaze focused

on the ground where the hem of her robe brushed grass, pine needles, and dark brown earth. He frowned at the sight of her dirty hem. None of his wives should allow their clothing to become soiled.

He led her back to the Temple, confident that Carrie followed him. No one would dare ignore his demands. He stepped aside so that she could open the door to his chambers and hold it until he entered. She closed the door behind them when she was in the room and he turned to face her.

"How may I serve you, Husband?" she said, her eyes still downcast as she lowered herself to her knees before him.

He withdrew the short leather flogger from his pocket and slapped the three braided thongs over his palm hard enough that he felt pain at the contact. "To serve my body is to serve the Light. Remove your clothing."

Carrie visibly flinched. "My will is yours, Prophet."

Neal raised the flogger and smiled as he thought of Lyra in Carrie's place.

He'd never doubted the range of his power and knew that Lyra would be back with The People one day. Mark and Adam would bring her to Oregon immediately and she would be taught her place.

Lyra would bear the child who would make Neal even more powerful than he already was.

CHAPTER *THREE*

Lyra clutched her backpack to her chest as her heart set in motion again. The cowboy gunned the El Dorado's engine as he shot away from Historic Bisbee, beneath the small overpass, and around the Lavendar Pit Mine. The street was wide enough for a short distance that the stranger beside her was able to pass several vehicles before coming to another underpass and then to the roundabout that would take them in any of four directions. She had no idea which turnoff the man was going to take.

Would she ever be totally free of the cult and Neal? How far would she have to go to escape them?

And who was this man who had rescued her from The People?

What about Mrs. Yosko?

Lyra jerked her cell phone out of her backpack, flipped it open, and dialed 911.

"What are you doing?" the cowboy asked in a sharp tone as they drove past Lowell and he swung the vehicle onto the roundabout.

When the operator answered, Lyra's voice came out

in a rush. "There's been a break-in at Mrs. Yosko's home." Lyra rattled off the address.

Before the operator could respond, Lyra snapped her cell phone shut. She threw a look over her shoulder again and saw the van bearing down on them. The van was close enough for her to see Mark at the wheel.

Lyra faced forward, her back tense against the seat as she looked at the stranger. "We're never going to outrun them."

"Trust me, honey." He glanced in his rearview mirror, then took the exit that would lead them through the lower part of Bisbee known as Warren.

Trust. Yeah.

She held her breath, praying a cop wouldn't stop them for tearing down Bisbee Road, which posted a 25-mile-per-hour speed limit. They had to be going at least 50.

Once they reached the residential area, the cowboy guided the El Dorado up and down streets she'd never been on. He wove in and out of neighborhoods, but every time she looked behind her the van would pop into view.

The man beside her rounded another corner, then shot up a street that she did recognize, the one that led up to the high school. When he neared the top of the hill, he swung into the high school's empty parking lot and gunned the engine so hard they practically flew out the opposite entrance.

The van's tires squealed behind them, but the sound was more distant now. Lyra looked over the back of the seat and saw the gap between their vehicle and the van was increasing. They rounded a corner and the van dis-appeared from view.

The cowboy tore along the street, whipped the steer-ing wheel, and entered a neighborhood they'd been through before. She continued to look over her shoulder. She held her breath, but as the cowboy charged down the narrow street, the van didn't come into view. "Did we lose them?" she asked, trying to catch her breath and slow her heart.

"Damn sure hope we did." Where the street curved, leading to another street, the cowboy brought the vehicle to a stop. They were hidden from view where they parked.

For a moment all Lyra heard was the purr of the en-gine, the heavy sound of her breathing, and the beating of her heart.

Her gaze met the cowboy's coffee-colored eyes. When she found her voice she said, "Thanks."

A droplet of sweat ran down the side of his face, and the scratches she'd left on his cheek looked red and still a little bloody against his tan skin. By the marks on his face and his bloody nose, he'd taken a lot because of her.

Why?

He rubbed his shirtsleeve over his face and blinked several times before looking at her. The pepper spray was probably hurting him like crazy.

"They sure want you bad," he said.

She frowned. In all the craziness, she'd forgotten she didn't know anything about the man who'd rescued her. "Who *are* you?"

He stared at her for a long moment. "The PI hired to track you down."

Lyra's heart thumped and she fumbled for the door handle with one hand while clutching her backpack with her other. The man grabbed her upper arm and she froze, her gaze locked with his.

"I'm not going to let them or anyone else hurt you." The man's grip tightened as she tried to jerk her arm away. "I'm trying to help."

She clenched the door handle and her knuckles ached. "You led them to me."

"I tracked you down this morning. I figured I'd find out if you wanted to be contacted by someone who claimed to be your cousin." His expression hardened even more. "I never planned to lead anyone to you. They must've followed me from my office."

"Neal Barker's not my freaking cousin." Lyra ground her teeth. "He's the leader of a cult called the Temple of Light. The compound is in Oregon, but he's been after me for five years."

The man relaxed his grip on her arm and let his hand slide away. Her flesh burned where he'd touched her, but not because he'd hurt her. He hadn't. Instead a kind of electrical energy sparked between them.

"What's your name?" she asked, softer than she'd intended.

"Dare Lancaster."

That was right. He'd told her when he'd arrived on her doorstep.

She leaned back against the car seat and a whoosh of air left her lungs as she stared straight ahead at a house painted pale blue with white trim. Its neat yard was a contrast to the weed-choked lot beside it.

After a moment, she turned her head and studied

Dare. His stubbled jaw was set, his eyes dark and narrowed. "You okay?" he asked.

She still fought for breath but managed a, "Yeah."

"You were lucky you didn't fall all the way down
those stairs," he said. "How's your ass?"

Lyra couldn't help a small laugh. "Hurts like hell."
She sobered. "But you—there's blood on your face."

Dare shrugged. "Just a hit to the nose."

"Thanks for helping me," she said quietly. "And
sorry about the cheek."

"My shins hurt worse." He winked. "You kick like a
mule."

Lyra managed a smile. "Shouldn't sneak up on a
woman."

The corner of his mouth quirked. "There's always
that."

"I've got to get out of here." Chills rolled over her
skin. "Anywhere. Can you drop me off at the bus station? If there's not a bus heading out soon, I'll hitch a
ride out of town."

"I'm not about to let you get caught again." He
drummed the fingers of one of his hands on the steering wheel. "We need to get you to the police. You can
get a restraining order."

"No!" Panic rose up in Lyra's throat like a flock of
birds. "You don't understand. That will mean nothing
to The People. They'll take me the moment I'm alone
and haul me to the compound in Oregon. I *have* to
leave Bisbee."

He studied her for a long moment. "I'll take you
someplace safe for the night. But first we'll head to my
ranch and ditch this thing. Sticks out like a sore thumb."

Lyra shook her head. "No. I can take care of myself."

Dare gave her a look of impatience. "I got you into this mess. I'm going to help you get out."

"*No.*" This time she put more emphasis on the word. Her backpack started to slide off her lap and she caught it by one of its straps. "How about dropping me off at a friend's house?"

"Do you have anyone you can trust?" he asked in a harsh tone. "Anyone who would take you in, someplace those cult bastards can't track you down?"

The word "trust" always made her stomach queasy. It had taken her time, but she had developed a few relationships with women who she thought of as friends. "Suzette, the potter," she started out slowly, "but she dropped one too many hits of acid in the sixties—not always there, mentally. Nicole, but she's on her honeymoon in Vegas." Lyra frowned, trying to come up with a solution. "Maybe Becca. She owns the small grocery store up Tombstone Canyon. She's always been helpful and nice."

"If you left behind an address book," he said, "it's likely they could track you to your friends."

Her eyes locked with his. "Then they'd be in danger." Her face went pale. "Mrs. Yosko! What if they go back and hurt her?" Tears bit at the backs of her eyes. Tears of frustration at the fact that she didn't know what to do and couldn't help Mrs. Y herself. "I've got to call her, at least to see if the police arrived." She flipped her cell phone open and started to dial, but Dare handed his phone to her.

"This is a secure line," he said.

She closed her own phone and reached for his. "Thanks." She dialed Mrs. Y's phone number. The elderly woman answered and Lyra's voice shook as she asked, "Are you okay?"

"Why wouldn't I be?" Mrs. Yosko said.

Lyra blinked and clenched the cell phone tighter. "I—well . . . the doors, the mess . . . have the police arrived?"

"They're here," the woman said. "Also got some men fixing the doors. Just a random breaking and entering, of course. The landlord understands everything perfectly, and insurance will take care of it all."

"I'm so sorry." This time Lyra couldn't help the tears in her eyes or in her voice. "I didn't mean for you—I should never have put you at risk. I just didn't think—"

"That's enough." Mrs. Y's voice had never sounded so sharp. "You did nothing wrong and I won't have you beating yourself up over it. You deserve a good life, and it's time you did something about it. It's time to stop being on the run."

Lyra couldn't think of a word to say, she was so stunned by Mrs. Yosko's words.

The woman's tone softened. "You take care of yourself. I expect to hear good news from you . . . soon."

"I'll miss you," Lyra said so softly she wasn't sure Mrs. Yosko could hear her.

"I'll miss you, too, girl," came the reply before she hung up the phone.

For a long moment Lyra stared at the cell. Finally Dare took it from her and flipped it shut. He studied her and then opened the cell and punched in a number.

"Lancaster here," he said when someone apparently

answered. "I need you to look into something called the Temple of Light. It's a cult out of Oregon. Might be in our county now, or at least a branch of it." Lyra's heart pounded with every word, and her eyes widened. "Find out whatever you can."

A pause, then Dare said, "Thanks," and snapped the phone shut.

"Why did you just do that?" Lyra's mouth was dry as she spoke. "Who did you talk to?" Her words nearly stuck in her throat as she added, "Do you really think they have a branch here?"

"That was my partner, Nick Donovan." Dare stuck his cell phone in a small holster at his side. He eyed her head-on. "When the man named Ryan Holstead contacted me, he mentioned being stationed in the Huachuca Mountains. There's no military station in those mountains. Fort Huachuca is on the other side of Sierra Vista. I want Nick to track them down. I need to know as much as possible about these sonsofbitches who are after you."

"Thanks, but it's not necessary. I'll be out of here before they can find me again." She had to force back more angry tears as she clenched her fists. "I should have planned better. I got so comfortable that I started to believe I was safe."

"It'll be dark soon." He glanced through the window up at the sky before looking back at her. "It ought to be safe enough then to head out to my ranch to grab my gear and change vehicles." He paused. "Why do they want you so bad?"

"Where's your place?" she asked instead of answering him.

"I have a little spread a good fifteen miles from here."

She couldn't take her eyes off his harsh profile. He looked like a real cowboy, tanned and weathered. Not just some guy who wore the gear. "A ranch?"

"Yep."

"I've never been on a ranch." Heaviness settled over her. "The People raised some livestock and vegetables. It was kind of like a farm, I guess. How do you know they haven't already gone there?"

"It's not easy to find someone in the valley if you don't know exactly where they live," he said. "Not too many people know where my place is, and it's not likely the bastards could find it. It would be damn near impossible to. They'd have to track down the right folks, who'd have to give detailed directions, which even then would take some time. A lot more time than I need to get in and out."

When it was dark, Dare drove the El Dorado out of Bisbee. Lyra remained silent and he focused on driving. They must have gone fifteen, maybe twenty miles when they reached a pair of open gates.

Panic seized Lyra's chest. She was alone. In the desert. Far from civilization. With a stranger.

She clenched the strap of her backpack and took a deep breath. Okay, her brain had short-circuited and she hadn't fully thought this thing through.

What was wrong with her? She was letting an absolute stranger take her out in the middle of the desert.

But he had saved her from The People. And she hadn't had a lot of choices.

Dare turned onto a rough dirt road and the tires

thrummed over a cattle guard before they shimmied on the ruts.

The El Dorado bottomed out and she saw Dare's frown in the glow of the dashboard lights. "Manny'll be pissed if I even scratch the muffler," he muttered.

They pulled up to the sprawling ranch house and her heart beat a little faster as they climbed out of the El Dorado.

It's going to be okay. Calm down!

A pair of border collies raised a ruckus and greeted Dare with enthusiasm. They sniffed Lyra and she jumped back just before she and Dare walked up the porch steps.

"Don't worry about the girls." Dare pointed to the ground at his feet. "Darby. Xena. Stay."

The dogs sat and looked up at him, but their tails still waggled like crazy, brushing the dusty ground in half-moon arcs.

After he opened the front door with a key on a ring filled with multiple keys, Lyra took a deep breath before walking into the ranch-style home. He closed the door behind them and she jumped again. She swallowed hard as she looked at Dare.

"Hungry?" he asked as he tossed his black cowboy hat on the seat of a recliner.

She pushed her hair out of her face. "Not really." She couldn't eat now if she tried.

"I'll make a couple of sandwiches after I see what I can do to get the rest of that pepper spray out of my eyes." He strode toward an archway, cast a look over his shoulder, and added, "Then I'll grab my things and we'll get on out of here."

While she waited, she took in the spacious living room. Newspapers and *Time* magazines were scattered over the top of a coffee table, along with a couple of hardbound books with worn bindings.

A straw cowboy hat rested on the back of a leather recliner that also had a denim western shirt draped over it. A couple of soda pop cans stood on an end table, and a large TV took up one corner of the room. She liked that the place had a lived-in look about it.

At the same time, she felt antsy, like bugs crawled over and under her skin. She rubbed her upper arms with her hands and rocked from her heels to her toes.

The People. The People had found her. She was on the run—again. She tried to fight the memories as her thoughts turned to the past, but she couldn't stop the images flashing in her mind. And she couldn't stop the old wounds from opening up again.

For so long she'd been angry at her father and hated her mother. If her police officer father hadn't died in the line of duty, she wouldn't be in this mess. If her mother hadn't been so weak, they would never have ended up in the Temple of Light.

Lyra clenched her fists. The memory of how she'd found out her father had died was so vivid, it would never leave her mind. She still remembered the faces of the police officers who had come to their home to tell her and her mother that Lyra's father had been murdered during a bank robbery. The way the two police officers tried to keep their expressions stoic. How bright the sunlight had been as it streamed through the windows. The scents of freshly mowed grass and her mother's roses coming in through the open French doors. The ticking of the kettle-shaped clock in the kitchen.

And the prickling of her scalp. The stinging of her skin. The unreality of it all, as if she were someone on the outside watching the scene.

It had taken her years to realize it wasn't her father's fault for getting killed in the line of duty and leaving her and her mother so that they ended up in the cult. But when Lyra was younger, she couldn't help but feel that if he had chosen a career other than being a cop, he'd still be alive and the Temple of Light would never have happened.

What Neal had done to her . . . She shuddered. Once in the cult the other men treated women and girls as subservient. The only reason Lyra hadn't been raped was the Prophecy. Underage sex and forced "marriages" for girls from ages fifteen to eighteen was the norm in the cult, something Neal encouraged. Ironic that the one thing that made her life a living hell, the so-called Prophecy, had saved her from being raped. He hadn't been allowed to touch her until she was eighteen, and he'd never had the chance because she'd escaped.

When it came to men, she'd learned to keep her distance, but here she was, her life and freedom in the hands of one tall, dark cowboy.

How could she put any trust in this man named Dare?

Goddamnit. She couldn't—no, she wouldn't—allow him to take control of her life in any way.

Dare walked into the living room, carrying a large duffle, and he'd washed all the blood off his face. His eye was red and one side of his face seemed a little swollen. The scratches from her nails were dark against his tanned skin.

A jolt of awareness shot through Lyra. Fear? Mistrust? Or something else?

"Let's go." He grasped her hand before she could react, and she winced at the contact. Her palms burned where the skin had been scraped off. Dare caught her pained expression and relaxed his grip on her just enough to examine both of her palms.

With a frown he said, "What did you do?"

"No big deal." She tried to pull her hands away, but he caught her by one wrist too easily. "Happened when I fell."

Without another word, Dare held on to her and led her into what appeared to be the master bedroom and to the adjoining bathroom. He closed the lid on the toilet and made her sit on it. After he retrieved a first-aid kit, he got down on one knee and proceeded to put antiseptic on her palms.

"The scratches on your face must hurt more." She shifted on the toilet seat. "It looks like you're going to have a heck of a black eye."

"I've had worse," he said without looking up from her hands.

While he cared for her wounds, strange feelings swirled through Lyra. As much as she had the urge to get up and run, she found herself quivering from the intimate act of him being so close and doctoring her palms.

Suddenly she barely felt the sting of the antiseptic. Instead she was keenly aware of everything about

Dare. His clean, masculine scent. The day's stubble shadowing his strong jaw. The way veins stood out along his forearms while he cared for her hands and the flex of muscle beneath his shirt. He had a hard, seasoned look about him, like he truly was a gunslinger from the Old West. He wasn't classically handsome. He was good-looking in a rough and rugged kind of way.

Her gaze settled on his firm lips and her belly quivered at the thought of kissing him.

She almost knocked herself upside the head with her free hand. Where had that come from? The trauma of the day must have scrambled her brain.

It was a few seconds before she realized Dare had stopped putting antiseptic on her palms. Her gaze slowly rose to meet his, and her cheeks burned at the fire in his eyes. Something hot and electric connected them.

"Come on," he finally said, breaking the spell she'd been caught in. His voice was low and hoarse as he added, "We've got to get you out of here."

Lyra cleared her throat as he took her by the wrist and helped her to her feet. She looked away from him. When she was standing, he grasped her chin in his large hand and turned her face so that she was looking right into his coffee-colored eyes.

"I'm not going to hurt you, Lyra," he said softly. "I don't blame you if you don't have a whole lot of trust in anyone. But I'll let you know right now that I'll do everything in my power to protect you." His gaze searched hers as he added, "Got that? So trust me."

She eyed him head-on as she pushed his hands away from her face. "I don't trust men. Period."

Well, hell, Dare thought. This wasn't going to work if he didn't find some way to earn her trust. He ground his teeth. He'd led the bastards right to her. He'd been had, and he'd been had good.

Why he felt such a need to protect this woman, he wasn't sure. Maybe it was the fact that he was the reason she was on the run because he had brought the men to her doorstep. Maybe it was because he'd let his partner on the force down and wasn't about to let Lyra down. Maybe it was the primal instinct to protect a woman in trouble. Maybe something about this woman was special.

Whatever it was, he really didn't care at this moment. He was determined to keep her safe, and he'd do everything in his power to make that happen.

Dare placed his hand against the T-shirt at her lower back and started to guide her through his house. His fingers burned where he touched her, and his groin tightened.

Damned if he didn't want her.

He shook his head. Jesus Christ. He'd better get his mind back on the job. The job he'd taken on the minute he'd led the cult members to her doorstep.

When they walked into his living room, Lyra paused to go to his floor-to-ceiling bookshelves. She picked up one of his framed photographs.

"Your family?" she asked, her gaze still on the photo.

"Taken at the ranch a year ago." Dare moved closer to her, keenly aware of her scent of roses and woman, and the primal lust she stirred within him. He pointed out each member of his family. "Mom and Dad on the porch swing. My brother, Josh, against the railing, my sisters, Kate and Melissa, sitting on the porch steps."

"And you with your shoulder hitched against the door frame." She looked up. "You're lucky."

Damn, she had a pretty face. "We have our moments. But I'd kick anyone's ass who messed with a one of them."

"Must be nice to have a family that loves you," she said softly. "That cares for you." He watched as Lyra placed the picture on the bookshelf and studied other photographs. "Are these children nephews and nieces?"

Pride rose in his chest. "All six. I'd do anything for those kids."

She nodded and trailed her fingers over a few books on the oak shelves. "Biographies, astronomy, Arizona history . . . and romance novels?"

Dare couldn't help a smile at her look of surprise. "My kid sister got me hooked on a couple of authors. They're good."

"They're just fantasy." Lyra shrugged. "I don't believe there's such a thing as happy endings."

With a frown, Dare said, "What did they do to you up in Oregon?"

"Listen. You have no idea what they're like." Lyra rubbed her arms again. "Nice family?" She gestured to the pictures and he could see her hand was trembling. "Helping me will put every one of them at risk." She put her hand to her forehead and clenched her eyes shut for a moment before opening them. Her expression became more panicked and she started looking around the room as if searching for something. "Everyone *I* know is in danger. I need to call them, warn them!"

"Hey." He grasped her upper arm. "They'll be all right. And we'll figure out something to get the cult bastards off your back." .

Lyra jerked her arm away. "What's wrong with me? I can't let you do this. It's unbelievable that I let you take me out here. Just drop me off somewhere and I'll hitch a ride."

This time he caught her by both arms and drew her to him. She tried to struggle as he brought her to his chest and cradled her in his arms. After she tried to get away from him, her muscles went limp and she felt the bone-deep exhaustion of the day. For that moment all the fight left her and she let herself sink against Dare. Let herself feel warm, safe, and secure, if only for a moment.

His masculine scent filled her, comforted her. She didn't know why, just that it did.

He smoothed his hand down her hair and murmured against the top of her head, "I won't let them hurt you, honey. I won't let them get you."

Something electrical started happening to her body when his lips brushed her hair. As if every nerve ending under her skin was charged wherever his body touched her.

She placed her palms on his chest and forced him to let her step away. When they drew apart, she felt a loss, like her body needed to be against his.

It must be everything that happened that day. There was no other explanation that made sense as to why her body was reacting to him.

Dare slipped his hands to her upper arms. "For tonight I'll take you to Tombstone. We'll spend the night in a motel there—we'll register under different names. I know the owner."

"Okay." She gave an exhausted sigh. "Tomorrow I hitchhike."

He lowered his head and clenched his hands tighter around her upper arms. "Tomorrow we come up with some kind of plan that will keep you from ever having to run again."

Lyra gave a heartless laugh. "Like that will ever happen."

"Trust me," he said softly, his gorgeous eyes fixed on hers.

Her mouth snapped shut. Then she said, "I just need to get through tonight. Then I'll decide what to do next."

"We'll talk about it in the morning." He gave a sharp nod. "Let's go."

Dare grabbed the bulging brown leather duffle and led her out the front door. She cast her gaze skyward for a moment. The stars were so brilliant here. She could see so many, just like the times her dad and mom had taken her out of Portland to the Cascade Mountains to go camping. She almost raised her hand like she had many times when she was a child and had thought she could touch the stars.

A deep, deep heaviness settled in her belly.

That was when her father was alive. When he would take her outside and show her the Big and Little Dippers and he'd tell her stories about them.

That was when she believed in her mom and had loved her. Before her father's death and her mother's choices had destroyed their lives.

Lyra's attention snapped back to the present as the Border collies greeted them and the automatic floodlights came on.

Dare watched the range of emotions that passed over Lyra's features before they went hard again. What was she thinking? What had she been through? If today was an example, this woman had been to hell and back.

He ordered the dogs to stay, then took Lyra to a shelter that housed his vehicles. He had a whole range of work trucks, an SUV, and one empty stall where the truck he'd driven to her house belonged. The assholes had slashed the tires. He'd have to have his foreman and one of his ranch hands take care of it when they returned Manny's car.

The night was cool as they strode across the hard-packed earth to the SUV. Even though his strides weren't hurried, he noticed Lyra had to double her steps to keep up with him.

The SUV was night black with dark tinted windows. A midsize model that he'd had specially equipped. Everything in it was high-tech, including the GPS.

Dare threw his duffle into the backseat, then held the passenger door open for her. "Get in."

She tossed her backpack onto the backseat beside his duffle, then buckled her seat belt as he shut the door with a solid thunk.

Dare strode to the driver's side door and, after removing his Stetson, swung his bulk into the seat and turned to set his black western hat on top of the leather bag in the backseat. He gave Lyra a long look before starting the vehicle. She appeared so strong yet vulnerable all in one.

He started the vehicle, then headed down the dusty road from his ranch. They reached the two-lane paved road and Dare swung the SUV onto it, heading north. Earlier they'd driven from the opposite direction. He glanced in his rearview mirror before looking back to the road ahead of him. No headlights behind, just pure darkness.

His own headlights flowed over mesquite and dry grass lining the road. A few red and white Hereford cattle grazed on the opposite side of a barbed-wire fence, their eyes glowing red in the lights of the SUV.

"No one's following us." Lyra had been looking over her shoulder. She turned back around and let out an audible sigh of relief before her words came out sharp and bitter. "For now."

CHAPTER *FOUR*

Neal paced the length of his large quarters and ground his teeth. He couldn't let his emotions get the better of him. Adam had just called again to say they couldn't find the PI's home. They'd only met a couple of people who knew him and said he lived on some kind of ranch, but they didn't know where it was in the valley. According to Adam, the valley was massive and it would be hell to track down one person's home or ranch.

Neal growled, then sucked in a deep breath. Scents of sandalwood and patchouli incense mingled with the smell of the vanilla candles burning at the small altar at one corner of his room. He released his breath and he moved toward the altar.

As he knelt before it, he bowed his head. "Forgiveness, Jericho, Lord of the Prophets, for my anger." A water glass always stood ready beside the pitcher next to the altar. He filled it and swallowed a hit of LSD, also known as Sacrament.

While he waited for the drug to bring him to his meditative state, he reached for the vessel of the Prophets and a baggie of what further helped him communicate with Jericho. Marijuana, in its purest and most potent form.

Once Neal had filled a bong half-full with water from the small pitcher, he tamped the dry leaves into its quarter-sized bowl and lit it. He brought the water pipe to his mouth and inhaled. Smoke filled his lungs, burned his throat, and he tasted the bittersweet taste of the weed on his tongue.

After holding the smoke as long as he could, he exhaled. A white stream poured through his lips and the scent of the leaf grew stronger in his room. He sucked on the bong again, then twice more.

He set the bong aside and sat back on his haunches, his hands folded in reverence for the Light. His muscles relaxed and his mind drifted to where Jericho would grant a vision to him, as he always had.

The First Prophet Jericho had been Neal's father's father. As Jericho had been fond of explaining, he had brought The People together when free love reigned and minds opened, allowing all who joined the commune to recognize the will of the Light. Jericho had taken multiple wives and fathered nearly thirty children, but his eldest son, Abraham, had been unworthy of succeeding his father. Jericho himself had taught Neal the way of the Light instead of teaching Abraham.

Jericho had passed on to the Light itself but still guided Neal through meditations and had instructed him on what his next step should be. Neal's father, Abraham, died not long after, during his own meditations.

Neal smiled. The strength of strychnine he'd laced

the pot and the LSD with had been more than enough
to rid The People of his incapable father.

The responsibilities of guiding The People had fallen
to Neal. He above anyone should rightly be Prophet over
all within his control and those who soon would be.

Colors began flashing in his mind as the present
came into view and the room swirled around him. He
had reached his meditative state.

It took only moments before he saw a younger version of Lyra—the first time he had laid eyes upon her.
He'd been recruiting new sheep for his fold and had met
Lyra and her mother, Sara, at a Portland arts festival
during one of his many magnificent sermons in an am-
phitheater. He had spoken with Sara afterward, but it
was the beautiful Lyra who had captured his attention.

The almost-fifteen-year-old girl's brilliant green
gaze had held a spark that attracted him at once. That
very night he had used the tools of the Prophets and
foreseen Lyra as his new First Wife after she turned
eighteen.

He hadn't understood Jericho's orders that Neal
wait until she reached that age, but he never questioned
the will of the High Prophet.

More important, Jericho told Neal that Lyra would
bear the new Messiah who would reach out to more people to gather them to the Temple of Light. The Messiah
would help Neal save the world from its demons. When
the new Messiah was of age, he would heal The People
and spread the realm of the Light around the world.

It had been necessary to bring the girl to the Light.
Immediately.

Of course it had taken some manipulation, but Neal had brought her and her mother into the fold.

For three years Lyra had lived in the commune, knowing one day she would serve the Light and The People as Neal's new First Wife. He'd had his other wives train Lyra in her responsibilities, instruct her in what would be expected of her as wife and servant to the Prophet. Neal had taken a firm hand in her training as well.

But she had vanished when she turned eighteen, mere days before he would have joined with her. "Escape" wasn't the right word for Lyra's disappearance. No one escaped the Light. The Light was always with them and protected the compound from potential intruders and protected The People from themselves.

But Lyra . . . Neal's body tensed as he remembered the day Lyra had . . . vanished. He'd been servicing one of his wives that evening and had followed with deep meditations when she left him to return to her tent. Hours later he went to Lyra's room to watch her sleep, perhaps to wake her and continue her education.

But she hadn't been in her bed.

At first he'd thought perhaps she had wandered to another part of the Temple, even though it was late. Yet within him he knew something was very wrong.

Within minutes he'd assembled a massive team of all the men in the commune. They'd searched every tent, every building, every square inch of the compound. It wasn't until Jeffrey returned with the dope that Neal determined where she'd gone. One of his tapestries from the Prayer Room was in the back of the truck with the drugs. And Lyra was gone.

Jeffrey had paid dearly.

More colors and light flashed through Neal's head as he meditated. The memories of that night and the days following swirled into nothingness as the present came to the forefront.

He saw Lyra as she must be now, five years later. A beautiful, mature woman ready to receive his semen and fulfill the Prophecy.

He saw everything so clearly. Lyra would come to him, not willingly, but she would come to him no less. He would join with her, then fuck her, filling her with his come. He would fuck her as many times as he had to until the new Messiah grew in her belly.

Neal smiled, feeling completely at peace. Lyra would come to him.

Soon.

CHAPTER *FIVE*

Everything had begun to feel surreal to Lyra, especially as she sat next to a virtual stranger and approached the town of Tombstone. The twinkle of lights was fairly sparse in the surrounding desert.

Her thoughts raced. She had to find someone to check in on Mrs. Y and make sure she got everything she needed. And Dixie—someone had to make sure she had her cat food the next time she ran out. Lyra would have to call Becca, who was probably the only one she could count on right now. But it was late and Lyra didn't want to wake anyone up.

While they traveled from the ranch to Tombstone, Lyra and Dare ate the roast beef and cheese sandwiches he'd thrown together before they'd left. She was surprised she was actually hungry and ate a whole sandwich. He ate two. She downed a good-size bottle of water, and he did the same.

Dare drove the SUV slowly through the small tourist town that was barely a blip on the map. She'd never been to historic Allen Street, and now it didn't look like she'd ever get a chance.

Lyra felt like she could crawl right out of her skin, she was so jittery and jumpy at the thought of The People spotting them. She forced herself to breathe. She was in a different town—albeit a really, really small town—and they were just going to spend *one* night at a motel, under assumed names. In the morning she'd head out and hitchhike to Tucson, where she could catch a bus to just about anywhere.

Dare guided the SUV into the parking lot of a U-shaped gathering of bungalows where a big, glowing yellow sign proclaimed *Tombstone Getaway.*

After they parked, Dare put on his Stetson, took her by the hand, and led her into the tiny lobby of the motel. She was surprised her palm didn't really hurt when he grasped it. Instead it tingled and she felt that strange connection with him that had her shaking her head. When they opened and closed the glass door of the lobby a bell jingled, startling Lyra.

An older man with a well-creased face, deeply tanned skin, large ears, and liver-spotted hands moved to the counter. "Lancaster," he said, before running his gaze over Lyra, then back to Dare.

He dug into his wallet and pulled out several bills. "Tonight it's Jameson." He handed the cash to the man, then stuffed the wallet into his pocket.

It was then that Lyra noticed Dare's gun tucked into the back of his waistband, against his black shirt. Jeez, why hadn't she noticed it earlier?

The man fished a brass key out from beneath the counter, then tossed the key to Dare. "Casita two, Jameson."

Dare touched the brim of his Stetson and Lyra followed him into the night. The parking lot was softly lit only by the big yellow sign. He unlocked and opened one door of the SUV and handed Lyra her backpack, which she hitched over one shoulder. He grabbed his duffle, shut the door, and locked it. The vehicle didn't chirp when he locked it—no doubt as a PI he wouldn't want to announce himself in any way. He took her by the hand and headed toward the casita that had a worn brass number 2 nailed to it.

"Wait." She brought them to a stop. "You got one room."

He gave her an impatient look before continuing to draw her along with him. "I'm not letting you out of my sight, honey. For one thing, I intend to guard you, and two, I don't trust you not to run."

Lyra ground her teeth. The man was too intuitive and protective. "How much do I owe you for the room?"

"Nothing."

"I pay my way," she said. "I don't mooch."

"I'm paying, so get over it," he said with an angry expression that caused her to snap her mouth shut. "This mess is my fault, so it's the least I can do."

When Dare opened the casita the door swung open and he flipped on the lights. Lyra wrinkled her nose at the smell of old carpeting and stale cigarettes.

"There's only one bed." She looked from the queen-size bed to Dare. "Where are you sleeping?"

The corner of his mouth quirked into a smile. "You'd make me sleep on the floor?"

"Or in the tub." After all that had happened to them in the last six hours or so, she was surprised she could return his smile.

He reached up and caressed her cheek with his knuckles. "You have the most beautiful smile."

A deep thrill ran through Lyra's belly and she fought the urge to move closer to him, to let him embrace her like he had earlier. Instead she stepped back and he let his fingers slip down her face before he tossed his duffle onto a chair.

Her hands trembled as she turned her back on him and set her pack onto another straight-back chair beside the door. She was alone in a room with a freaking stranger! A stranger who made her feel something more than she should be feeling right now.

With a huff of air that caused her bangs to flutter at her forehead, she unfastened and raised the flap of her canvas backpack and tried to ignore her awareness of the man. It had to be a reaction caused by the day's events.

She jerked a T-shirt out and turned to find Dare with no shirt on, his Stetson, boots, and belt tossed onto the chair with his duffle, and the top button of his Wranglers undone. Her gaze moved up from his waistband to his well-muscled chest. He had a large scar on his right shoulder. She could just imagine how it would feel to run her palms over his smooth, tanned skin as she kissed that scar. She'd move her fingers up higher to his neck and into his dark hair—

Her eyes met Dare's and her heart beat faster. She bit her lower lip and clenched her T-shirt in her hands. He raised his hand and slipped his fingers into his hair, ruffling it in a way that made him look even sexier.

She cleared her throat. "I think you'd better sleep in the bathtub."

S irens screamed.
    Too far away!
    Dare rounded one side of the warehouse while his partner crouched behind the open door on the driver's side of the cruiser.

"Get your ass over here, Lancaster," Franklin said just low enough that only Dare could have heard.

He and Franklin had responded to a simple trespassing call at an old building on the south side of Tucson and had come upon what looked like a serious drug deal. The moment they'd realized what was going down, Franklin called for backup.

They'd managed to keep from being seen and eased away from the doorway to the building. Franklin made it back to the cruiser before Dare.

"Cops!" came a shout from inside the warehouse.

"Shit," Dare said under his breath.

He heard a shot behind him. He swung around into a crouch, his arms straight out, gripping his Glock with both hands.

At the same time he recognized two facts: Franklin was lying facedown in a pool of blood, and a man was swinging his aim from Franklin to Dare.

Without a moment's hesitation, Dare shot the bastard in the heart.

The man dropped.

Dare shouted into his shoulder radio, "Officer down! Officer down!"

Keeping low, he bolted toward Franklin. Adrenaline

pumped through Dare's body and he dived for the cruiser.

Shots whizzed over his head.

Before he reached Franklin, something slammed into Dare's shoulder with enough power to knock him flat on his back.

Excruciating pain tore through him, almost blinding him.

Despite the pain, he held his arm close to his chest and managed to scoot behind the cruiser's door, beside Franklin.

The screeching of tires coming to a halt on the asphalt, the earsplitting wail of sirens, and the shouts of men and women officers told him the cavalry had arrived.

But as he looked down at his partner, the hole in Franklin's head and the man's blank stare told Dare it was too late.

D are opened his eyes to find his body covered in sweat. He brought his right hand up to rub his left shoulder. The pain radiating through his old wound made it feel as if it had happened yesterday rather than seven years ago. His disorientation cleared almost immediately, but the recurring nightmare lingered on.

He'd slept on the floor by the bathroom in the bungalow he shared with Lyra. A cramp spasmed in his lower back and his head felt like it was going to split. Lyra had given him the bedspread and three of the four pillows, and he'd found another blanket in the closet. That had done nothing to make the floor in the least bit comfortable. Not that he'd expected them to.

Still in his jeans, he rose. He tilted his head from side to side and the bones made a light popping sound as the movement relieved the crick in his neck. He ran his palm over his stubbled jaw. He felt like hell.

Dare turned to look at the empty bed. All that was on it was a couple of twenty-dollar bills.

I pay my way, echoed in his head.

Lyra wasn't anywhere in the small room.

Her backpack was gone.

"Fuck!" He nearly slammed his fist against the wall, just bringing his knuckles short of the painted bricks.

Instead, he strode across the room and jerked open the casita door. She hadn't quite closed it—probably to keep him from hearing her leave.

Of course she wasn't outside. Not where he could see her, anyway.

That Goddamn nightmare. It had been so intense he hadn't heard the slightest sound she'd made, which wasn't like him.

In moments he'd pulled on a T-shirt, slipped his belt through the loops, yanked on his boots, slid his Glock into the back of his waistband, and shoved his Stetson on his head. He ignored the cash and stuffed everything else into his duffle, grabbed his SUV keys along with the room key, and stormed out of the room.

Goddamnit. He had promised himself he would protect her. Not let anything happen to her. She was going to get herself killed like Franklin. And Dare couldn't stop it.

Something settled hard and deep in the pit of his gut. He'd failed again.

But he wasn't giving up until he knew for sure he couldn't find her.

After tossing the morning clerk the room key, Dare unlocked his vehicle and climbed in. He fired it up, backed out of the parking lot, put it in first, and stopped at the entrance. Lyra would probably be hitching a ride to Tucson, so he'd start out heading that way. If she wasn't on the road, still trying to hitchhike, he'd never find her.

Just before pulling out of the parking lot, he glanced at the convenience store catty-corner from the motel.

Lyra was climbing into the passenger seat of a beat-up blue compact car. Relief combined with frustration made his head ache even more. He had the brief inclination to charge across the street and block the car's exit, but he didn't know what Lyra's reaction would be, and the last thing he wanted was for someone to call the cops.

Dare narrowed his eyes as he waited for the car to slip into the nonexistent traffic. Instead of taking a right and going toward St. David and Benson, which would lead her toward Tucson, the vehicle made a left, heading in the direction they had come from last night.

Dare clenched the steering wheel.

Was Lyra going back to Bisbee?

He scowled before the thought occurred to him that Lyra might be going to Sierra Vista, backtracking a little before heading to the largest town in the county. She just might have taken the first available ride and was counting on catching a bus or hitchhiking from S.V. to Tucson. No two ways about it, she had to find a ride, maybe even to El Paso or Phoenix.

Dare guided his SUV onto the small highway meandering through Tombstone, keeping back far enough that he hoped he wouldn't be noticed but could still keep the car in sight. He had already memorized the car's license plate number.

Not much later, the car turned at the exit that would take them to Sierra Vista. There was no way Dare was going to lose them now.

It crossed his mind that Lyra could no doubt take care of herself and would make it cross-country without his help, while running from the cult.

But that gut feeling he'd had since meeting her wouldn't let go. On so many levels he felt the need to help this woman and keep her safe. Hell, he barely knew her. But he wanted to protect her while finding some way to get the bastards off her back—for good.

L yra leaned her head back against the headrest of the passenger seat. "I can't thank you enough for giving me a ride."

The brunette shrugged a shoulder. "No problem. You don't look like a killer, and I can always use the company." She had large brown eyes and enough freckles on her face and arms for six people.

Lyra hoped she could trust this woman, too. She sighed at the word "trust" again and clenched the straps of her backpack. "It's just as hard to hitch a ride with a total stranger, too. In the past, I've caught rides with women. I especially don't trust men."

"Don't you have that right." The brunette tossed her a smile. "What's your name?"

"Janet," Lyra said without hesitation. She'd used that name when she'd hitchhiked fifteen hundred miles to Tucson from Sandy, Oregon. Once in Tucson she'd lived on the streets until she saved up enough money from selling her artwork to hitch rides to one of the smallest towns she could find to hide in, a place that was also an artists' community where she could sell her metalwork and live off the income.

"I'm Doris." The forty-something woman kept glancing from the road back to Lyra. "Why are you hitchhiking?"

It was Lyra's turn to shrug. "Time to move on."

"Where are you headed?"

Lyra paused. "San Francisco."

Doris seemed fine with Lyra's brief responses. The woman turned out to be pretty chatty, which was a relief to Lyra. She wasn't in the mood to talk. While Doris rattled on about every man she'd dated in the past year, Lyra's thoughts kept returning to Dare. She couldn't get her mind off the man—and it wasn't just that he'd saved her from The People. No, if she was being honest with herself, she'd felt a deep, dangerous attraction to the man. His dark hair and brown eyes, the fluid way he moved, the finely muscled chest she'd seen last night. And his scent and the memory of how it had felt to be in his arms when he'd comforted her.

Get with the program, Lyra! It was just one of those rescuee-falls-for-rescuer kinda things.

Lyra sat up straighter in her seat. It was still early and she hadn't had a chance to contact her friends to help Mrs. Y or to make sure the elderly woman was okay.

"Where do you want me to drop you off?" Doris said, breaking into Lyra's thoughts.

To her surprise, they were already rolling through

the eastern part of Sierra Vista. "Wal-Mart." Lyra gestured to the store on their left.

"Wal-Mart it is." Doris drove to the large chain store and pulled up in front of the entrance.

"Let me pay you for my share of the gas," Lyra said as she started to open the flap of her backpack. "It's so expensive now."

"*No*," Doris said with enough emphasis to startle Lyra into looking at the woman. "I was coming here anyway and you were great company."

"Thank you." Lyra returned the woman's smile as she pulled on the door handle and pushed the car's door open. "You don't know how much I appreciate the ride."

"Not a problem."

Lyra climbed out and shut the car door before taking a few steps back. She slipped her arms through the handles of her backpack and hitched it up, waved goodbye, and headed straight into the store.

It had been the kindness of strangers that had helped her get away from The People to begin with. Even then she'd been through some pretty rough times, but she'd had some help. Only this time, the cash she had in her pack was enough to help her start a new life somewhere else. She'd have to live on ramen, macaroni and cheese, and water, but she could afford to rent an apartment until she started selling her artwork again, as long as she didn't go anyplace too expensive.

That ruled out New York City.

Inside the store, she grabbed a shopping basket and first thing headed for the aisle with the hair dye. She'd

have to find everything to make her look like the fake
ID she'd paid a lot for just in case she had to go on the
run again. She'd need it to buy a ticket to board the bus.

Lyra rushed through the store, grabbing what she
needed. It didn't take her long to choose a nice shade of
red temporary hair dye and a few makeup products—
she'd never been one for makeup, so that was something that had really made her look different on her
ID. She found big sunglasses, a yellow tank top, and a
matching pair of shorts.

She practically ran to the back of the store and
picked out a pair of jogging shoes so her old ones
wouldn't be recognized. She even remembered to snag
a pair of scissors and some bubblegum. At the last
minute she ran to the food section of the superstore and
picked up a Danish for breakfast.

Groaning with disappointment, she realized she was
going to have to give up her backpack. She sighed.
She'd had the thing since her days on the streets—it
was one of her first real possessions. And it was just
perfect for all of her art tools, her cell phone, and
everything else she kept.

Lyra pushed her cart to the section where the store
displayed several rows of backpacks. A pink Barbie
pack made her laugh as she thought about carrying that
around. Yeah, no one would guess it was her, but she
didn't think she could live with a picture of a doll on a
bright pink pack.

Eventually she settled on a sturdy yellow backpack
that went with her new look. Why not? It would func-
tion well for what she needed.

As she paid for the items, her hands trembled, even

though she doubted any of the cult members would be in the store at that moment. When she finished the transaction, she took her purchases into the ladies' restroom, brushing by one shopper and entering the largest stall. Within a few minutes she'd changed into the yellow tank top and shorts and changed her shoes. Her new backpack bulged by the time she had transferred all of her clothes into it along with her other possessions. She'd have to get rid of the shoes—she just didn't have room for those to fit. She stuffed her wad of cash and fake ID into a pocket of the pack and made sure she zipped it.

After she peed, she came out of the stall. Thankfully, the restroom was empty. She threw away her old shoes and with a sad sigh tossed away her old pack, too.

She placed her new pack and purchases on the floor and snatched the scissors out of the bag of purchases. Lyra grimaced as she carefully hacked off a good six inches of her hair so that she now sported a bob instead of having it a little over shoulder-length. Just as she tossed the hair into the garbage, a woman with two children came into the restroom and Lyra jumped. The woman was too busy with the toddlers to even notice Lyra.

Still, she chose to work on her makeup first before she would dye her hair. She applied a thick layer of foundation, a heavy dose of blush, and used blue eye shadow, black mascara, and red lipstick. One thing she'd learned was that she was probably least likely to draw the cult's attention by dressing in loud colors and wearing bright makeup, because they'd expect her to be subdued like she'd always been.

When she was finished applying the makeup, the woman came out of the large stall with her children, washed her hands and her children's without looking at Lyra. Finally the woman left with her kids and Lyra skimmed through the directions on the bottle of hair dye.

If she didn't want any stains, she'd need to protect her hands and her neck. She dragged one of her old T-shirts out of her backpack to put around her neck to keep the dye from getting on her tank top. Then she emptied out the two shopping bags, jamming the makeup and scissors into her backpack, but left the sunglasses out on the shelf on the countertop beside the sink.

Lyra wrapped her hands in the now-empty plastic shopping bags, grabbed the bottle of dye, leaned over the sink, and poured the entire contents of the bottle over her hair. With her hands covered by the bags, she managed to work the dye through her hair. Someone came into the bathroom while Lyra was rinsing the excess out, but she didn't look up and prayed it wasn't a store employee.

After she rinsed her hair, Lyra threw away the bags and dye bottle. She rubbed the T-shirt that had been around her neck over her hair to get out most of the water and any remnants of the dye. She wiped up the mess on the countertop, then tossed the T-shirt. An elderly woman came out of a stall and gave Lyra an odd look but just washed her hands and dried them beneath the hand dryer.

Thank goodness there was a dryer. When the lady left, Lyra twisted the metal nozzle so that the air would blow upward instead of down and proceeded to dry her hair the best she could.

Finally finished, she took a deep breath, turned, and looked into the mirror.

As she'd expected, a virtual stranger looked back at her. Her red hair fell in a smooth, if not a little uneven, cap down to chin-level. Her makeup was bold and her clothing bright. She picked up the pair of sunglasses and slipped them on. Dang, even she wouldn't be able to recognize herself.

One more thing would help alter her appearance. She dug a pair of socks out of her bag and padded each cup of her bra. She smiled when she looked at her reflection again. Now those were a pair of breasts. She unwrapped a piece of bubblegum, popped it in her mouth, and started chewing. *Ewwww.* Talk about too much sugar, and the watermelon flavor—ick. But she continued to chew it with her mouth open until the sugar dissolved and she was able to blow bubbles.

She dropped the rest of the gum into her backpack and slung the pack over her shoulder. Jeez, she hoped no one would think she was stealing anything. At least she had the receipt to prove she'd purchased everything in the backpack and what she was wearing.

Lyra straightened her posture, took a deep breath, smacked her bubblegum, and walked out of the bathroom, her chin tilted up. Like she'd expected, no one paid attention to her—the place was too busy with people coming and going. The loud chatter of voices rang in her ears.

When she stepped outside the automatic doors, sunshine warmed her face and she smiled. A new look brought on a feeling of self-confidence she hadn't had before. From behind her sunglasses she scanned the

crowd, looking for a likely candidate to give her a ride
to the bus stop.

From the corner of her eye she spotted a black SUV,
and her heart stuttered. If she didn't know better, she'd
think it was Dare's vehicle.

It *was*!

Damn it!

How had he found her? He must have followed her
from Tombstone.

Lyra didn't look his way, just blew another huge
pink bubble and let it pop over her mouth and the tip of
her nose. When she spotted an elderly woman Lyra
sucked the bubble back in, forced a smile, and strode
into the parking lot with as much confidence as she
could. The entire time she walked toward the woman,
Lyra felt prickles up and down her spine as if Dare
were looking right at her.

She reached the woman and clenched her new backpack tighter in one arm. She gave the woman a little
wave with her free hand and made her smile brighter.
"By any chance could I get a ride to the bus stop? If it's
not out of your way?"

The woman studied Lyra for a moment with keen
blue eyes. "All right," the woman finally said. "Just as
soon as I get my bags in the trunk."

"Thanks." Lyra kept her smile cheerful, but her
body vibrated with tension as she chatted and helped
the woman load her purchases into the back of the
green sedan. When they were ready to take off, Lyra
climbed into the passenger seat clutching her backpack. Not once had she looked Dare's way.

Why was he following her, anyway? He couldn't help her. He was a stranger, and she really had no clue why he seemed to want to protect her. She could take care of herself.

And if she could get out of this parking lot without the cowboy PI recognizing her, that would just prove herself even more.

Dare glanced at his watch, then back to the entrance of the store. He'd seen Lyra go in a good twenty minutes earlier. What was taking her so long? He hadn't followed her in, afraid he'd lose her in the big store and she'd be out of there before he had a chance to track her down.

Instead he watched the entrance, waiting for her to reappear. Countless people walked in and out of the store, and his practiced eye swept over each and every one of them. Once he saw a blond woman with a similar build and height as Lyra, but then he got a good look at her and shook his head.

Dare watched mothers with toddlers in tow, boys with pants so big and long the hems were ragged, and teenage girls with skirts that were way too short.

He'd sure never let *his* teenage daughters dress like that if he had any. If he ever found a woman to settle down with. For some reason his thoughts turned to Lyra and he imagined she'd make a great mother and wife. He shook his head. Where did that thought come from?

Another mother holding the hands of small children, one on either side of her, walked out of the store.

The mother was followed by a redhead wearing bright yellow clothing and large sunglasses. The woman had generous breasts and long legs and blew big bubbles with her chewing gum. She paused before continuing after the mother of the toddlers.

Next a young woman with *huge* boobs and a tiny waist came out arm-in-arm with an older man who had silver-gray hair and a crisp shirt and slacks. She paused to kiss him on the lips, laughed like a schoolgirl, and they continued walking across the lot. Looked like someone had a sugar daddy.

For some reason Dare's attention was drawn to the redhead, who had stopped to help an elderly woman load her trunk with her purchases. The redhead had a bright yellow backpack slung over her shoulder. He glanced at the front doors of the store before looking back at the redhead. He caught sight of her smile as she talked with the woman.

In that instant he knew it was Lyra. No one had a smile as beautiful as hers.

Dare shook his head and couldn't help a grin of his own. *Clever girl.* He had come so close to not recognizing her. Hell, she'd even made her boobs look bigger.

The green sedan pulled out of its parking space. Dare waited until the car was almost out of sight before bringing his SUV around to follow it. If Lyra had spotted him, she'd be on the watch for him if he came too close.

Regardless if he couldn't keep up, he was pretty sure where she was headed now that she'd changed her appearance.

* * *

After sucking in a deep breath, Lyra tried to relax. She glanced at the side-view mirror and smiled when she saw Dare's SUV still parked near the entrance of the store. Ha! She'd fooled even the PI.

Feeling a little lighter at heart—yet at the same time somehow disappointed—Lyra did her best to be talkative. The woman seemed a little tense at first but gradually warmed to Lyra on the short ride to the bus stop. This time Lyra didn't ask if she could help pay for gas. After she climbed out of the car, before she closed the sedan's door, she dug in her pack and found a five-dollar bill.

She tossed it on the car seat and said, "Thank you."

The woman protested, but Lyra closed the door, smiled, and waved before striding around the corner of the building. She opened a glass door and walked into the small bus station.

Lyra hugged the backpack to her chest using one arm as she stood in the short line to get her bus ticket. With her free hand she opened one of the zippered pockets just enough to dig out more cash for the ticket and to grab her ID before zipping the pocket back up again. Trying to relax was futile as she stood in line waiting for her turn. She casually looked around the lobby of the bus station. No sight of any of The People. She kept her sunglasses on in case.

Still she felt like something was crawling up her spine.

When she purchased her ticket to Phoenix, the clerk only casually looked from Lyra's ID to her face before taking her cash and handing her the ticket.

She left the air-conditioned chill of the bus station lobby to enter the July sunshine and sat on a sun-warmed bench to wait for the bus. The green bench smelled like it had been newly painted. Between that and the exhaust from passing cars, she got a headache.

Okay, while she waited she could eat her Danish and have time to make the calls she had needed to make since last night. She slipped her hand into her pack, felt around, and grabbed the plastic-wrapped apple Danish. After setting her pack on the bench beside her, she opened the package to eat her breakfast. She managed to keep her fingers from getting sticky and got up to toss the wrapper into a nearby garbage can.

A droplet of sweat rolled down her neck and between her breasts from the heat, and her hair started to stick to her moist forehead. Sierra Vista was a few degrees warmer than Bisbee.

She gave a wry smile. *But it's a dry heat.*

Lyra plopped back onto the bench and reached into her backpack for her cell phone to make her calls to Becca and her other friends. Her grip on her pack slipped. All of her art tools and the small treasured tin she'd made from her artwork tumbled out and onto the concrete.

"Crap!" The friggin' Velcro hadn't held on one of the side pockets. Lyra scooted off the bench, bent down to pick up the tin and the few tools she used for her metalwork, and stuffed them back into the pack—this time inside.

She stood and had started to sling her pack over her shoulder when a large hand caught her by her upper arm.

Lyra went rigid as she was jerked against a hard, wiry body.

A sick feeling dropped to her belly as Mark said close to her ear, "It's about fucking time, Lyra."

CHAPTER SIX

L *et. Me. Go."* Lyra punctuated every word while trying to keep her tone controlled. "I'll scream so loud everyone on the block will hear me."

Mark pressed something hard and small against her lower back. Her heart slammed against her breastbone. Chills scrabbled up and down her spine, more intense this time than when she thought she was being watched earlier.

"I've had men waiting at every bus stop in the county," he continued. "Wouldn't have recognized you if you hadn't dropped that tin out of your backpack." He moved his hand from her arm to slip into her short hair, and his breath warmed her ear as he moved his lips closer. Her skin crawled. "Wonder what Neal will think of your new look. I'm pretty sure he won't be too happy, and you'll probably get your ass whipped for it."

Heat bubbled up inside her and she started to shake. Not only did fear course through her body, but she felt hot, raging fury at the man behind her, along with anger at her own stupidity.

"Come on." Adam moved into her line of vision and she saw that he was pretty banged up. Probably from the fight with Dare. Adam's gaze darted from side to side. "We've gotta get her out of here."

She didn't want to die, but would that be preferable to returning to Neal?

No. She'd get away from them. She'd change her appearance again. Shave her head even. One way or another, she'd escape and stay out of their reach.

Mark moved his arm down to her shoulder and kept his body close and what she assumed was a gun between them.

Heart pounding and mind racing, Lyra clenched the handle of her pack and walked with rigid steps around the corner of the building. The moment they moved into the deserted parking lot and stood beside the van, Lyra kicked her heel against Mark's shin as hard as she could. She caught him by surprise and whirled away from his grip.

She went stone cold and absolutely still when she saw Mark pointing a gun at her, his bruised face purple with anger.

"I don't care if you live or die," he said, his voice trembling.

Confusion flowed through Lyra and she blinked. Wasn't he one of the stupid believers? He was one of the very few who knew about the Prophecy—at least that had been the case when she lived in the Temple. Why would he want to kill her now?

"Mark . . . ," came Adam's concerned tone. "Just get her into the van."

"Adam, this Prophecy crap is crazy. You know it." Lyra backed up against the van door, her eyes on the gun. "Tell Mark to let me go."

A black blur whirled in front of her as a man rammed his booted foot against Mark's gun hand.

The gun went flying, landed on the asphalt, and skittered across its surface.

Relief shot through her. *Dare!*

Fury rode Dare like a mustang fighting for his territory. Dare plowed his fist into Mark's jaw. The man's head snapped to the side. Dare swung his leg out and swept Mark's legs out from beneath him so that the bastard fell hard onto the asphalt.

Goddamnit. If Dare hadn't been caught in a clog in traffic caused by an accident on his way here, he would have had Lyra before any of this happened.

The other man, called Adam, jumped onto Dare's back. In a quick movement, Dare flipped Adam over his shoulder. The man landed on his back with a grunt of pain.

At the same time, Lyra had dropped her pack and bolted across the asphalt for Mark's gun.

Mark scrambled to his feet and dived for Lyra.

She cried out as he caught her by the ankles and brought her down hard on her belly and chest. Her sunglasses went flying and she spit out her bubblegum.

Lyra stretched her fingers just far enough that she grasped the butt of the handgun. Mark grabbed her by her waist, drawing her closer to him.

She twisted in Mark's grip, flipped over, and pointed the barrel at Mark's head.

"I really don't give a crap what happens to you," she said in a harsh voice. "It's obvious this is self-defense, and I have a witness to prove it." Her arms didn't even tremble as she held the gun with both hands. "A local PI is going to have a lot more clout than a dirty sonofabitch like you." She gave him a cold smile. "Not to mention I'm beneath you, so the angle of the shot will prove that I'm defending myself. Don't think for a moment I won't."

That's my girl, Dare thought as he drew out his own gun and aimed it at Adam.

Mark gave Lyra a furious, vicious look as blood dripped from one corner of his mouth. He smeared the blood across his cheek with the sleeve of his shirt. "The cowboy may have saved your ass again, bitch, but next time—we've got something special planned for you."

Lyra couldn't help the cold encasing her heart at his words. By the look on his face as he pushed himself to his feet, she knew he meant every word. No, this wasn't the end. This was just a delay.

Dare appeared at Mark's side, and before she knew it, he slammed his fist into Mark's jaw.

Mark staggered sideways and shook his head. More blood spilled from his mouth, and his teeth were coated in red as he regained his balance and growled. His braid was partially undone, and a chunk of loose hair crossed his face.

"Out of here." Adam grabbed Mark by the sleeve and gestured to the street. "Car."

From the corner of her eye, Lyra saw an old station wagon pulling into the parking lot.

Mark didn't take his gaze off Lyra as Adam guided him into the passenger seat of the van.

Lyra ran to a nearby dumpster and flung Mark's gun into it, so the people in the car wouldn't see it. She saw Dare putting away his gun.

The next thing she knew, Dare had her by the elbow, her pack in his free hand. He practically marched her to his black SUV and lifted her into the passenger seat before she had a chance to climb in by herself. He threw her backpack at her feet, then slammed the door.

Sweat plastered her hair against the side of her face and she felt like her makeup was melting. Her breathing came hard and fast as she collapsed against the seat. The gun dug into her lower back.

Mark and Adam drove their van out of the lot, then her gaze landed on the couple exiting the station wagon. The man and woman gave her and Dare curious looks. Lyra glanced away.

Dare slid into the driver's seat of the SUV. His grim expression and the fire in his eyes told her he was pissed. Beyond pissed.

Damn. She'd been so sure she could take care of herself, and here she was, relying on this stranger again.

He didn't start the vehicle. Instead he gave her a long, hard look. His eyes darkened and his lips tightened into a thin line.

Before she knew what was happening, Dare grabbed her by cupping the back of her head and pulled her roughly to him. The console pressed against her belly.

Lyra gasped as he smashed his lips against hers and gave her a hard, fierce kiss. His tongue plunged into her mouth and he kissed her like he was conquering her, then owned her. She pressed her palms against his chest and tried to push away, but he clenched his hand in her hair and drew her tightly to him. She gripped his T-shirt in her fists.

And then she began to give in. And to give back as good as he was giving.

She was drowning.

He smelled so good. Tasted so good. Of battle, fire, and passion.

Slowly the kiss became less angry and more sensuous. Lyra's breasts ached and her nipples hardened. When Dare reached into her T-shirt and pulled out one sock and then the other, she shivered at the contact of his hand against her flesh. After he tossed aside the second sock, he slipped his hand into her bra and rubbed one of her nipples with his thumb.

Lyra moaned against his mouth. Her head was practically spinning as she moved her hands from his chest, up his neck, and into his hair that was damp with sweat. Her sex throbbed like mad, and electric sensations zinged through her belly.

He moved his hand and thumbed her other nipple and she thought she'd lose it. The tingling between her thighs increased so much she felt like she'd explode. She'd given herself orgasms before, using her fingers, but she knew it would be so much better—out of this world—to experience a climax with Dare.

Suddenly he jerked away from the kiss and she wanted to draw him back to her. His eyes still had an angry spark to them, but it only made her want him more.

"Don't ever leave like that again," he growled. "You need protection, and I'm damn well going to be the one to give it to you."

"If you kiss me like this every time I take off," she said, trying to catch her breath, "I might just do it again. And again."

His features relaxed and he eased his hold on her hair while slipping his other out from her tank top. He cupped her face in both hands and gave her a soft kiss that sent more electric thrills to her belly. She'd never wanted someone so badly as she wanted Dare at that moment.

The mere thought shocked her to her core.

She'd never wanted any man until him. She'd never trusted a man enough to let him get close to her. Trusting a man enough to have sex with him—never.

The wild sensations coursing through her body right now were telling her differently.

She let her hands slide down from his hair to his chest, and his skin burned her fingers through the T-shirt. She snatched them away and clasped both of her hands in her lap. The look he gave her told her he more than wanted her, too.

He glanced from her long enough to dig the keys out of his pocket, jam them into the ignition, and start the SUV. He gave her a long look that caused butterflies to zip through her belly before he turned his attention to driving out of the parking lot and into traffic.

"They're likely to look for a vehicle like this one at all the hotels," he said. She thought his voice shook a little, and his knuckles were white as he clenched the steering wheel. She was surprised at the pleasure she felt when she realized it was because he wanted her. "We'll ditch this one for something different."

Dare's heart pounded, and he tried to take his mind

off of what had just happened between them. He
wanted her with such intensity it blew his mind. But after what she'd been through—she had to be ready.
She'd have to want him as much as he wanted her.

After driving up and down various streets to be sure
they weren't being followed, Dare headed to a car dealership off the main drag. He cut to the chase as soon as
he walked into the showroom. He told the floor manager exactly what he wanted and how much he was going to pay. The manager didn't argue or try to haggle
when he saw how serious Dare was and that he didn't
have time to mess around. The transaction for the
black, low-slung sports car with dark tinted windows
was finished within an hour and a half. Part of the deal
was that the dealership would keep Dare's SUV in the
back after detailing it.

The powerful engine of the sports car roared as
Dare shot through traffic, just barely keeping the vehicle ten miles over the speed limit. He continuously
kept his eye out for anyone who might be following
him, but his and Lyra's luck held.

It was a nice hotel with a restaurant and room ser-
vice, and Dare could use a good meal right about now.
This hotel, a far cry from the casita they'd rented in
Tombstone, was luxurious in comparison.

Lyra had handed him the cash for the night's stay
when they were in the car. He didn't argue with her
take-charge attitude. The woman didn't look like she
was one to be messed with right now.

After Dare checked in, he went out to the car and
grabbed his bag and Lyra's backpack out of the trunk.
She walked beside him into the hotel without talking.

When they reached the room, they slammed the door shut, tossed their bags on the floor, and just looked at each other. They stood just inches apart, and Lyra's heart pounded.

He took the step that brought them together and he cupped her face in his hands. She caught her breath as he brought his mouth to hers.

Since she'd left the cult she hadn't let a man touch her in any way . . . until Dare.

This time he brushed his lips back and forth over hers and she trembled. When the pressure increased he remained gentle, almost tentative. His tongue entered her mouth and she tasted him. Such a masculine flavor. She followed him, letting him teach her how to kiss. How to really kiss. Those few teenage fumbling attempts before the Temple of Light were nothing compared to having a man like Dare kiss her.

The contact in the SUV had been so filled with fire and emotion from the fight with Mark and Adam. The kiss she and Dare had shared had been a release of all the intensity of what they'd experienced. His way of telling her he was in charge now, that he was going to take care of her.

She had responded with matching need. Primal need that had taken over all her senses.

And now she wanted that fire, wanted whatever he could give her. Dare drew away and she licked the moisture from her lips as she looked up at him and he smiled down at her. So sexy, so sensual.

He reached up to tuck her short hair behind her ear and his smile slipped away as he said, "We have some talking to do."

Lyra rubbed her hands up and down her upper arms, warding off a sudden chill that took away the warmth of his kiss. She moved out of his embrace and toward the window.

"Uh, honey." Dare walked up behind her, took her by the shoulders, and backed her away from the window. "Can't take any chances. You could be seen." He turned her to face him. "How did you end up in the Temple of Light?"

She drew away from his grip. For a long moment she just looked at him. He waited with an expression that told her he wasn't going anywhere and that she wasn't, either, without them having this conversation.

Finally, she said, "My dad died just before I turned fifteen." The memories played over in her mind like they always did when she thought about her father's death. "Momma was lost without him. She'd always been kind of spacey and not all together. Momma was definitely not self-reliant. She was also easily swayed and into New Agey kinds of things."

Lyra turned her back on Dare and closed her eyes for a moment. She felt only the cool air of the hotel room against her skin and the soft hum of the air conditioner. "Momma's father died when she was eleven. Stepping back and looking at it from the outside, from what I saw growing up, I think my dad replaced what she had lost and she clung to that need for a father figure."

When Lyra opened her eyes, she swallowed down the rising panic that always came from thinking of The People. "My mother and I met Neal before Daddy's death, at some kind of program she dragged me to in

Portland. Where we lived . . . before. I can't remember the sermon clearly," she continued, "but he talked about the 'Light' and how we could all work together in harmony and serve the Light. How we would be the blessed children and leave behind all that was evil in this world. Some bull like that."

Everything around her blurred as the memories came harsher and faster. "Not long after Daddy died, the next thing I knew Neal was taking my mom and me for a ride. I had no idea that it was an actual cult until we got there. Once they had us in the commune, there was no way out."

She felt the heat of Dare's gaze on her back, but she didn't want to look at him while she talked about it. "Armed guards along the inside and outside the fence," she continued. "No one got in that Neal didn't allow, and no one got out except for the men who were his leaders of the Light. Like Mark and Adam."

Her mind turned to the reason why she and her mother had ended up in the commune. "I think Momma was so dependent on others that she grabbed onto what Neal offered her. He was a strong figure, a male she wouldn't be intimately involved with, and he represented what Momma thought she needed. At least that's what I've come to believe as I've grown older."

Lyra flinched at the memory of the three years after they were taken into the cult. "Of course Momma was totally brainwashed and lost touch with reality." Lyra clenched her fists and gritted her teeth. "I *hated* it. I hated Neal. I hated my mother for taking me there. When I figured out there was no way to escape, I pretended to go along with his crap."

"How did you get out?" Dare's voice came from behind her, low and soothing, and bringing her slowly back to the present.

"I was desperate to get out of there before Neal—" She swallowed, nearly choking at the thought. "I got really lucky. Neal was off with one of his wives and I followed Jeffrey to where the cult kept their vehicles.

"I'd overheard earlier that he was going into Portland for supplies." She began pacing the room as she continued, rubbing her hands up and down her arms. "It was dark and I'd grabbed a black tapestry out of the Prayer Room and wrapped it around myself, inside out. I snuck into the back of Jeffrey's truck. I hid myself behind some crates and made sure every inch of me was covered.

"When he parked, it was in a dark alley and there were some men on the driver's side. They talked about making an exchange, money from the cult for drugs—LSD, crack, marijuana." Tremors ran through her body at the memory. "When I realized I was in the middle of a drug deal, I was so scared I'd get caught. But I was on the opposite side of the truck bed, and while they made their deal, I dropped the tapestry and slipped out of the truck. As soon as I was far enough away, I ran. All I had was the twenty bucks I found on Neal's dresser," she said, "and the freaking robe he forced me to wear.

"The only thing I've always felt guilty about," she said as she paced, "was leaving my mother behind, even though I hated her for what she put me through. But I knew she would be fine. I wouldn't have been fine once Neal got his hands on me."

"What did you do next?" Dare's tone was quiet, concerned.

"I stole some clothes and hitchhiked to Tucson, which seemed far enough away without having to worry about cold and snow. I lived on the street, in homeless shelters, always moving, and working odd jobs." The memories of those days were a mixture of pain from what she went through to survive and a feeling of freedom from having escaped the Temple. "I worked my way up from being homeless to making out all right. I was lucky, too, that after a while a nice woman helped me get into a women's shelter so I didn't have to live on the streets or in homeless shelters anymore. I kept creating my artwork and saved every penny I could to start a new life."

"You're amazing." Dare's hands gripped her shoulders from behind, stopping her in midstep. He began massaging her neck with deep, even pressure of his thumbs. "How old were you?"

"Eighteen when I left The People," she said, still tense beneath Dare's skilled fingers. "Five years ago."

She pulled away from his massage as she turned to face him and tilted her head back to look into his eyes. "Your turn."

Dare slid his hands down to hold hers. "What do you want to know?"

"First of all," she said, keeping her voice dead serious. "How did you get a name like Dare?"

The corner of his mouth quirked and she knew he hadn't been expecting that question. "My first name's Jake. Dad started calling me Dare when I was a kid. I was something of a show-off, especially in front of girls." He rubbed his thumbs over her knuckles. "I never refused a dare. Like to have gotten myself killed a time or two."

A smile crept across Lyra's face. "I can picture you pulling all kinds of stunts."

"Jumping barrels with my bike, fences with my horse, driving my car a hundred miles an hour, playing high school football like the devil was after me—stuff like that." He shook his head. "Broke my leg once, my foot another time, and my right arm twice. Ended up with a lot of scars. It's a wonder I'm still alive, all the crap I pulled."

Lyra withdrew from his grasp. She moved to the bed, perched on the edge of it, and braced her hands to either side of her hips. "There's something I'm very curious about. How did you find me?"

Dare sucked air through his teeth and paused a moment before replying. "The man who came to my office had a piece of your artwork. I happen to have a friend who has some similar work, so I checked with him to see where he bought it."

Lyra stared at him head-on. "Everyone knows me as Linda in Bisbee. So how did Suzette know to send you to me?"

"A wild hare," he said. "Didn't think it would hurt to check to see if you were one and the same."

She raised her chin. "Bet you didn't expect to get a faceful of pepper spray."

He found it hard to hold back a smile. "Sure as hell didn't."

Lyra closed her eyes and tilted her face to the ceiling. So much pain filled her beautiful face that Dare wanted to take her in his arms and caress away the hurt. To protect her from ever being hurt again.

He moved to the chair beside the desk and sat, not five feet from her. He leaned forward and propped his forearms on his thighs as he spoke. "Tell me why they want you so bad."

"It's stupid." Lyra opened her eyes and stared toward the window. "And embarrassing."

"You can tell me." He tried to relax, but the tension in his body wouldn't let him. He knew this wasn't going to be good.

Lyra shook her head, her expression miserable. "I can't," she whispered.

"I need to know, honey," he said softly. "I can't help you if I don't know what you're dealing with."

A deep, shuddering breath wracked her body, and she looked down at her hands. "When I lived with The People, Neal, the Temple's Prophet, said Jericho—the First Prophet—visited him in a vision." She turned her gaze to Dare. "Jericho told Neal that he would take a wife who would bear his son, the next Messiah. And Jericho told him that I was the one who would carry that child."

Her words slammed into Dare with the force of a two-by-four. "Shit."

"Isn't that the truth." She fisted her hands, her expression furious. "When I was eighteen he planned a joining ceremony where I would become his new First Wife. He has a whole bunch of wives, but I was supposedly the *Chosen*." Tears glistened in her eyes, and she clenched her hands so tightly her knuckles were bone white. "That's when I ran away." She sniffled. "In one way I was lucky, because the Prophecy said I had to be eighteen before Neal had sex with me. Most girls in the cult are married off to men when they're fifteen—or else they're pretty much raped."

Fury pumped through him and Dare barely resisted slamming his fist into a wall after hearing what the bastard had put Lyra through—was still putting her through. Not to mention all the other girls and women in the cult. He pushed from his chair by the desk, strode to Lyra, and settled on the bed beside her. He pulled her against his chest, drawing her tight within his embrace.

Lyra wrapped her arms around his waist and clung to him for comfort. Comfort she'd never had and needed more than she ever realized.

Hot, painful, humiliating memories flooded Lyra's mind, memories that she wanted to shove out and never think of again. But she couldn't quite force out the images that had haunted her for years.

"There's more, isn't there?" Dare stated.

She pressed her cheek against his shirt and nodded. "I don't want to talk about it. The memories hurt too much."

"Honey, I need to know." He brushed her hair and gripped her tight to him. "And I think it's something you need to get off your chest."

Lyra couldn't look at him and kept herself pressed up against him. He held her tight and continued to stroke her hair, and she almost felt like everything would be okay.

The words slipped out before she could take them

back. "He used to make me—he used to make me watch."

Dare went completely still. "Watch . . . what?"

"He would bring in one of his wives and make," she swallowed hard, "he'd make me watch him having sex with her."

Dare clenched his hand in her hair and his entire body went so rigid he felt like steel against her. "The fucking bastard made you watch," he repeated, his voice so harsh it would have scared her if she wasn't so sure his anger was directed at Neal and not her.

Lyra held on to Dare tighter, afraid she might fall without the strength of his embrace. "He said it was to train me in how I should act when I was his new First Wife." Tears fell easily now, and her cheeks were completely wet. "Sometimes he would flog them as punishment for one reason or another. Sometimes he would flog me," she added in a whisper.

"And." She whispered her next words. "And he made me take him in my mouth."

She turned so that she was face-first against Dare's chest. "I've never been able to get those memories out of my mind."

"Goddamn sonofabitch." Dare gripped her so tight she almost felt as if she would break.

Dare moved to the bed and sat on it, drawing her onto his lap and holding her like he'd never let her go. For a long time he held her as she cried.

Hiccups wracked her body as her tears started to lessen. "I'm afraid, Dare. I'm so afraid."

Anger raged through Dare with the force of a wildfire burning an entire forest. What the sonofabitch had done to Lyra—Dare was beyond furious. So furious he didn't know what to say at that moment.

Tears had soaked through Dare's shirt, warming his chest as she cried. "I'm so tired of running," she continued. "I just want a normal life. I don't even know what that is." She tilted her tearstained face to look at him. "I won't be caged again. I won't be forced to have that man's child."

Heat magnified throughout Dare's entire body at the thought of what the cult leader had forced her to do when she was a teenager. No way was Dare letting the assholes get their hands on her. He wasn't letting her out of his sight.

Lyra continued to cry quietly against his chest. "I'm so tired. I don't want to run anymore. I don't want to run."

Dare gently stroked her hair, trying not to tremble with the force of his anger, letting her get it all out. "I won't let the sonsofbitches get their hands on you. I promise."

She pushed away from Dare and wiped tears from her eyes with the sleeves of her shirt. "Damn it." She gave another sniffle and pushed her hair out of her face. "I hate crying."

Dare took her chin in his hand and forced her to look at him. "You've been through a lot. Don't get all over yourself for the way you're feeling right now."

Lyra's lips trembled like she was trying to smile. "Who'd have thought you'd be such a sweet man?"

Dare grimaced. "Promise you won't tell Nick."

Lyra laughed and brushed tears from her eyes with the backs of her hands. "He's your partner, right?"

"Yeah." Dare frowned as his mind churned through their options. "I've got to find some place to hole up until we figure this thing out."

"I don't want to be an inconvenience." Her eyelashes felt wet against her cheeks when she blinked. "I just need to get away from here. Far away. I could go across the country. Boston maybe, or Daytona Beach. Anywhere that would put as much distance as possible between me and them."

Dare shook his head. "There's got to be a way to get them off your back for good."

Lyra gave a long drawn-out sigh. "Fat chance. You've only gotten a taste of them. Neal Barker will never stop hunting me." She wiped her eyes again. "I can't even get a driver's license. Or a credit card, because I know they can track me down that way. I can't live a normal life. Whatever normal is."

Dare drew her onto the bed so that they were lying on the bedspread with their heads on the pillows, her back to his chest. He gripped her around her waist and held her as close as possible, trying to give her every bit of comfort he could.

She sniffed and shivered a few times before she gradually began to relax against him. Eventually her breathing became deep and even, and he knew she had fallen asleep.

Even as she slept he had to fight back rage that continued to burn through him. He stared at the room's window. He saw nothing but his bare hands around the neck of a man's throat, wringing the life out of him.

It was a long time before Dare could relax and let just thoughts of Lyra fill his mind. Everything about her stirred something in him. Her bravery, her rebelliousness, her determination, and her softness.

A primal urge rose within him. He wanted to protect Lyra with everything he had. He wanted to replace bad memories with good. To give her something special. To treat her like the beautiful, extraordinary woman she was. She deserved so much better than what life had dealt her.

One way or another he was going to make sure she never had to run again.

CHAPTER *SEVEN*

W hen Lyra woke, she startled. She was alone in the hotel room bed with a blanket draped over her. The sky outside the window had grown dark, but soft light lit the room.

Tantalizing smells met her nose, and her stomach growled. Roast beef, perhaps, and potatoes?

She rolled over and pushed herself up at the same time she saw Dare sitting in an armchair, studying her. He was reclined with his body stretched out, his booted feet crossed at his ankles, and his hands folded on his belly. He looked absolutely delicious.

"Ready for dinner?" he asked with a gentle smile.

Dried tears made Lyra's face feel tight, and her eyes burned from crying. But for some reason the sight of Dare made everything else vanish and she was able to smile back at him. "Starving," she said as she noticed the valet cart with silver domes, no doubt covering the source of those mouthwatering smells.

Dare got to his feet and extended his hand to her. She let him draw her up so that she could swing her feet over the side of the bed and then stand.

"First I need to wash my face." She released his hand

and instantly missed the warmth, the sense of security, it had given her for just those few moments. She had a hard time breaking the link that seemed to connect them as her eyes locked with his. Finally she managed to get herself to move. She walked away from him, into the bathroom, and closed the door behind her.

When she saw her appearance in the mirror, she groaned. Her mascara and eye makeup were smudged and she felt like a melted wax mannequin. Seeing her newly dyed and shortened red hair was still a shock as she studied her reflection. With a shake of her head, she turned on the cold water and splashed it over her face. The water felt so good and bracing, and she felt a little more like her old self.

After she'd used a washcloth to scrub off all the makeup and had used the toilet, she washed and dried her hands before opening the door and going into the bedroom. Dare had his shoulder hitched up against the doorway, his arms folded across his chest, as he watched her come out of the bathroom. Their gazes met and she took a deep breath.

He looked so yummy she could have eaten him instead of the dinner. The mere thought made her warm inside, and her cheeks flushed with heat.

She broke away from their eye contact and turned to the room's table, where he'd arranged the meal and dinnerware. "You didn't have to wait for me," she said as she moved toward the table and sat in one of the chairs.

She'd been right—roast beef. Baby red potatoes with other vegetables were arranged beside the beef, and a bread roll perched on one side of the plate. Condiments sat in the middle of the table, along with two dessert plates of double chocolate fudge cake and glasses of iced tea.

"How'd you know all of my favorites?" She smiled at him as he took the chair opposite hers.

His sexy grin made her belly flutter as he settled in and picked up his knife and fork.

During dinner they talked about baseball and basketball—turned out they both loved the sports. Dare was a huge Arizona Diamondbacks and Phoenix Suns fan, while Lyra was into the Los Angeles Dodgers and the Seattle Supersonics. She and her father had been rabid fans while she was growing up. For some reason talking about the sports with Dare felt good, and she only felt a little sadness over the loss of her past.

With baseball they argued about the best pitcher in the league and who would take the World Series. With basketball, hands down Michael Jordan was the best player ever and seemed like a heck of a nice guy.

While they ate dessert, they discussed their favorite movies and movie stars. When Dare reminded her of scenes from an older movie, *Analyze This*, he had her giggling over the time the mob boss Paul Vitti said to Dr. Sobel, "Want I should clear your schedule for you?" And it struck her even funnier as she remembered the time Dr. Sobel said, "You don't hear the word 'no' very often, do you?" The mob boss replied, "Yeah, I do, but it's more like, 'Please . . . noo . . . noo.'" She'd watched it at Becca's on DVD not too long ago and hadn't laughed so hard in ages.

Dare's favorite movies were action/adventure, and Lyra preferred futuristic and fantasy. Neither of them was into "chick flicks," but they both enjoyed a good comedy.

By the time they'd polished off the dessert, Lyra was feeling pretty good. Great conversation with a sexy man and double chocolate fudge cake—she was *so* there.

After calling room service, Dare pushed the cart containing all the empty dishes next to the door in the hallway, then shut the door behind him.

When he turned back to Lyra, she suddenly felt awkward and shy.

"It's getting late," he said, not taking his eyes from hers.

Lyra nodded but couldn't talk because her throat had gone dry and she couldn't think of a word to say. Her heart pounded and crazy sensations zipped from her belly to her sex.

By the look in his dark eyes, Dare felt the same tension that now filled the room. It was electrifying.

When he walked toward her, she found herself moving, too, until she met him halfway.

For a long moment she stared up at him. His penetrating gaze made her feel like he was inside her, a part of her.

Dare brought his hands up to her face as he lowered his mouth closer to hers and she felt his warm breath on her lips. She wanted him to kiss her so badly that she couldn't wait. Didn't wait.

She slipped her hands up and around his neck and brought him down at the same time she tipped her head up, closed her eyes, and pressed her lips against his. Dare groaned and opened his mouth, and she slipped her tongue inside. He tasted so good. Of chocolate cake, iced tea, and male. He smelled of sunshine and warmth, a warmth she wanted to wrap around herself and never let go.

When he drew away, she opened her eyes and licked her moist lips, still tasting him on her mouth and tongue. A thrill rolled around in her belly as his erection pressed against her. Her nipples were so hard they ached, and she felt shivery and jittery.

Dare lowered his head again and bit her lower lip. She cried out as he thrust his tongue into her mouth again. His stubble abraded her soft skin, making her feel even more raw inside and out.

Lyra moaned and he answered her by sucking her tongue into his mouth. He moved one of his hands into her hair and clenched a lock of it so hard that the pain of it turned into a sweet kind of pleasure.

While his mouth literally ravaged her, his free hand slid up her thigh, beneath her tank top, and to her breasts. He pinched one of her nipples and she groaned from the desire that grew in intensity from his touch.

"Take off your shoes," Dare murmured against her mouth before he trailed his lips to her jawline.

Lyra didn't hesitate. She toed off each shoe, kicking them across the room.

Dare continued taking a lazy path with his lips down her neck to her cloth-covered nipple. Lyra held on to him as he nipped at her breast through her tank top and she found herself wanting him to hurry. Wanted so much more than just kissing and touching.

For the first time she wished she was wearing some kind of sexy underwear. Lace, satin, silk. Anything but the simple white cotton hip-huggers she wore and the plain white bra.

He hooked his fingers in the sides of her shorts and panties and began to tug down on both as he moved his mouth lower. The thrill in her belly was sending moisture to her panties and she caught the scent of her own musk. Heat burned in her cheeks at the thought that he probably smelled it, too.

She braced her hands on his shoulders as he slowly pulled her shorts down. He paused to nuzzle her light brown curls and she gasped. Just having him touch her there was turning her inside out.

It was all too slow. Something inside her wanted everything faster. Needed him in so many ways she couldn't begin to fathom. It was then she realized how she'd grown to trust him in such a short amount of time. Everything he'd done for her, everything they'd shared, just made her want him more.

When her shorts were at her feet, she paused from embarrassment at being naked in front of him but sucked in her breath and swallowed her shyness. She stepped out of her shorts and he stripped off one sock and then the other. He moved back up her body, kissing his way up the inside of her thigh, flicking his tongue out in the curls on her mound, and up until he was standing again.

Lyra's heart rate was going nuts as he brought his mouth to hers in a powerful kiss. At the same time he slipped his thumb into her folds and stroked her clit. Lyra cried out and broke the kiss as her hips jerked against his hand.

"You're so sweet." Dare moved his mouth to the

hollow of her throat and groaned. "I've got to taste all of you."

Taste her? Before she had a chance to realize what he was doing, he swept her up in his arms, gripping her ass in his big hands. She wrapped her thighs around his waist and held on to his neck as he strode straight for the bed.

He settled her on her back on the bedspread and straddled her legs. The denim of his Wranglers scraped against her thighs, exciting her even more.

Dare's look was dark, intense, focused. He was almost rough as he helped her out of the tank top and her bra, revealing all of her. Lyra's belly quivered and she grew wetter. She fought back another wave of shyness as her nipples puckered, achingly tight, beneath his gaze.

"You're so beautiful." His eyes focused on her chest as he lowered his head and captured one nipple in his mouth.

Without even realizing what she was doing at first, Lyra tilted her head and arched her back, thrusting her breasts higher. Dare groaned and gripped her pale globes in both hands while moving his mouth from one nipple to the other and back. She moaned and trembled beneath him. She slid her hands into his hair and clenched it in her fists as he licked and sucked her breasts.

When he released them and moved his mouth to the hollow of her throat, she almost sobbed.

"Spread your thighs," he murmured as he knelt between her legs.

Heat flushed her cheeks and she parted them a little.

He gripped her thighs and pushed her legs wide as he licked a trail to her navel and down to her mound. All she could do was writhe, small cries emanating from her throat. It was all something she'd never experienced, and she was just short of begging for more.

She found herself holding her breath as he nuzzled her curls and she heard him inhale deeply. "You smell so good," he said, his voice as rough as gravel in a box.

He placed his palms on the insides of her thighs and spread her wider yet. Lyra bit her lip, waiting for his next move.

"I want you, Dare." Heat flushed Lyra's entire body. "Don't make me wait."

Dare chuckled and nuzzled her mound again. "That's my girl."

Parting her folds with his fingers, he ran his tongue along her slit from a sensitive spot between her anus and her folds all the way to her clit.

Lyra cried out and clenched the bedcovers with her hands as she felt his mouth on her. Ohmigod. She'd never expected to feel something so incredibly wonderful as this. The feelings grew even more intense as she watched his head between her thighs.

He licked and sucked her clit while thrusting his fingers in and out of her channel. She couldn't help how wild she went beneath him, the sensations almost too exquisite to bear.

She climbed higher toward climax. She had to come, and she had to come now. But Dare moved away from her clit to drive his tongue into her channel.

"Don't stop." Her voice was so hoarse she could barely hear herself. "Please, don't stop."

A satisfied expression crossed his rugged features before he buried his face against her folds.

Lyra cried out again, this time longer and louder. He was taking her to a peak that she'd never been to before. Never like this. He licked her harder, driving her on. She could feel her climax winding like a spring in her belly and she knew at any moment she was going to lose all control.

Dare sucked her clit, and the world around her burst into a rainbow of colors. Sparks exploded behind her eyes and she screamed loud and long. Her head spun with the power of it and her hips thrashed against Dare's face.

He didn't stop, though. He kept licking and sucking, continued thrusting his fingers in her channel. Shock waves rolled through her body.

Soft whimpers and moans came from her throat in between each spasm of her core. "No more. I can't take any more."

She heard a soft chuckle and then he kissed the inside of her thigh. "I would never have taken you for a screamer."

Would she ever stop blushing? As hot as her face was, she knew she must be bright red.

He eased up so that he was lying beside her and pulled her toward him so they were face-to-face. He hooked one denim-clad thigh over her naked hip and rubbed his erection against her.

Her body still pulsed and throbbed as he traced her lower lip with one finger. "I love the way you screamed when I made you come."

More heat warmed her cheeks. But right now she

had something more on her mind. She couldn't wait to see him naked. Couldn't wait to feel what it would be like to have his cock inside her. From what she felt pressed against her belly, he was big. She wanted to stroke him, feel his length in her palm, to please him like he had pleased her.

She moved her hand to his belt buckle, and her fingers brushed his erection through the denim.

Dare's cock jerked against her touch. He sucked in his breath and caught her hand in his large grasp. "Not tonight."

Lyra looked at him, her eyes wide with surprise. "What do you mean?"

He released her hand and traced his fingers along her jawline to her ear, a sensual movement that made her shiver. "You've just had a hell of a day. You need rest."

"But—"

He silenced her with a hard kiss that caused mini spasms to go off in her core again. She tasted herself upon his tongue, smelled her juices on his lips.

When he pulled away, he wiped the moisture away from her lower lip with his thumb. "When I make love to you, I want you to be sure that's exactly what you want. After the last couple of days you've had, you need time to be sure."

Warmth crept through Lyra, a different kind of warmth that spread through her chest. The kind of warmth that came from being able to trust someone. Someone who might actually care for her needs over his own. "Are you sure?" she whispered.

"No." He groaned and pushed himself up from beside

her. "I'd better get my ass away from you and take a cold shower. My self-control is running on empty."

Lyra watched him as he eased off the bed. He was so sexy, so powerful looking. He studied her naked body beneath the glow of the lamplight and shook his head. "You get some sleep."

"You can sleep on the bed tonight," she said with a little smile. "I won't make you sleep on the floor."

Dare winked and turned away. She watched him stride to the bathroom door. He paused in the open doorway and looked back at her. "Go on now. Get some sleep, beautiful."

Lyra continued to stare at the door long after he closed it. She'd wanted him so bad, and she knew he'd wanted her. But he'd had the strength to step back when she would have charged forward.

He was right. She wasn't thinking clearly now and her life had been turned upside down and inside out.

Lyra groaned. The orgasm made her feel kind of floppy and relaxed. She barely had the energy to go to her backpack and jerk out a T-shirt. After she tugged it on, she climbed beneath the covers. The sheets felt cool against her skin, and Dare's unique scent surrounded her. She tucked a pillow under her head and breathed deep, as if drawing him inside her. She was so relaxed and so tired that in moments she faded off to sleep.

D are gritted his teeth and rubbed the old wound on his shoulder as he stepped into the shower. The day's activities had caused a small flareup of pain, but it wasn't much.

He started to switch the water to cold but instead let the warm water beat against his back. He closed his eyes and fisted his cock, picturing Lyra's lush body. Her breasts were perfect, her nipples large and raspberry red, and he loved her full curves.

It had been all he could do to walk away from her tonight.

He continued stroking his cock, imagining he was thrusting into her beautiful pussy. He pictured himself driving into her hard and fast. He'd loved the little whimpers and moans she'd made while he licked her clit.

A groan rose from his chest as he moved his fist faster, stroking his cock from balls to tip. He could hear the smack of flesh against flesh, the smell of their sex, the cries spilling from her lips.

Dare climaxed with another loud groan. He opened his eyes, braced his free hand against the shower wall, and watched his come spurt on the tile. He eased his hand up and down his cock until the last drop of semen spilled from him.

And even then he wasn't satisfied. He wanted Lyra with a passion that surpassed anything he'd ever felt for another woman. He braced his other hand against the tiled shower wall and let the warm spray flow over him.

At that moment, Dare knew he was in deep shit.

CHAPTER *EIGHT*

N eal clenched one fist at his side as he spoke this time with Mark on his cell phone and was told the news of Lyra's second escape. Neal's bare feet sank into the plush carpeting while he paced the length of his large room.

He called on Jericho and the Light to give him patience.

"We almost missed her at the bus stop because she cut her hair, dyed it red, and piled on the makeup," Mark was saying with an angry edge to his voice. "She dropped a few things out of her backpack and that's how we spotted her."

Neal fought for calm as he held the cell phone between his shoulder and ear and went to his altar and lit a joint. "Lyra changed her appearance?" he said slowly.

"She doesn't look anything like she did before," Mark said.

"Bitch," Neal growled. "I'll teach her a lesson once you get her to Oregon."

"The cowboy got in the way again, at the bus stop." Mark's voice sounded even more furious.

Neal frowned at the hostility in Mark's tone. It wasn't

like him to react this way, especially when it came to discussing Neal's future First Wife.

"You seem to be forgetting your place," Neal said. "You fucked up and lost Lyra. You should be on your knees right now."

Mark quieted on the other end of the line. "I apologize, Prophet."

Neal pressed the phone harder against his ear while bringing the joint to his mouth with his free hand. His fingers trembled with the force of his anger. He sucked in a long drag before releasing the smoke. "Are you sure Lyra and the PI aren't at any of the local hotels?" A slow burn rose in his chest that wasn't caused by the weed. "Absolutely?"

"It's big, but not that large of a town," Mark said, his tone lower and more respectful. "I had all of our available men check every hotel and ask to see if a woman matching her description had checked in. No luck. We searched the hotel parking lots for his SUV. We've got the plate number, too. She has to be hiding someplace else."

Neal let a long silence hang in the air to let Mark know how pissed he was. He took another drag on the joint. "If you don't find her," he said in a slow, measured tone as he released the smoke through his nose and mouth. "You have my promise you'll regret it."

He was certain he heard Mark swallow at the other end of the line. "I know I've disappointed you, the High Prophet Jericho, and the Light." Mark's tone changed so that there was a slight tremor in his voice. "We'll get the mother of the new Messiah."

Now that Neal was easing into a meditative state

with the pot, a thought occurred to him, no doubt the
Light telling him what would aid them in getting to
Lyra. "Find out who her friends and acquaintances are.
Learn what you can and a way to reach her. Get through
to her. When you've done that, call me and I'll give you
more instructions."

A sound of relief came across with Mark's words.
"We'll do it right away. In the name of Jericho and the
Light."

"Succeed and you'll be my second in command,
Mark." Neal had said the same to Adam, but neither
man knew that he'd made promises to both—promises
he didn't intend to keep.

"I'll take care of it," Mark said, this time with a
smack of satisfaction to his voice.

When Neal snapped the cell phone shut he ground
his teeth again but forced himself to calm down and his
muscles to relax. The marijuana was already helping
with that. He snuffed the joint in the bowl he used for
an ashtray and slipped the phone into a pocket of his
robe before striding out of his room, down a long hall,
to the room that contained the best computer and surveillance technology available.

It wouldn't do for The People, other than his most
trusted sheep—the incompetent assholes—to know
there was this kind of sophisticated equipment within
the compound. Part of belonging to the Temple of the
Light was abandoning all material possessions, including any technology. The followers also had no clue
about the surveillance cameras monitoring his compound, not to mention his outside activities that helped
make him a very rich man.

Jericho and the Light, of course, expected Neal to use this technology to protect The People as well as the wealth he continued to amass. He even owned his own private jet, along with a luxurious beach house on Cape Cod that he visited every now and then.

Using his hands, Neal drew back his long hair so that it hung straight down his back as he strode into the room that housed the computers and other instruments they needed. "Have you searched every available source to find new traces of Lyra?" he snapped at Larry, the technological guru who'd been monitoring security of The People for several years.

"She's still a ghost." Larry's double chin and his paunch gave away the fact that he ate more than his share of provisions. While the rest of The People were fed by carefully rationing food, Larry ate whatever he wanted, whenever he wanted. Neal had decided it was a small price to pay for a man who was a genius when it came to this tech crap beyond Neal's knowledge.

"Idiot." He ground his teeth as he met Larry's small gray eyes. "You should have found her years ago."

Larry's throat worked as he swallowed. "She's been careful. Over the past five years I've continued to check the records of every motor vehicle department in every state, and she's never gotten a driver's license. She's never applied for any kind of credit—at least not under her real name. She has a Social Security number, but I've never been able to locate her using it."

Neal growled, fighting the urge to slam his fist into the side of Larry's head. But he couldn't. He needed the fat bastard too badly.

"Father." Jason's voice broke through Neal's thoughts

and he relaxed as he turned toward his eldest son. He was a man of twenty-five, and Neal was grooming him to be the Messiah's first when it was his time, once Neal passed on to the Light.

"Jason." He went to his son, smiled, and wrapped one arm around his shoulders. Pleasure always stirred in Neal's heart when he was around the young man who reminded him so much of himself. "Good news?"

Jason gave one quick nod as Neal stepped away. "The Colombians have agreed to the exchange. Marijuana and cocaine for the shipment of AK-47s."

"Good." Neal smiled, showing his pleasure. His son was a man worthy of his future position within the Temple of Light. "We'll have Gretchen make us a gourmet meal to celebrate," Neal added.

Jason grinned, and Neal's heart warmed even more. Jason had always been special, from the moment his mother birthed him. Despite the bitch's crying and begging, Neal had taken the boy away at once to raise him in the Temple. A nanny had breast-fed and taken care of the boy. Neal had spent as much of his free time as possible with his son to groom him for his special place among The People.

After Neal passed on, Jason thought he was to be the next Prophet. Long before Neal left to join the Light, Jason would see the necessity of letting the Messiah take the lead.

Neal and Jason had a tight bond and nothing could break it.

The only child who would outshine Jason was the new Messiah.

The child who would bring forth the coming of a new age. A time when the word of the Light would be known everywhere and when the Light would be worshipped by all.

CHAPTER *NINE*

Lyra's fifteenth birthday had come and gone. Now she knelt beside her mother, next to their dirty white tent, as they both shucked ears of corn in their commune at the base of Mount Hood. Wind tore at Lyra's coarse cotton robe and dust kicked up in her face. The tent flap snapped in the air and corn husks tumbled over one another. She gathered them into a pile before picking up another ear of corn.

Smells of roasting corn and beef stew made her stomach growl, but she ignored it. She wanted to ignore everything. The backs of her eyes stung from tears she wanted to cry, but she refused to.

How she hated this place and her mother for bringing her here.

"Lyra."

The sound of the Prophet's voice made her jerk her head to look up at him.

Instead of spitting at him like she'd prefer to do, she kept her voice calm. "Yes, Prophet?"

He held out his hand and gave her a smile that turned her stomach. He always turned her stomach, no matter what he did or said. "It's time we begin to teach you, to train you to fulfill your destiny."

My destiny?

Shock vibrated under Lyra's skin and she glanced at her mother. With no sign of emotion on her face, Sara looked at Neal Barker, the so-called Prophet.

What was Neal talking about? Why didn't her mother react? What was going on?

Knowing she had no other choice, Lyra bit down on her tongue to keep from telling Neal exactly where he could put his hand. Instead she reached up and let him draw her to her feet and looked into his blue eyes. He was much taller than she was. His palm was smooth beneath hers because he didn't do manual labor like the rest of The People.

Lyra did her best not to flinch at Neal's touch, and she lowered her gaze and her head like all of The People were supposed to do around him.

He took her by the shoulders and guided her toward the Temple.

Her heart beat even faster when he called to one of his wives, Selma. The black-haired, slender woman joined them and walked side by side with Lyra, both of them now behind Neal with their heads lowered.

When they reached the Temple, they entered the foyer, right in front of the Prayer Room, the only room she'd ever been to in the Temple. Instead of entering the room through the set of doors directly in front of them, Neal went to the right, down a long hallway, and through a large door.

Selma closed the door behind them while Lyra just stared around the room, her eyes wide. She didn't think she'd seen any place so luxurious in her life. The burgundy carpet was so deep and plush her dusty feet sank into it. A massive bed took up the center of the room. Mirrors and oil paintings graced the walls. An altar, bureaus, and even a crystal chandelier dangled above the bed, and a fountain gurgled in one corner.

"Lyra." Neal's commanding voice jerked her attention to him. "Sit on the bed."

Her heart jackhammered so hard her chest hurt. She could barely get her feet to move as she obeyed. Once she was seated on the thick, velvet comforter, she clenched her hands in her lap.

"On your knees, Selma." Neal motioned to a spot in front of him, and the woman quickly did as he asked and kept her gaze lowered. He turned to Lyra. "One day you'll be my First Wife and duties will be required of you in the name of the Light."

A buzzing started in Lyra's ears and she began to tremble.

"Remove your robe, Selma," he said, and the woman followed his direction without hesitation.

Lyra turned away from the sight of the naked woman's body, but Neal's harsh order forced her to look at the pair. "You will watch, Lyra. You will not turn away from me again. Do you understand?"

She gave short, jerky nods. Oh, God, what was he going to do?

Lyra moved her hands to her sides and gripped the bed's comforter. Dizziness swept over her as she watched the scene in horror. The buzzing in her ears was so loud she didn't really hear Neal's instructions to Selma. The naked woman was on her knees, her upper body stretched out so that her face was against the carpet and her hands were straight above her head.

Neal knelt behind Selma. He took his dick in his hand, positioned himself, and thrust into the woman. He began pumping in and out of her. Selma didn't make a sound as Neal used her.

The desire to puke rose up in Lyra and she had to clench the comforter tighter to keep from clapping her hand over her mouth.

Because Neal was watching her. The entire time he kept his gaze on Lyra until he finally jerked and his jaw tightened. For a moment he held still, then he slid his limp dick out of Selma's body and got to his feet.

"Leave us, Selma," he said, still watching Lyra.

After the woman had scrambled to her feet, dressed, hurried out the door, and quietly closed it behind her, Neal approached Lyra. He was still naked and his dick was hardening again. When he reached her he leaned down and grasped her fist.

"Place your hand on me," he commanded.

Lyra and her hand didn't want to obey. Her body trembled harder and she struggled to open her fist. Neal gave a noise that sounded like an angry growl, and she forced herself to grasp his erection. The moment she felt the sticky penis, she lost it.

She leaned over and puked all over his burgundy carpet.

Lyra jerked awake with a small cry and a tremor in her body. It took her only a moment to orient herself, especially when Dare squeezed her tighter to him.

"You all right, honey?" Dare stroked her hair behind her ear. His touch and the way he was pressed against her back almost comforted her. Almost.

"Fine." Her voice sounded rusty and like she'd been crying. Lyra pulled herself out of Dare's embrace and scrambled out of bed.

Dare had worn only his jeans, and when he sat up in bed her gaze was drawn to his torso as his muscles flexed with his movements. His hair was rumpled and the shadow of his stubble was dark. "Don't bullshit me."

A flash of irritation caused Lyra to narrow her eyes. "I said I'm fine." She spun and snatched her pack up from the chair she'd left it on and marched into the bathroom, shut the door, and locked it.

After the water was at the right temperature and she'd stripped off her T-shirt, Lyra stepped into the shower. She tipped her head back, letting warm water wash over her face and her body. Some of the remnants of her dream and the exhaustion from the past two days slid away with the water, circling around her feet and down the drain.

But the dream came back to her, haunting her.

Neal had backhanded her so hard after she'd thrown up that she'd nearly blacked out. He had jerked her to her feet by grasping his hand in her hair and had forced her into the bathroom, where he had her wet a couple of towels. He dragged her back by her hair to the spot where she'd thrown up and then made her clean up the mess. The whole time he shouted at her, telling her he would beat the crap out of her and that he would drug her if she did that again.

At that moment she hadn't cared. She'd rather be cleaning up her vomit than touching him.

But he wasn't through with her.

After she finished cleaning, Neal had led her into a small room inside the large Temple, in the opposite direction from his room. A blue glow lit the room, making Neal's features sharp, and he had looked like she thought the devil would. There had been monitors and computers—things that weren't allowed in the commune—and no people were around.

As calm as if the scene before hadn't happened, Neal had pulled her onto his lap, held her by her waist, and explained her "destiny." How she was to join with him when she was eighteen and become his new First Wife. How he would impregnate her so that she would carry the "new Messiah." How that child would grow to adulthood and lead his disciples and The People to spread his message around the world.

Neal's penis had grown hard beneath her buttocks, and he had slid his hands from her waist until they parted her robe and his palms rested on her still-developing breasts.

Terror had risen within her with every word he spoke, and she couldn't stop shaking. The walls of the small room seemed to close in on her. The acrid smell of plastic and new carpeting, mixed with Neal's odor of marijuana, had caused bile to rise up in her throat. It had been all she could do to force it down and not throw up again.

She couldn't show any more of the intense fear pounding in her body or she knew he would drug her. He had said he wouldn't "join" with her until she was eighteen because that's what the "Prophecy" had told him. She was "the Chosen."

Lyra closed her eyes and let the hot shower water beat on her face. If only she could get those memories out of her mind.

Oh, he hadn't forced her to have intercourse with him, but he did demand that she take off her clothes and give him fellatio. He had thrust into her mouth so hard she had gagged each time. When he came he made her swallow his semen and she almost threw that up all over him. But the memory of that powerful backhand, the threats of beatings and drugs, had made her keep it all inside until after he left her room. Most of the time she would run into the adjoining bathroom and retch into the toilet.

And she had cried. And cried.

Lyra shook her head beneath the shower's spray, bringing herself back to the present again. *No, no, no! I won't go back to him. I won't!*

Tears flooded her eyes to be washed away by the warm water. The urge to heave became stronger and stronger and she shuddered with the need. Somehow she forced it back. She opened her eyes and moved so that her face was no longer under the spray. As if to burn away all the memories of what he'd done to her, she turned the shower knob until the water was hotter and then hotter yet.

She tried to concentrate on other things, like washing her hair. She worked out some of the temporary dye, but she knew it would be a good two weeks before it was all out. She'd just have to be a redhead for a while.

Her thoughts kept returning to the nightmare, and her stomach felt like a sandstorm was there, stinging and harsh inside her.

Lyra closed her eyes for a moment before opening them. She took a deep breath and finally pushed all thoughts from her mind. She concentrated on soaping her body, the clean scent invigorating her senses but burning her skinned palms. Her ass still ached from when she'd fallen, but the pain was really no big deal.

When she finished her shower and toweled off, she slipped into a clean T-shirt and a pair of jeans she drew out of her backpack. She brushed her teeth, then scrubbed her face with a wet washcloth. Her hair hung wet and limp around her face, so she used the hotel blow dryer and her brush to dry it into a smooth bob. Now she just looked like herself again, except with short red hair instead of longish blond. She sighed. So much for her disguise.

That thought only led her back to the dream, and her stomach churned again.

After she stuffed all her belongings into her pack, she took a deep breath and let herself out of the bathroom. She was done with nightmares and thinking of the past. She was prepared to face the day.

Dare was reclining on the bed, still only in his jeans, his hands clasped behind his head. From the sound of it he was apparently watching a news program, but he turned his attention to her when she walked out of the bathroom. She tossed her pack on the floor beside the door as she looked at him.

"Morning, beautiful." He rose and swung his legs over the side of the bed. She met him halfway across the room and he took her by her upper arms and brushed his lips over hers.

"I'm sorry for being so cranky," Lyra whispered. "It was just a bad dream."

He drew back and looked down at her. "Hey. No apologies necessary."

"Thank you." She managed a little smile. Dang, but she liked this man. More than liked him. "Time to take your own shower, cowboy."

He rubbed his knuckles across her cheek. "Good try."

His hand against her skin felt so good. "What do you mean?" she asked in a husky voice.

"You'll take off again as soon as I turn my back," he said as he stroked her.

"I'll stay." She raised her crossed fingers. "I promise."

He shook his head.

Her lips turned up in a broader smile, and she held out her little finger. "Pinkie swear?"

This time he raised an eyebrow.

"Raise your hand like mine," she said. He gave her an odd look but obeyed. She crooked her finger around his and squeezed. "I pinkie swear to you that I won't leave. 'K?"

"Uh-huh," he said as he released his finger from hers.

"Really." Lyra placed her hands on her hips. "Kara and I always used to do that and we never broke our promises to one another." Sadness rolled through her and her shoulders slumped. "She was my best friend . . . before."

Dare took her head in his hands and pressed a kiss to her head. "Be right back." He released her, grabbed his duffle, went into the bathroom, and shut the door behind him.

Leaving her completely alone. Alone to do whatever she wanted.

Lyra forced herself to look away from the door of their hotel room. She'd promised. Other people had made so many to her and had broken them. She tried to always keep hers. When she left him yesterday morning, she hadn't made any kind of promise. This time she had.

Dare was in the bathroom, door closed, trusting her. He trusted her.

She wondered about how strong and determined he was to keep The People away from her . . . and how that made her feel safe.

While she heard the shower run, she sat on the edge of the bed and watched the news. She half-expected to see a picture of herself as a missing person with Neal claiming she was mentally unstable and kidnapped or something. She wouldn't put it past him.

Lyra grabbed her cell phone and hit auto-dial for each of her friends. Becca's store answering machine picked up, so Lyra left a message for her. When she called Nicole's bed-and-breakfast, she was told that Nicole was still on her honeymoon, but Lyra went ahead and left a message and tried to make it sound non-urgent. There was no answer at Suzette's shop or her home. Mrs. Yosko didn't pick up the phone, and Lyra didn't bother to leave a message, since the elderly woman never listened to her voice mail anyway.

A tight knot formed in Lyra's belly. She felt so helpless and didn't like the feeling at all.

When Dare came out of the shower he was fully dressed, his hair combed, and she caught the wonderful scent of his spicy aftershave. He studied her for a moment before he said, "Hungry?"

CHAPTER *TEN*

After they finished the large brunch of omelets, hash browns, yogurt, and fruit they'd ordered from room service, an insistent chirruping sound came from the small holster on the side of Dare's belt. "Hold on," he said as he reached for his cell phone.

He forced his eyes away from Lyra's to his cell and checked the caller ID. It was his partner. Dare flipped open the phone and put it to his ear. "Donovan."

"Those Temple bastards have been asking for you," Nick said, a hard edge to his voice. "Got word from Manny."

"I figured." Dare glanced at Lyra and she gave him a questioning and concerned look before he tore his gaze from hers. "I've got to get the client someplace safe."

"Use my place." Nick had built his home within the Mule Mountains surrounding Bisbee and kept it so private that only God and Dare could find him. "I'll be here until I leave for your surveillance case for Letty Johnson," Nick said, "and then I've got a run to make. Get your asses on the road."

"We're out of here."

"By the way, Manny said you'd better not have bottomed out his El Dorado," Nick added with amusement in his tone.

"Uh-huh." Dare snapped the cell shut and shoved it into its holster. His gaze met Lyra's again. "Get your things."

Her heart started that now-familiar thrumming as she grabbed her shoes that lay at the foot of the bed. From her pack she pulled out a clean pair of socks, shoved her feet into them, then into her running shoes.

Running. I'm so tired of running.

When she had her worldly possessions with her, she slipped her pack over one shoulder, blood rushing in her ears. Even though she didn't think they were in immediate danger, she had a jittery sensation inside her that made her feel like she'd had too much caffeine.

Dare caught her by the shoulders and steadied her. "It's okay, honey. You'll be fine."

She bit her lower lip before saying, "It's not fine. Neal and the others are nuts and they won't stop till they find me. I'm endangering you just by the fact that you're helping me."

He cupped her cheeks and brushed his lips over hers. "Trust me," he murmured.

There was that word again.

Still, Lyra sighed against his mouth. She wanted to melt and sink into him, believing that everything *would* be okay. But in her heart she knew that wasn't the case. As long as she was alive, Neal wouldn't stop hunting her down.

They checked out of the hotel and climbed into the black sports car. She glanced around the parking lot, then the road, as they drove onto the main street. No sign of The People.

She turned back to Dare, and he said, "There's no way they'll find you at Donovan's." Then he tossed her a grin. "Of course I'll have to blindfold you so you can't tell anyone where he lives."

Lyra smiled at his teasing, but then her mind began to race. Her words spilled out as fast as her thoughts surged through her mind. "I've still got to find out if Mrs. Y's okay. I need to see if Becca or Suzette can care for Mrs. Yosko—"

Dare squeezed her leg with one of his big hands and she shut up and looked at him. "Everything will work out," he said before he put his hand back on the wheel. "Just relax."

Relax? How could she begin to relax?

"You said you hitchhiked, which you did yesterday." Dare took his gaze off the road for a moment. "Hitchhiking is dangerous, especially for a woman."

Changing the subject, was he? Lyra rolled her shoulders. Okay, she'd try to relax for now.

"It was like life or death to me," she said after a moment. "I couldn't let Neal do what he planned, couldn't let him touch me." She shuddered. "Any more than he already had. I picked and chose who I rode with. Only women who appeared to be on the soft side—no one who looked like she'd been on the street awhile. Also elderly women or elderly couples, and mothers of small children. I was amazed at how many people helped me. Once I hit Tucson I decided to stay awhile, until I got on my feet."

"You were smart. But it was still dangerous."

"I did what I had to do."

Dare was silent for a moment as if churning it all over in his mind. "I saw some of your artwork at your house. You've got talent."

Heat touched her cheeks. For some reason a compliment coming from him meant more than all she'd heard from her customers via Suzette. "When I was a kid my mom was into everything artsy. I thought it was so cool how beautiful works of art could be created from strips of old tin cans, metal lunch boxes, aluminum, and other things." She smiled. "I loved making aluminum insects out of soda pop cans and designing other creatures made of tin."

Dare couldn't help but smile, too, from the warmth the conversation brought to her tone. "What else have you created?"

"Bowls, mugs, ornaments, geckos and other animals, boxes, briefcases, trunks, and so on." She paused before continuing, "But what I really like making are free-form pieces."

Dare nodded, urging her to continue.

"When I was a teenager, my favorite things to make were roses. I was really good at them." Her eyes took on a faraway look that he saw when he glanced at her again. "I haven't made a rose since my father died. They were his favorites, too. I had a whole colorful bouquet that I'd made for him." Her voice quieted when she continued, "Of course, once Neal took us in with The People, everything was left behind or sold. He took all the money we had 'in the name of Jericho and the Light.'" Sarcasm laced the last words.

Dare reached over to squeeze one of her hands,

which was braced on her thigh. Her skin felt cool to his touch and he rubbed his thumb on her knuckles, wanting to give her what warmth he could. He drew away and put two hands back on the steering wheel.

"Like I told you, my artwork was how I made some of the money that helped me get on my feet," she said. "I'd dig tin and aluminum cans and things out of garbage dumpsters, then make whatever I could. There was a nice old lady at the weekly bazaar in Tucson who would let me sell my things with her paintings and didn't charge me commission. I was able to buy clothes and food, and gradually began to save everything I could."

Dare's blood boiled as he thought of Lyra being forced to live on the street when she'd escaped the cult.

"Eventually I made enough that I was able to afford to take a bus out of there. Big towns were too obvious, so I chose a little tourist town I'd heard about where I could sell my art, Bisbee. I rented a room at Mrs. Y's," she continued. "Suzette, who designs pottery, lets me sell things in her shop on consignment. Mrs. Yosko recommended her."

Lyra's skin tingled when she looked at him, taking in his well-cut, tanned features, but she wondered why his jaw had just tightened and why he'd narrowed his gaze as she told him her story.

"Tell me about your childhood," he said after a long moment of silence.

She leaned back against the seat and stared straight ahead, yet didn't see anything but what was in her mind. "Memories of my childhood through my teens are jumbled up. I think because of what I went through in the cult." The lock of her hair across her cheek suddenly irritated her and she shoved it behind her ear. "I remember things like doing all kinds of different artwork with my mom from the time I was a little girl until . . . well, until. My dad took me to the county fair each year and to lots of spring-training baseball games."

Just the memory of him calling her by his nickname for her, Angel, made tears prick the backs of her eyes. "Momma and Daddy took me to Multnomah Falls on Larch Mountain. The waterfall is over six hundred feet high and is absolutely breathtaking." She held back a sniffle. "That was the last thing we did as a family before Daddy died."

Lyra scrubbed her palms on her jeans, then winced from the pain. "Daddy was pretty cool," she said. "Momma wasn't so bad, but when she took me into the Temple of Light—I've never been able to forgive her."

She inhaled, then sighed. "When I became a teenager I got a little rebellious and snarky. I stopped doing things with my parents, and just wanted to spend time with my friends." A spunky spiral-curled blond-haired girl popped into her thoughts. Lyra hadn't thought of Kara until she "pinkie swore" with Dare. Her heart twisted. "We left everyone without saying a word. Momma just went along with Neal and took us to the Temple of Light and left the real world behind. My aunts, uncles, cousins, and friends probably don't even know what happened to us."

Lyra glanced at Dare. He kept his eyes on the road. She still felt bad about the scratches on his face, but she enjoyed watching him. She liked the way his coffee-colored eyes would lighten when he smiled and darken when something pissed him off. The way his brown hair curved slightly over the neck of his denim shirt. It was so sexy seeing him with his shirtsleeves rolled up and the golden hairs on his arm against his tanned skin. And his hands. Such long, strong fingers gripping the steering wheel. What he could do with those hands . . .

She cleared her throat. "What about you? I've told you a lot about my life, but you haven't shared much of yours."

Dare gave her a casual look, then focused on his driving again. "Pretty uneventful growing up on a ranch."

Lyra shook her head. "Sure. If you don't count the times you nearly killed yourself with all those stunts."

He grinned. "There is that."

She picked at a loose thread on her T-shirt, then forced herself to stop. "Tell me more."

His hands flexed on the steering wheel. "Like I said, I grew up on a ranch with Mom, Dad, and my brother and sisters, Josh, Kate, and Melissa. I'm the oldest and Dad wanted me to take over the ranch when I was older.

"I always wanted to be a cop, though. So I went to college for a couple of years and majored in criminal justice. I entered the police academy when I was twenty-one, then was on the force in Tucson for a few years."

The thought of Dare being a cop brought back memories of her police officer father and she bit the inside of her lower lip. "Why did you leave?"

Dare was silent for a moment. "My partner was killed in the line of duty." His jaw tightened. "I let him down."

"I'm sorry," she whispered. And she was. She hurt for Dare's partner. She hurt for her father. She hurt for Dare. "What did you do next?" she asked to get away from that part of the conversation.

"Decided to run my parents' ranch when they retired," Dare said. "Josh and my sisters had all gone their own ways. I started my own private investigation firm not long after because I couldn't get away from the need to help people. My foreman works the ranch and I run my business from Bisbee. My partner works mostly out of his home."

"So what about your future now?" She cocked her head. "You run a ranch and you're a PI. What else do you do? What do you want?"

He gripped the top of the steering wheel with one hand as he drove, while the other rested at the bottom. "Outside of camping and fishing with my brother and father, visiting my sisters and my nephews and nieces, and dating here and there, my social life isn't exactly what I'd call jumping.

"But I'm pretty sure about one thing." Dare glanced at Lyra. "I'd like to settle down and have a couple of kids. Just waiting for the right woman."

Her cheeks burned at the way he looked at her before he turned his attention back to the road. She cleared her throat. "I don't believe in the right man or woman."

Dare sighed and her thoughts turned to what was happening in the here and now. "You really don't think The People can find us at your friend's place?"

He shook his head. "Nick's private as hell and doesn't have any close relatives. I'm pretty much the only one who knows how to get to his place." His lips twisted into a smile. "He doesn't even take his women there."

Lyra cocked her eyebrow at that. "His women, huh?"

"Nick's not one for a serious relationship. Likes to

keep to himself." Dare glanced at her. "He used to be in Special Forces but doesn't talk much about it. Hell, he doesn't talk about it at all. I think the war—stuff he saw—might have sewed him up tight inside."

"Have you had any serious relationships?" Lyra asked before she could stop herself.

"A couple. Still friends with Catie, but Elena headed off to Mexico with a guy she'd been screwing. Haven't seen her since."

"I'm sorry," Lyra said quietly. "I think."

He raised his brows and cast a look her way.

She gave him a small smile. "If she was sleeping around on you, then she didn't deserve you to begin with."

Dare cracked a grin. "I like your way of thinking."

Comfortable silence hung between them for a while. Lyra took a deep breath, stared out the window, and saw that they were climbing back into high desert, the mountains on the opposite side of Bisbee. Lots of oak, mesquite, manzanita, and cedar trees made up the scraggly forest on either side of the highway. She didn't do a lot of traveling, preferring to stay where she felt safe. It was greener along the roadside, and unlike the lower desert, where they'd just come from, one couldn't see too far. "He lives around here?"

"Yep." He glanced in the rearview mirror. "Good. No one behind us."

The next thing she knew, Dare was aiming the sports car toward a stand of trees and a steep drop-off from the highway. Lyra gasped and gripped the door handle so tight her knuckles ached and her injured palm burned like fire. They were going to plunge off the mountainside!

In a quick maneuver, Dare whipped the car around the stand of trees and onto a road that had been nonexistent from the highway. It didn't even look like a road. Barely two ruts that caused the car to pitch and rumble as he drove. It was a wonder if he wasn't beating up the sports car.

Lyra let out a long exhale, released her death grip on the door handle, and sank down in her seat. "You scared the crap out of me."

"Sorry." Dare swung the vehicle around more trees where there didn't appear to be a road. They followed a brief dirt road and then whipped around in the opposite direction from where the other road was going and vanished behind more trees.

Everything seemed to blur by. "Your friend must be paranoid."

Dare laughed. "He likes his privacy."

"He sure has it."

They passed nothing but trees, bushes, and more trees and bushes until Dare pulled up to a grove of them and stopped the car. She wasn't surprised when he said, "Grab your gear. We're at Nick's."

She reached behind her for her backpack, which had slid to one side of the seat, likely from all the twisting and turning. "That Nick must be one weird guy."

Dare snorted. "I'll be sure and let him know."

Lyra grabbed the handle of her pack. "Don't you even go there."

When they had their stuff, he made sure the car was locked. "Just In case someone came by."

Like that could ever happen. She could imagine the guy who lived here as a recluse with a beard and a neurotic look in his eyes.

Lyra followed Dare around the copse of trees, and at first she didn't see the cabin. She had to do a double take. It was built onto the side of the mountain and made of wood that blended well into the trees, a large cabin with a three-car garage. Interesting. She had to admit the sprawling "cabin" was beautiful, all glass and wood. Clean breezes carried the scent of oak and wildflowers . . . And the smell of freedom.

They climbed up a porch and he flipped through the keys on his key chain until he found an odd-looking silver key. When they reached the door he poked the key into an even odder-looking lock. She stepped back when she heard a high-pitched beeping sound. Dare pulled out the strange key and pushed the door open.

Once they were finally inside and walked through the entryway, she was shocked to see how enormous the home was. A great room with an open-beamed ceiling opened up the whole area, and big skylights highlighted the furniture in forest greens, maroons, and navy blues. Throw rugs were scattered across gleaming wooden floors. An entertainment center took up a good portion of one wall with a huge plasma-screen TV, and a wet bar was off to the side. Through a large archway to the right she saw an expansive kitchen with copper-bottomed pots hanging from a rack above a kitchen island. To her left was a smaller archway with stairs and a sturdy oak handrail.

Dare hung his Stetson on a rack near the door that had a couple of other western hats on it, then headed to the archway to the left. She grabbed onto the rail as she followed Dare down a set of polished wooden stairs that opened up into a spacious hallway. "His home's too neat to be a guy's place."

"Nick's a neat freak." Dare looked down at her with amusement in his eyes. "Just don't touch anything and you'll be safe."

"Well, that's encouraging." As they reached the bottom of the stairs Lyra hefted her pack higher, then walked down the wide hallway with Dare. "So this Nick guy is a weird, paranoid neat freak."

A huge man stepped out into the hallway a few feet in front of them.

Lyra gasped and came to an abrupt stop.

"Nick." Dare continued walking and reached out to grasp the man's hand and shook it.

She barely heard them exchange words of greeting as she looked at the man, taking in his vivid blue eyes and drop-dead gorgeous features—yet he had a harsh, unyielding look to him, too. He wore a tight black T-shirt that showed a physique even more powerful than Dare's, and that was saying something. Nick's blue jeans fit him snugly, and he had incredibly muscular thighs. He wore cowboy boots that were scuffed and obviously well broken in.

When she managed to close her mouth, her gaze finally met his piercing blue eyes. "Weird, paranoid freak?" he said in a deep Texan drawl.

"Ummmm . . ." Lyra swallowed and her face was so hot it must have been brilliant red.

Dare slapped Nick on the back. "She's got you pegged."

Nick raised an eyebrow. The way he was looking at her made Lyra want to fall straight through the floor. Then the corner of his mouth quirked into a grin and she almost dropped her backpack.

He raked his gaze over Lyra from head to toe. "One room or two?"

Heat flushed through her again and she was thankful when Dare said, "Two."

Nick turned and escorted them down the hall. She couldn't help but notice what a fine ass the man had— almost as nice as Dare's. Nick showed Dare where to stow his stuff in one room. Lyra bit her lower lip as she followed Nick alone to the next door.

He paused in the doorway before she could get by and he glanced in the direction of Dare's room before looking back at her. "Doubt you'll be needing the room, sugar," he said in his drawl. "But you can put your gear in here."

Lyra didn't know which emotion she felt more at that moment. Embarrassment at what he'd caught her saying or anger at his assumptions. *Sugar, my ass.*

What she ended up feeling was relief when he moved out of the doorway and let her pass.

"Lunch in thirty minutes," he said, and turned away. "Don't be late."

The moment he was out of the doorway, Lyra shut the door—perhaps a little *too* hard—tossed her stuff on a chair, and plunged face-first onto the quilted bedspread. She groaned. That would teach her to make assumptions.

CHAPTER *ELEVEN*

Carrying the scent of pine and cedar, wind whooshed through the trees surrounding the compound, sounding like the roar of the ocean. Neal's robe flapped around his ankles and his long hair whipped against his face as he strode through the ordered maze of tents with one single-minded purpose.

He was so pissed at his men's failures to capture Lyra that he knew exactly who to extract payment from.

When he reached Sara Collins's tent, Neal found the woman where he'd expected. Lyra's mother was sitting beside several other women, knitting clothing for her daughter's baby.

Before Sara had the opportunity to look up, Neal grabbed a handful of her graying hair and yanked her to her feet. Whatever she'd been working on tumbled to the ground. He forced her to follow him through the compound while he maintained a grip on her hair. Her feet tangled in her robe and she stumbled, but Neal's hold on her didn't fail.

When he reached a larger tent, he dragged Sara through the flap. He released her hair and backhanded her so hard she fell face-first onto the canvas floor.

She didn't move. Didn't make a sound. Smart bitch. Knew she couldn't move until she had permission and she'd be punished if she so much as whimpered.

After they stepped into the almost bare room, Neal said, "On your knees. Facing me."

Sara slowly pushed herself to her knees and scooted around until she faced him but didn't look up.

"I'm beyond pissed at your daughter," Neal said.

He planted his sandaled foot straight into Sara's midsection and she flew back, her head striking the hard floor again.

Sara's eyes closed. Blood dripped beneath her nose and onto her lips. The skin around one of her eyes was swollen and would probably turn black. At one time Sara had been confused and actually asked to leave when Lyra disappeared. But Neal had taught her a lesson that day, too. Once with the Temple of Light, there was no leaving.

"When Lyra is home, you're going to help me keep her here. If she leaves again, you *will* be punished." Neal smiled. "Severely. She's going to fulfill her destiny as mother of the new Messiah."

Neal added softly, "And when he's old enough, the Messiah will be by my side and he will lead our people so that all will know the power of the Light."

The flap of the tent rustled. Neal startled and turned. His son stood behind him, an expression of shock on his pale features as his gaze locked with his father's.

Fuck.

How much had his son heard?

Jason's voice trembled as he asked, "What did you say, Father?"

Shit. "Nothing." Neal cleared his throat as he went to Jason. He clapped his son on the back and gave him a winning smile. "Are the men assembled?"

The shock on Jason's face finally faded to an expression of calm and his color returned. "Yes, Father."

"Very good." Neal gave his son a nod of approval. "Is everything ready for Ryan's punishment?"

"Yes, Father," Jason replied. His face had become a mask, no expression on his features, and he sounded almost like a robot when he said, *Yes, Father.*

Neal turned to Sara and scowled. "Get back to work."

Sara's words came out as a croak. "Yes, Prophet."

Neal ducked out of the tent, followed by Jason, then Neal and his son walked side by side toward the back of the compound.

"One thing I have yet to teach you," Neal said as he walked with his son, "is how to control The People." He looked at his son, who glanced at him. They were of equal height, so he looked right into his son's gaze before turning back to their path. "I feed their addictions, their obsessions."

"What?" Jason said. "How?"

"Take Mark for example." Neal ruffled the hair of a little girl who was about five before he continued walking. "I pulled him off the street. He was a drug addict."

Jason narrowed his eyes when Neal glanced at him. "But Mark doesn't do drugs," Jason said.

"Exactly. I have given him a new addiction, a new obsession." Neal paused for impact. "Me."

This time Jason came to a full stop and Neal faced his son. "What do you mean, Father?"

Neal clapped one of his hands on Jason's shoulder. "He relies on me, worships me even. He desires no more than to please me and to be my second."

Jason looked as if he was going over Neal's words in his mind. "I see. Control the people's addictions, and control them."

Neal gifted his son with a broad smile and squeezed his shoulder before dropping his hand away. "I'll teach you how to control every man in the Temple of Light."

They began walking again and Jason gestured toward the arena. "What's Ryan's addiction?"

"His is simple," Neal said. "He's an alcoholic."

Surprise edged Jason's reply. "But no alcohol is allowed anywhere in the compound."

"I ensured that Ryan got his whiskey." Neal scowled. "Until he fucked up."

Jason cleared his throat. "What about me? What's my addiction? I don't smoke. I don't drink. How do you control me?"

A slow burn mixed with an unidentifiable ache rose within Neal. He clasped Jason's wrist and studied him with a calculating expression. "You're my son. You're like me. We have no addictions."

Without waiting for a response, Neal released Jason's wrist and continued walking toward the arena, letting the lie settle between them. His son was addicted to praise and the willingness to do whatever it took to get that praise from his father.

When they arrived at the large, open arena, all but the entryway was filled with the men and boys, children of the Light.

An X-shaped cross headed the far end of the arena.

Disbelievers might call it a Saint Andrew's cross, but it was in fact one of the symbols of the Light.

Strapped face-first to the cross, naked from the waist up, was Ryan Holstead, the asshole responsible for involving the PI, and the reason Lyra had managed to escape. Twice.

Jason stopped inside the ring of male spectators.

Neal paused and looked at his son. The boy was so handsome, like himself. "It's time you show your leadership qualities," Neal said. "The men need to see that you are my eyes and ears when I'm occupied with other matters, and that you'll deal out punishment when it's necessary."

Jason paled again. "What do you want me to do, Father?"

"Come." Neal walked from the crowd to the open arena. Jason hesitated, then followed.

When they stood within feet of the sonofabitch, Neal saw Ryan trembling so hard his body twitched. Neal said just low enough and close enough that only Ryan could hear, "You may have cost us the future of our people."

"I live only to serve the Light." Ryan sounded as if he was crying.

Good.

"You have displeased the Light," Neal said loud enough that his voice boomed and reached the males of all ages surrounding them.

He turned and saw his men with stoic expressions on their faces. The only males who weren't attending were the armed guards surrounding the perimeter fence and stationed at the gate. From where they stood in front of the fence, men wearing fatigues and bearing AK-47s and M249s faced the crowd. More armed guards were stationed on the other side of the fence. The people were protected from the inside out.

The Light's believers remained silent, so silent that only the occasional low of a cow and clucking of chickens could be heard.

"Our brother has committed a most heinous crime against the Light and all we have faith in and believe in." Neal let his powerful voice resonate through the crowd. "He must be taught a lesson."

Neal gestured to Joe, who immediately stepped forward, grasping a long black bullwhip in one fist. He bowed when he offered the whip to Neal, grip first.

He gave Joe a curt nod, indicating that he should return to his place in the crowd. The man bowed again and did as he was silently ordered to do.

Keeping his expression grim, Neal turned to his son and offered him the whip. Jason hesitated, his face even paler. When he finally reached for the whip, Neal saw that Jason's hand shook. Neal frowned. His son was twenty-five and this task should be performed without a second thought. Perhaps he hadn't been firm enough in his son's education.

When Jason fisted the whip, Neal turned his attention to the crowd. "Jason is officially my first in command. If I am unavailable to deal with situations such as this, from this point on, Jason will."

He nodded to Jason, whose expression was stoic, but his lips tightened in a thin line and his face was as pale as wax. He bowed to Neal, then faced Ryan's back.

In the open arena, the heat of the July sunshine beat

upon Ryan's pale flesh and sweat trickled down his spine and into the gap between his skin and his jeans.

Neal stepped away to give Jason room to perform his task. He had been trained in the use of a bullwhip since he was a child.

Jason clenched his empty fist at his side. His other fist gripped the bullwhip. His jaw tightened. For too long of a moment he didn't move, and Neal narrowed his gaze. To show any weakness wasn't acceptable. He would have to discuss that fact with his son. Later.

Jason extended his arm. He hesitated again.

With a sudden look of determination, he snapped the whip at Ryan's back, breaking the man's skin. Blood welled from the bright red welt. A stifled moan came from Ryan. He knew his punishment would be far more severe if he cried out.

Jason struck Ryan again.

Too slow.

Then again.

And then Jason began whipping Ryan hard and fast, as if Neal's fury were his own.

Neal watched his son's face, which had gone from pale to scarlet. Anger burned in his eyes, and he bared his teeth.

Ryan's skin became a bloody mass, but Jason didn't stop.

"Enough," Neal said.

It was two more strikes of the bullwhip before Jason stopped. Ryan's sobs were low enough that Neal barely heard them.

But Neal was more concerned with how hard his son's

body shook. The sweat running down his crimson face. The rage in his eyes. The heaviness of his breathing.

Neal turned away from his son and addressed the crowd. "Manuel and Ernie, cut the man down. Take him to his wife to be treated."

Without bothering to look at the men who passed by him, Neal continued speaking to the crowd. "We are blessed to be the children of the Light and to learn from our mistakes."

"Praise the Light," one man called out, and the others followed until the mob shouted in unison, "Praise the Light. Praise the Light!"

CHAPTER *TWELVE*

L yra freshened up by washing her face and combing her hair. For the first time in a long time she was conscious about the way she looked and the way she was dressed, and she wished she had something nice to wear that was clean. As usual she wore faded blue jeans and a loose T-shirt tucked into her jeans. It was the same sort of outfit she wore when she worked.

Lyra grimaced when she thought about the fact that she was going to have to face Nick. Nothing like calling her host a weird, paranoid neat freak. For him to hear her say it was enough to make her want to crawl under the bed.

And then to find out the guy was drop-dead gorgeous. *Whoa.* He sure didn't look anything like she'd expected. But then, appearances weren't everything. The so-called Prophet, Neal, was good-looking.

The thought of Neal made her stomach churn like it always did, and she had to force thoughts of him from her mind. She'd take being embarrassed in front of Nick any day to being anywhere near Neal.

Lyra checked her cell phone for the time and saw that it was completely dead. She pulled out her charger, found a wall outlet, and plugged it in before setting it on a table in the corner of the room. She wanted to try calling Mrs. Yosko again, but the phone was so dead it would have to be charged at least a little before Lyra could get it to power up.

She glanced at the phone by the bed. Would Nick mind if she used it? She'd ask.

If she didn't hurry, no doubt she'd be late to dinner—Nick was probably a time freak, too. She rubbed her sweating palms on her jeans before she opened the bedroom door and headed upstairs.

When she reached the spacious great room she found it was empty, but heard male voices coming from where she'd seen the kitchen when they'd arrived. She hooked her thumbs in her jean pockets to have something to do with her hands and casually walked into the archway of the kitchen. It was huge. As she'd seen earlier, a pot rack hung from the ceiling over the island, and the perfectly shiny copper-bottomed pans reflected the track lighting. The cabinets were mahogany or cherrywood and the walls were a pleasant shade of taupe. The black granite countertops seemed to stretch endlessly, and all of the appliances were aluminum and of the finest quality. The guy had taste and obviously had money, too.

Dare acknowledged her with a nod and a smile but continued talking with Nick. She took a moment to observe both men as Nick arranged taco shells on a platter. They were two of the best-looking males she'd had the opportunity to study at one time. Rugged good looks, solid, muscular builds, and dark hair. Nick's brilliant blue eyes were narrowed as Dare spoke.

She forced herself to shift her thoughts away from gorgeous men to food. The aromas of beef, cheese, and onions made her stomach growl loud enough that she caught the attention of both men.

"Hungry?" Nick switched off a burner and raised an eyebrow.

"Smells good." She managed to meet his eyes. "Can I help with anything?"

"Taken care of." He reached into one of the high cabinets to the right of the stovetop and drew out three plates made of the kind of pottery Suzette created. As a matter of fact, when Lyra glanced around the kitchen she saw a lot of the same work, from the salt and pepper shakers to canisters. "Go ahead and make your own tacos," he said.

Lyra still felt embarrassed as she moved closer and took one of the plates from him. She dropped two crispy taco shells onto her plate from a tray by the stovetop. "Did you buy your dinnerware from that little pottery shop on Main Street across from the southwestern restaurant?" Lyra took the heavy-gauge serving fork from him and began plopping seasoned shredded beef into her shells.

"Suzette's," Nick replied as he handed Dare a plate. "I custom ordered all my dinnerware from her."

After piling five taco shells on his plate, Dare took the meat fork from Lyra as she moved on to the cheese, onions, tomatoes, lettuce, and salsa. "She sells some of my work in her shop," she said.

"I know." Nick took his turn at making his own tacos, piling five shells on his plate like Dare had. "I bought a few of your things when I picked up my order.

The pieces I bought were the ones that led Dare to Suzette's and then to you."

Her cheeks heated. She wasn't sure if she should be thanking him, considering that it was his purchases that brought The People to her door.

"Um, thanks for buying some of my things," she went ahead and said. She moved to the table in the kitchen nook, which was set for three, with place mats and cloth napkins in pottery napkin rings that matched the dinnerware. The napkins matched the place mats. Was this guy for real?

When they were seated around the table, each with a glass of iced tea, Lyra couldn't help asking what had been on her mind since they arrived at Nick's home. "If no one knows where you live, how did you build this place? Get well water and electricity?"

"Hired a contractor and his team." Nick gave her a direct stare, his eyes narrowed. "Then I had to kill them."

Lyra had just taken a bite of taco and choked. She dropped the taco on her plate as she started coughing. Dare rubbed her back while she gulped some iced tea.

When she looked up, the skin around Nick's eyes was crinkled in amusement and Dare was shaking his head, his mouth curved into a grin.

"Donovan paid them really well to forget he existed," Dare said. "The electric company has the meter near the highway, and he gets his mail in town."

For the rest of the meal, Lyra kept her thoughts to herself and ate her tacos, afraid she'd say something stupid. Nick and Dare talked about a new surveillance case for a woman named Letty Johnson.

"I'm leaving to get right on it after we finish taking a look at those aerial maps," Nick said after he crunched a mouthful of taco and swallowed. "Mr. Johnson supposedly gets off work at the courthouse some nights at eight, but when I checked with a clerk, she said he always heads out right at five. Never fails."

"Should be an easy mark." Dare wiped his hands with his napkin. The two men had devoured their five tacos in the same amount of time it had taken Lyra to eat two. "Asshole gets off early, screws another woman, then gets home late and tells Mrs. Johnson he worked into the night." Dare scowled. "A woman deserves better than that kind of cheating scum."

"Yep." Nick pushed back his chair, stood, and grabbed his plate and fork. "The photos should be interesting."

"You really take pictures of people having affairs?" Lyra couldn't keep her mouth shut as she grabbed her own plate and stood. "Like on TV?"

Dare gave a low laugh and Nick raised an eyebrow as he said, "How else do you expect me to prove he's fu—" He cleared his throat. "Prove that he's cheating with another woman?"

"Oh." Would her cheeks ever stop flaming around this man? "Must be, um, interesting work."

"Most of the time surveillance is pretty boring," Dare said as they carried their plates to the sink. "Not much exciting about sitting in a car or tailing the mark. Especially when they don't follow a regular schedule. The guy Nick will tail could go straight home tonight, and he'll follow him tomorrow, possibly the next day and the next, until he catches the S.O.B. at it."

"Dare, though," Nick said as he looked directly at her, "becomes a little too involved with his work."

"Shut up, Donovan," Dare growled. "I do my job."

Nick faced Dare head-on. "Let's just say at times you forget it's not personal."

Lyra's skin went hot. She was one of those people Nick was talking about.

Dare took a step closer to Nick, his hands clenched at his sides. Nick just shook his head and went back to cleaning the kitchen.

When Dare looked at her, Lyra turned away and kept her eyes averted. Somehow she'd forgotten she was just another person he'd felt the need to protect.

When they finished putting away the leftovers as well as cleaning up the dishes, table, and countertop so that everything was absolutely spotless, Lyra followed Nick and Dare down the flight of stairs.

Nick paused and looked from Dare to Lyra, and his hard gaze rested on her. "She stays here."

Dare rubbed his hand over his afternoon stubble. "She's okay, Donovan."

For a long moment Nick looked at her.

"She needs to see," Dare said. "It's possible she can help us."

Nick's eyes never left hers. She held her breath. He finally nodded and turned away.

She and Dare followed Nick as they went all the way to the end of the hallway and down another staircase. Their footsteps were loud against the wooden floor as they walked along a different hallway and into what must be the master bedroom. It was huge and masculine with its polished wood floor, thick wood furniture, taupe and brown bedding and furnishings.

But when they went into his large walk-in closet, hair at her nape prickled. Everything was close around her. Too close.

Lyra shook her head and took a deep breath. She could do this. Whatever it was, she could do it.

At the back of the confined space, she thought she saw Nick push something on the wall. She nearly jumped when a piece of the hardwood floor rose up a couple of inches, then slid to the side. Nick immediately climbed down a set of metal stairs. When she glanced at Dare, he gestured for her to follow Nick. Her body tingled and she felt a little light-headed. The fact that they were in a closet made her feel a bit on the claustrophobic side, but going down into a room below the closet? She closed her eyes and opened them again. She could do this.

Lyra sucked in a deep breath and positioned herself so that she could grab the metal handrails. They were cold beneath her palms. She slowly headed down the steps into the low-lit room.

When she reached the bottom, she turned and her stomach dropped. A room filled with computers and monitors. Different from Neal's, yet the same.

Huge monitors, computers, electronic maps, and a zillion other high-tech gadgets filled the place. Blue light flickered throughout the dim room, and she was so overwhelmed by it all that her head spun.

She was barely conscious of Dare coming up behind her until he kissed the top of her head. She shivered and goose bumps prickled her skin as she looked up at him. He lowered his head and gently brushed his lips over hers and smiled.

The tension in Lyra's muscles increased despite his closeness and gentleness. He rubbed both her arms, then released her to walk to where Nick was waiting. The other man had a hard, impatient look.

When she heard what they were talking about, her stomach turned to lead. Lyra's feet seemed to take her to Dare's side of their own accord. Her heart pounded and her throat grew dry.

"We can get him for underage sex," Dare was saying, "as well as polygamy. Most of all, I'm pretty sure from what Lyra talked about that they could be running drugs."

"If that's the case, then we'd have something to put them away for a while," Nick said. "If we can just figure out a way to prove it.

"When I looked into the cult after talking with you, I gathered some info and found out the Temple of Light's satellite compound is here," Nick was saying as he and Dare pored over a large map that looked as if it had been taken from the sky. The map was against a lit background so that it could be read more easily, and the glow reflected against Nick's and Dare's faces. "We didn't get a clear shot because of the weather and the trees," Nick said. "We'll work on it."

Dare nodded, his jaw tight.

"They're building their new compound at the base of the Huachuca Mountains." Nick used a pencil and pointed to the location. "Here's the perimeter fence, and they appear to be well guarded. All of these shapes are probably tents where the cult members live, and these dots are the cult members. From the intelligence I've gathered so far, they've set up satellite compounds all over the U.S."

The Temple of Light really was here. And the cult had spread across the country.

Sweat dampened Lyra's forehead and she felt like hot needles were pricking her skin. All she could do was stare at the map, yet her head swam and she didn't see it. With satellite communes everywhere, she probably couldn't ever run somewhere they wouldn't find her.

"This other map is of their compound just outside of Sandy, Oregon," Nick was saying.

She shuddered at the mention of the place she now thought of as hell. Was Neal still there? Or was he here, in Arizona, now?

Lyra wrapped her arms around her belly. Images, smells, and sights filled her mind.

The nightmare of when Neal had told her about being the Chosen was like a fist slamming into her belly. Everything was vivid, like it was happening all over again. He had taken her into a room like this one and told her of her "destiny." He had touched her breasts. Had forced her to touch his penis.

Bile rose up in Lyra's throat and she clapped her hand over her mouth. In the distance she heard a male voice, and then two strong hands grabbed her upper arms.

"No!" She struggled to get away from the hands. "I won't. I won't!"

The strong hands shook her and her head fell back.

The dim room came into focus and she saw Dare's eyes fixed on her, his jaw tight. She immediately went limp, her knees giving out on her.

Dare drew her into his embrace and held her. "It's all right, honey," he murmured against her hair. "Everything will be all right."

Hot tears leaked from her eyes and dampened his shirt. Her entire body trembled. "It's not," she said against his chest. "It will never be over."

She pushed him away, looked around the room, and trembled all over. "I've got to get out of here. Got to get out of here."

Lyra didn't know how she made it back up the stairs and out of the high-tech room. All she remembered was Dare taking her to her bedroom and helping her out of her shoes and jeans so that she had just her T-shirt and underwear on, and then he tucked her under the sheets and quilt.

Dare scooted onto the bed behind her, on top of the quilt, all but his boots on. He molded his body against hers and wrapped his arm around her waist. She trembled even as he held her tight and whispered soft words. "I'll never let them get their hands on you, Lyra. Never."

Her voice shook. "You can't stop them. No one can."

"I can, and I will." He squeezed her tighter. "Now rest."

Lyra didn't think she would be able to relax, but eventually she slipped into dreams filled with images of being taken back to the compound and Dare coming to rescue her on a great black horse.

• • •

Anger seared Dare's veins and he could barely contain himself as he held Lyra. He wanted to go after Neal Barker so badly that his body ached with it. He'd slam his fist in the bastard's face for what he'd done to Lyra, and he'd feel the satisfaction of Barker going down as he hit him again and again.

For a long time Lyra remained tense in his embrace, her breathing short and choppy. But eventually her body relaxed and her breathing slowed and became deep and even. Every now and then she would jerk as if she was dreaming or having a nightmare. He nuzzled her hair and breathed in her sunshine-and-roses scent.

It was only early evening, but the room was dark thanks to the closed wooden shutters and the fact that he'd turned off the lights. Lyra had been through so much in the past three days that she needed to rest.

For a long time he held her as she slept. Finally, when he was fairly certain she wouldn't wake, he slipped from the bed, careful not to disturb her. He settled into a chair in the room. He braced one elbow on an arm of the chair and stroked his jaw as he studied Lyra. Her features looked relaxed, and he hoped her dreams would be peaceful.

How could they stop this Neal bastard from going after Lyra anymore? What could possibly stop him and keep her from being on the run?

Dare ground his teeth. With the information Lyra had given him, they had enough info to get Neal Barker in deep with the law if they could prove it.

How could they get the law into the main compound

to expose any of this? And if Barker was put away, how long before he was out and after Lyra again?

Nick had headed out on his run by the time Dare left Lyra's bedroom. He made his way back to Nick's surveillance room to take a look at the satellite map of the Oregon compound again. When he was in, he moved to the table in the center of the room and switched on the light beneath the maps. He studied the main compound intently, frustrated that everything on the map wasn't better defined. They couldn't formulate a plan without knowing every bit of the layout of the compound and the position of the guards.

They'd have to figure a way to get him. Too bad the S.O.B. wasn't in Arizona.

He clenched his jaw, tempted to crumple the map into a ball and toss it across the room. Better yet, put his fist through a wall. What the cult leader had done to Lyra . . . Goddamn. Everything she'd gone through, Dare had no idea. Different scenarios churned through his mind and every one of them made him want to knock the shit out of Neal Barker. Repeatedly.

A plan. He had to come up with a plan. Other than storming the main compound with a small army, he was clutching at straws.

He flipped the light off so that the table no longer lit the map, then turned to the stairs. His boots rang against the metal as he made his way up. When he was in the closet he found the hidden button and closed the surveillance room. He strode up the series of stairs and hallways to Lyra's room. Her door was open, and when he slipped into the near darkness he saw that she was no longer in bed.

Damn. He shouldn't have left her alone.

Dare made his way upstairs to the great room and found Lyra sitting on one of the couches in the dim lighting. She was clutching a pillow and curled up in just her T-shirt. She looked so beautiful with her tousled hair and her sleepy expression.

Soft country music played in the background. A slow song started up and Lyra startled when he said, "Dance with me."

CHAPTER *THIRTEEN*

As Dare approached her, Lyra felt a thrill deep in her belly. There was something in his eyes, something in the low timbre of his voice when he'd asked her to dance.

She'd never danced before—at least not since junior high school. She started to tell him so, but before she could say anything he was already at her side. He took her hand in his and helped her to rise.

The moment she was up, he wrapped her in his embrace and she sighed. He smelled so masculine and felt so good, his body warming her through her T-shirt. The soft country song surrounded them as he held her close and they began slowly moving to the music. There was magic in the music, magic that wove through her thoughts and around their bodies.

She slipped her arms up his neck and into his thick hair and felt his erection against her. Sensations sizzled from her belly to that place between her thighs, and she melted more fully against him. Through the thin material of her bra and T-shirt, her hard nipples rasped against his shirt, adding to the complete feeling it gave her to be in his arms.

"Honey, what you do to me," Dare murmured against her hair. "Every time I see you, I want to touch you. I want to hold you. I want to make love to you."

Lyra let out a soft sound of surprise and looked up into his eyes. For a long moment he held her gaze as they swayed to the music. Then he lowered his head and softly brushed his lips across hers. She closed her eyes and sighed into his mouth. He nipped her bottom lip, causing her sigh to turn into a moan.

Dare slipped his tongue through her lips and explored her, teasing her by tangling with her tongue, then running his along the edges of her teeth. She wanted to taste him fully, and she matched his kiss. What started out as slow and gentle became more intense, more needy. He slid his hands from her waist down to cup her ass and press her even tighter to him.

Lyra's heart pounded harder and faster. He tucked her head beneath his chin and held her. She'd never felt such a sense of safety, security, like nothing could ever hurt her. With Dare it would be easy to let herself go. To let herself believe that everything would be okay.

She tilted her head up, bumping his chin. He moved his head back and their gazes locked. They continued to move slowly to the beat of the song as they looked at each other.

"Do you get this close to all the women you help?" she asked, a little tremor to her voice.

Dare stilled and they no longer moved with the music. His eyes grew dark, almost like a storm shadowing the sky, and his expression no longer relaxed. "Don't even begin to think like that. You are special."

Lyra tried to look away, but he took her face in his hands and brought her around to look at him again, and she said, "There's nothing special about me."

"Everything about you is special." He pressed his lips to her forehead. "Honey, I've never met a woman like you. You're strong, smart, beautiful."

She tried to shake her head, but his hands kept her still.

"Look at what you've done, what you've been through," he said. "You lost your father. You ended up in a dangerous cult, and the bastard subjected you to shit no one should have to go through."

Tears burned her eyes and she opened her mouth, but Dare wouldn't let her say anything.

"You escaped. You were homeless but brought yourself out of poverty. Despite everything you've been through, you've made friends, you've made a good life for yourself." He moved his hands from her face and stroked her hair. "You are special, Lyra Collins. And don't you ever think you're not."

She buried her face against his chest and clung to him. He was so solid, so real. She barely knew him, yet her heart was opening up to him. How could she let that happen? Dare held her tight. He asked nothing from her, just gave.

She tilted her head to look up at him again. "Thank you," she whispered.

"I shouldn't be touching you like this," he said as he drew back.

"Why?" She kissed the curve of his neck and felt his warmth against her lips. He smelled so good.

"With everything that's happened to you," he said

with a low groan. "You need time to rest, time to sort your thoughts."

Her lips met his again, then she pulled away and smiled. "Right now my thoughts are perfectly sorted, Dare Lancaster."

He pressed his mouth to her hair and she felt the rise and fall of his chest as he inhaled deeply. "You'd better think long and hard about what you're saying. What you're doing to me."

"And what you're doing to me," she said softly. "I can't help it. I don't *want* to help it. What I want is you. That's not going to change no matter what happens. No matter how much you tell me I need time." She raised herself up on her toes and brushed her lips against his in a whisper-soft movement. He groaned against her mouth. "What I want, what I need, is you," she said.

Dare pressed his lips to hers and the intensity of his kiss took her breath away. He wasn't gentle. His kiss was hard, dominating. The stubble on his jaw was rough against her face as he moved his mouth back and forth against hers.

His big hands squeezed her ass cheeks. He began to move his palms a fraction at a time over the flare of her hips, to the indentation of her waist, and farther up until his fingers rested just below her breasts.

Lyra tightened her hold on his hair as he kissed her, held her. She prayed for him to touch her nipples, and when he brushed his thumbs over them she thought she was going to lose her mind. She arched into him and he rubbed her nipples harder.

She couldn't stop kissing him, didn't want to stop

kissing him. They were so close she felt the pounding of his heart against her chest, the throb of his pulse where her arm rested on the curve of his neck.

Dare raised his head and dragged in a deep breath. Her lips were moist, and her face felt warm from where his stubble had chafed her. Her breathing had quickened and her heart was pounding.

He rubbed his mouth over her lips again. "Are you sure?"

Lyra smiled and brought her hands from his hair to cup his stubbled cheeks. She reached up and gave him a light kiss. "Nothing could change my mind. I want you, Dare."

The expression on his face was almost tortured, like he couldn't wait any longer. It made her want to smile inside, to know that he wanted her so badly he could barely control himself.

"Let's get downstairs." He parted from her, took her hand in his, and drew her to the stairs. "I'd rather not have any interruptions."

She couldn't help a small laugh. "Nick said he didn't think we'd be needing two rooms tonight."

Dare grinned and kissed the top of her head. "When it comes to you, I think I'm an open book."

They started down the stairs and she squeezed his fingers as she looked up at him. "Me, too."

When they were in his room he firmly shut the door and locked it behind him. "Nothing short of an explosion is going to interrupt us," he said with a sexy grin that made her melt.

He led her to the bed and guided her so that she sat on the edge, looking up at him. The quilt felt soft beneath her thighs, and the floor was cool under her bare feet. For a guest room it was large, with big, bold furnishings and a bed that was perfect for lovemaking. The lighting wasn't too bright, but he turned on the bedside lamps and then flipped off the switch for the overhead lights and it was far more romantic.

Lyra swallowed down a burst of nerves that caused her to tremble. She wanted him to come to her, to touch her, to taste her. Yet at the same time something tight gripped her belly. This would be it. This would be the man she'd lose her virginity to.

She trusted him enough to give it to him.

Dare was incredibly slow and deliberate in his movements. He went to his leather duffle, where it perched on one of the cushioned chairs. The sound of the zipper was loud in the quiet room. He reached in, felt around, and pulled out a box. For some reason her cheeks heated when she saw that it was a box of condoms.

"Prepared?" she said.

"For you." He moved to the nightstand, opened the box, and let the packets spill onto its surface.

"Um, wow." Her gaze met his as he came back to stand over her. "You have that much stamina?"

He grinned that sexy grin again and placed his hands to either side of her hips, bringing his face close to hers. "For you," he repeated.

"Then be with me," she whispered against his lips, and he kissed her softly, gently. He brought his hands to the hem of her T-shirt and tugged it upward, exposing her sturdy plain white bra. *One day silk and satin,* she promised herself.

Same as last time, he didn't seem to care what she

was wearing when he pulled her T-shirt over her head and tossed it on the floor. She took a deep breath as he kneeled and lowered his mouth, and licked her through the cotton of her bra. Lyra moaned as he sucked each nipple so that the material was wet and cool when he removed his mouth. He moved his hands smoothly beneath her arms to her back, where he easily unfastened her bra. He slipped it off her, and when he tossed it aside the bra landed on one of the lampshades.

"Nick wouldn't approve of you throwing things around the room," she said with a grin.

He gave a low laugh. "That makes it even more fun."

Lyra didn't have time and definitely didn't have the presence of mind to respond, because he began licking one of her nipples with his warm tongue, then sucked her nipple into his mouth. She slipped her hands into his hair and tilted her head back. Soft moans came from her throat with every suck and nip of his teeth.

He moved to her other nipple, and the one he'd just licked and sucked felt cool without his mouth on it. She sighed with pleasure as he brought one of his hands up and began rolling the nipple between his fingers.

When he moved his mouth from her breast to her belly, she sighed with disappointment at him leaving her nipples, yet excitement that his mouth was traveling toward her mound. He rubbed his nose against her cloth-covered sex and she heard his deep inhale.

"I love your scent," he said as he raised his head and gripped the elastic waistband of her cotton panties. "And I already know how good you taste."

A rush of heat whooshed over Lyra. He drew back

so that he could ease her panties down, over her hips and legs to her feet. When he reached her feet he lightly massaged them before pulling the panties over her toes and flinging them so that they hooked over the bedpost.

She couldn't help a small giggle, but it quickly turned into a gasp as he scooted her up the bed so that she was lying on her back with her head on the pillows. Dare had his denim-clad knees to either side of her thighs and his hands braced beside her head. He brought his mouth to hers and kissed her, and his shirt felt rough and erotic against her nipples.

Lyra had to touch him. She reached down and cupped his cock through his jeans. He felt so hard and long beneath her hand. Was it only yesterday that he'd given her the most incredible orgasm she'd ever had? So much had happened in the last three days that her head spun with it. But she knew this was right. Everything about Dare was right.

"Get naked." She pulled away from his kiss, and she was so turned on she could barely speak. "I want to see you with nothing on."

Dare didn't stop looking at her as he eased off the bed. He unsnapped his Western shirt and flung it onto the floor, and she sighed. His smooth chest was marred only by the large scar on the front of his right shoulder, and she wondered how he'd gotten it.

His biceps flexed with every movement he made as he unhooked his belt and whipped it out of the belt loops. He held both ends together and snapped the belt on his hand. He had a wicked look in his dark eyes. "You do know that if you're a bad girl I'll have to punish you?"

Lyra raised her brows. "Do I get to spank you if you're a bad boy?"

He laughed and tossed the belt aside. "Guess that puts us at a stalemate."

She smiled and watched him toe off his boots, then take his socks off. "You know you're taking too long."

The look in his eyes darkened. She bit her lower lip as he shimmied out of his jeans. His erection was a hard outline against his white briefs. The moment he pulled his briefs down, his cock sprang out, long and hard. Big enough that she worried if he would fit inside her.

When he was completely naked she took a moment to study him. He was so large and powerful she actually felt small in comparison, and she'd never felt small before.

His movements were smooth as he eased onto the bed beside her so that they were facing each other. "You're beautiful," he said as he trailed his fingertips along her waist to her hip. "The moment I saw you walking up your stairs carrying those groceries, something twisted in my gut."

She couldn't help but tease him. "Then you got a faceful of pepper spray."

Dare grinned, but it vanished as he clamped his hand on her ass and pressed himself so tightly against her that his erection dug into her belly, and her breasts were smashed against his chest. A frisson of fear mixed with excitement caused her to shiver. How bad would it hurt?

"You smell so good." He nuzzled her neck and her hair. "Always like sunshine and roses. And woman."

Lyra's body was so sexually charged that every word he said sent more vibrations through her.

He moved his hand between them and slipped his fingers into the folds of her sex. "Damn, you're wet."

Tingles prickled her skin. Whether from embarrassment, fear, desire, or the feel of him stroking her clit, she wasn't sure. Probably all of it. He thrust two fingers into her core, and she gasped as he caught her off guard. She began to ride his hand instinctively, wanting more than his fingers but taking what he was giving her right now.

She wrapped her palm around his erection and lightly squeezed. Everything about this moment, about this man, was beautiful, and all the horrors of her past evaporated like mist beneath the rising sun.

As she touched him, she marveled at how *he* felt in her hand. Hard steel encased in soft velvet. He closed his eyes and groaned as he pumped his fingers in and out of her and she slid her hand up and down his cock.

Dare opened his eyes and held her gaze. He withdrew his fingers from her channel and grabbed her hand, not letting her caress him anymore. "Don't think I'll last much longer at this rate," he said in a voice so rough it was almost harsh. "It's all I can do to keep from spreading your thighs and making love to you so hard you'll see stars."

More warmth swept through Lyra. "That's what I want." And she did. Oh, how she did.

Dare kissed her long and hard as he grabbed her ass and pulled her tight against him. His cock was so hard and she was so ready. More liquid pooled between her thighs, and she didn't think she could take much more erotic torture.

The feeling of butterflies going berserk in her belly became stronger as he rolled her onto her back. He knelt between her thighs, grasped his erection in one of his hands, and rubbed her folds with the head of his cock. Lyra trembled beneath him.

This is it. This is it.

Dare took a deep breath and sat back on his haunches, just looking at her for a moment. He reached over to the nightstand, grabbed a packet, got the condom out, then threw the package on the floor. While she watched, she bit her lower lip as he slowly rolled the condom down his cock. Her heart beat faster to know he was going to be inside her, all of him, in just moments.

His expression was so serious when he looked at her again. "Are you a virgin, honey? I don't want to hurt you."

Heat rushed to her cheeks as she nodded. "I—I just need you. I'll be okay."

"I want you to remember this," he said when he placed the head of his cock at the entrance to her core. "I don't want you to ever forget our first time."

"How could I?" she whispered as she slid her hands down his back. "I'm with the one man who's rocking my world."

Dare's jaw tightened and he slowly pushed inside of her.

"Ohmygod, ohmygod." Pain seared her as her gaze met his. "Stop. Just a moment. Please stop."

He held completely still, his expression filled with concern. "I'm sorry, baby. Do you want to change your mind?"

Lyra shook her head. "No. I'll be okay. I'm ready for more."

Her eyes watered and she bit her lower lip as he inched his erection deeper inside her channel. It hurt so bad she couldn't help a couple of tears from slipping down the sides of her eyes.

When he was fully buried within her, he held still and kissed away her tears. While he moved his lips to hers and gave her a gentle, sweet kiss, her body had time to adjust to his length and girth.

After a few moments he drew away and she smiled. It was starting to feel really good with him inside her. "Do it now. I want it."

He began a slow, even stride, moving her body with every thrust, rocking her world, just like she'd said. It hurt at first, but the beginning sensations of pain became such extreme pleasure that she lost herself to it.

She slipped into a trance. A trance of pleasure, of feeling, of being.

"Look at me." The gruff voice came from above her and she pulled herself back from the Otherworld she'd found herself in for those few moments. "I want to see your eyes while I take you for the first time."

Lyra's whole body was on fire as her gaze locked with Dare's. She squirmed beneath him, then wrapped her legs around him and crossed her legs at her ankles. She wanted him, wanted to keep him close.

Dare grunted as his thrusts became harder and faster and it felt impossibly better and better. He surprised her by raising her legs up and putting them over his shoulders. To her shock and pleasure she felt him even deeper. It felt so good.

Stars started to spark inside her mind, and she found it harder and harder to maintain her focus on Dare's eyes. Her whole body vibrated like it was going to explode. His jaw was tight and he looked like he was gritting his teeth. Sweat rolled down the side of his face and fell onto her breast, and she knew she was going to lose it.

"I'm going to come." His strokes were long, deep, fast, his voice hoarse and tight as her legs clamped him over his shoulders. He brought one of his hands between their bodies and stroked her clit in time with his thrusts. "Come with me."

Tingles erupted where he fingered her into sparks all over her skin, and those stars in her mind became brighter and brighter. She lost focus and couldn't see Dare's eyes any longer. She tilted her head back. Her orgasm coiled so tightly in her belly that it was only going to take a few more strokes of his cock and his fingers, and she'd be gone.

Dare brought his lips to hers and kissed her so hard she felt his teeth against hers. He thrust his tongue into her mouth and fingered her clit harder. His kiss and touch shoved her over the peak, past reason, past thinking. She cried out against his mouth, and when he raised his head she was still crying from the exquisite sensations.

"That's it." He thrust three, four, five more times. "That's it," he barely managed to get out before he shouted, his voice filled with triumph and power.

The sound of his cry made her body throb even more, and she couldn't stop from bucking against him. Dare's cock pulsed inside her channel, and she felt herself grip him tight with every spasm. She didn't want it to end, yet she didn't know if she could take any more.

With one last groan, he lowered her legs from his shoulders and rolled onto his side. He brought her close to him, his thigh hooked over her hip, and her face resting against his chest. His breathing was hard and ragged, and his heart pounded beneath her ear. Her own heart thrummed just as hard and she was having a hard time catching her breath, too. She sucked in the scent of sex, sweat, and testosterone. His body felt slick and warm against hers, and for some reason that made her hot for him again.

Dare squeezed her tight before relaxing his hold, and he seemed almost reluctant to do so. He nuzzled her hair, his chest moving with the breath he took, and he released a deep sigh.

"I've never trusted a man." She swallowed, finding the words hard to speak. "Until you."

He pressed his lips to her forehead. "Thank you for this, for trusting me."

"Thank you for making my first time so special." She smiled. "I feel wonderful inside and out."

Dare cuddled her close to him. "You wore me out, woman. I'm so tired I don't think I could move if I tried."

She gave him a wicked grin as she ran her fingernails down his chest, and her eyes met his. "What about all the other condoms?"

Dare's mouth curved into a smile at Lyra's words. Despite the fact that he felt like every bone in his body had melted, his cock was stiffening. So that was what mind-blowing sex was like.

Lyra ran her finger down his chest and reached up to kiss him lightly. "Hmmmm?"

He responded by rolling onto his back and bringing her with him. She giggled as he brought her on top of him, so that she was straddling him, and his cock was nestled beneath the folds of her pussy. "I can handle all you can dish out." He hoped he could. What she did to him was incredible. It wasn't just the sex, it was something deeper, more primal, something gut-level.

With a quick movement, he slipped off the condom and disposed of it in the wastebasket between the nightstand and bed.

Lyra pushed herself up by bracing her hands on his chest, then rose up with her palms on her thighs. "What am I going to do with you?" she said as she rocked her folds over his cock. She looked so beautiful, her short red hair tousled, her lips swollen, and her skin pink and moist from perspiration. The smell of her musk about drove him out of his mind.

"I'm going to take you again," he said as he braced his hands on her hips.

She shook her head and grinned. "Not yet, cowboy. I'll let you know when I'm ready to ride."

"Oh yeah?" He slid his hands up to her breasts and cupped them in his palms. He liked how they were large and overflowing. "Maybe this cowboy is ready for a ride now."

Lyra tipped her head back and moaned at the feel of his hands on her breasts. When he pinched both of her nipples she gave a little cry, and more moisture flooded from her and onto his cock nestled against her folds. She had to take control of the situation.

She leaned forward and met his gaze as she brought her hands up and placed her palms over his strong fingers. "Stop distracting me."

He slid his hands from her breasts and settled them at her waist. "From what?"

"From this." She reached up and brushed his hair from his forehead. "I want to touch you."

Dare's grip on her waist tightened as she trailed her fingers down the side of his face, over his coarse stubble, and to his firm lips. He took one of her fingers into his mouth and sucked, causing her to gasp in surprise and pleasure. She pulled her finger from his mouth and trailed it down his jaw, the wetness of it mixing with the sweat of his skin.

She leaned forward and her nipples rubbed against his chest. Inhaling his incredible scent, she moved closer yet and pressed her lips to his face and began flicking her tongue along the same trail her fingers had taken. His skin was salty and she said, "Mmmmmm, I love how you taste."

Dare grabbed her ass cheeks and squeezed as her lips met his. She was glad he let her take the lead as she nipped at his lower lip, then slid her tongue into his mouth. She lightly sucked on his tongue, and he squeezed her ass tighter, as if restraining himself. He moved his mouth in time with hers, a gentle kiss that she felt ripple throughout her body. It made her want to have him inside her again, but she wanted to play, first. She was a little sore, yes, but the pleasure far outweighed what small amount of pain she had felt.

She moved her lips from his and kissed his skin along his jaw to the curve of his neck and down to the scar on his shoulder. She pressed her lips softly against it and raised her head to look at him. "Another macho wound?"

Dare's features darkened and she knew at once she'd hit on a sore subject. "From my days on the police force," he said, and she sensed he didn't want to talk about it anymore.

Lyra reached up to kiss him again, wanting to wash away the memory of whatever painful experience had caused that wound.

She reached over to the nightstand and took one of the foil packets in her hand. As she lightly trailed one corner of the packet down his chest to his abs, she gave him what she hoped was a sexy grin. "Ready for a ride, cowboy?"

The rumble in his chest vibrated through her fingers. She brought the condom packet to her mouth and caught the edge with her teeth. With her eyes focused on his, she slowly ripped opened the package, taking her time, making him wait.

He narrowed his eyes, and his fingers dug into her ass cheeks. "Hurry up, woman."

Lyra cocked a brow. "Woman?"

Dare growled and she grinned, but she slipped the rubbery soft condom out of the package and tossed the foil onto the floor. She scooted back so that she straddled his thighs and she had access to his very erect cock. He had to release her ass but stroked her thighs with his fingertips.

Intent on teasing him as much as she could, Lyra placed the condom on the head of his erection and rolled it down as slowly as possible.

He groaned and grabbed handfuls of her hair. "If you don't stop teasing me, I'm going to buck you off and fuck you my way."

The thought of him taking her like that, and the way he said "fuck" sent a thrill through her belly. "Later, cowboy," she said.

Dare released his grip on her hair as she rose up and positioned herself just over the head of his cock. Her eyes locked with his as she slowly eased down his length and took him deep inside her.

She held still for a moment, unable to move. *Oh. My. God.* She closed her eyes for a moment as his cock filled her hard and deep. He stretched her so big and she felt the bite of soreness again. Yet she could come just from the feel of him inside her.

"Lyra . . . ," he said in a husky tone.

She opened her eyes, arched her back, and started riding him. The sensations were wild as she moved up and down on his huge erection, trying to keep a slow and even pace. He reached up and pinched her nipples, and she gasped as the thrill of his touch went straight to where they were connected.

Lyra rose up and down at a faster pace. She was taking him so deep. He had a tight hold on her hips and he began bucking to meet her movements. Her eyes met his again and he had a fierce expression, his jaw taut as he slammed up into her. He put his thumb on her clit and stroked.

Her orgasm began to swirl within her like a tornado the harder he touched her clit. She braced her hands against his hard chest, her arms and legs quivering, as she continued to ride him. That tornado raged, swept her up, and threw her into the storm. She cried out as her body felt the thunder and she saw the lightning.

With a sob she collapsed against his chest and he moved his finger from her clit. "God, that was wonderful."

Her core continued to throb around his cock as he brushed her hair from her face. "I'm not done yet."

She raised her head and managed a smile. "Bring it on."

Lyra cried out as he flipped her over onto her back, his cock still inside her, his hips between her thighs.

Dare had never felt such an intensity to come in his life. The woman had taken him to an incredible orgasm already, and yet she'd made him want her more than ever.

He paused to bite and suck each of her nipples, driving himself crazy by holding back his own climax. Her skin tasted salty, and when he kissed her full on the mouth, driving his tongue inside her, her wonderfully sweet flavor caused him to draw in his breath.

With a slow rocking motion he began to thrust into her. He was driving himself crazy by taking his time. He slipped his arms under her knees, widening her thighs so that he could bury his cock deep, feel her up to his balls.

Tears streamed from her eyes and he paused. "Are you all right?"

"Don't stop." She gripped his hips. "This just feels so good."

Dare thrust into her, slamming his hips into hers. She was so slick and wet. His balls hit her pussy with every thrust and added to his need to come. The sensation in his groin was almost painful. He ground his teeth and drove into her harder and harder.

Lyra's body shook and she bucked beneath him as she cried out with another orgasm. The spasms of her core around his cock were too much. It tossed him over the edge, throwing him into her so deeply, he felt as if he was a part of her, as if they were one.

This time when he rolled them both onto their sides, she murmured, "You rode me hard, cowboy, and I'm saddle sore." She snuggled against him. "The other condoms can wait. For now."

CHAPTER *FOURTEEN*

When Lyra woke in the morning she definitely felt sore and well used. Her back was to Dare now, her body spooned against his and his arm gripping her tightly around the waist. Beneath a thin sheet, his thigh rested on hers. She loved waking up with him like this. She'd never felt so wanted, so protected.

And content. She didn't want to move from his arms, didn't want to face what the day held for them.

"Morning." His low rumble sent a thrill through her as he kissed the top of her head.

"A very good one—with you," Lyra said softly, and snuggled against him. She would have loved to turn around and have him kiss her thoroughly, but she probably had morning breath and had to brush her teeth. And after all that wild sex, she also needed a nice hot shower.

"Time to get up." He slipped his hand from her waist to cup her breast. "Unless you have a better reason to stay in bed."

She held back a moan and gave a small laugh instead. "I think the shower is where I need to be."

Dare nuzzled her neck. "Shower sex. Works for me."

Lyra laughed louder and slapped at his hand. "I need to get my stuff out of the other bedroom." She drew away from his warmth, slipped off the bed, turned, and took in the sight of him. He had propped himself up in bed with his head in one hand. He was so good-looking with rumpled hair, dark stubble on his face, and the sheet draped over his hips. And the way he was looking at her . . . it made her feel sexy and beautiful.

She forced herself to head into the bathroom to grab a towel. When she had wrapped herself in a nice thick, fluffy one, she glanced at the mirror and groaned. Talk about bed-head! She did her best to finger-comb the short red mop so that it didn't look quite so wild.

Lyra returned to the bedroom, shook her head, and grinned when she saw their clothing scattered all over the place, the bedclothes rumpled, and the quilt on the floor. The towel was snug around her body as she unlocked the door. "Nick would have a cow at this mess," she said just as she opened the door and almost stumbled right into the man himself.

Her face immediately turned so hot that she knew she was bright red. "Um, good morning," she said.

Nick propped his hand against the doorway and glanced over her shoulder at the room. He raised one of his eyebrows as he moved his gaze down Lyra from head to toe before looking at her flaming face again. "It appears to be," he said in a deep bass rumble.

Dare's voice held amusement as he said from behind her, "Out of the lady's way, Donovan."

Nick stepped back. Lyra hurried through the doorway

and practically ran to the bedroom next to Dare's. Her towel slipped as she opened the door and she panicked as she grasped the cloth tightly in one hand while hurrying into the room. She couldn't shut the door fast enough behind her.

She threw herself face-first on the bed. Again. *Damn, damn, damn.*

L ooks like she's a wild one," Nick said as he propped his shoulder against the doorway and looked at Dare with a glint in his eyes.

Dare ran his fingers through his hair and held back a grin. "Stop scaring the crap out of Lyra."

"What's the fun in that?" Nick shrugged. "Breakfast will be ready in twenty minutes." He closed the door behind him.

Dare swung his legs over the side of the bed, got to his feet, and stretched. He felt like he could take on the world after his night with Lyra. Just the thought of her made him hard again. Even though he'd suspected it, the fact that she'd been a virgin still floored him. But when he thought about her life, it made sense. She hadn't been able to trust men. He almost couldn't believe she'd given that trust to him, along with her virginity.

He grabbed a towel out of the bathroom and draped it around his hips before heading to the adjoining room. When he opened the door he heard the shower running and steam escaped the bathroom in a light fog. He closed the door, dropped the towel, and made his way into the bathroom.

When he opened the shower stall door and stepped inside with her, Lyra yelped in surprise, swung around, and punched him in the arm. "Don't scare me like that!"

Dare caught her by her shoulders and captured her mouth with his. Lyra sighed when he raised his head. "You win," she whispered as her big green eyes looked up at him and water from the shower rolled down her cheeks. "You can scare me like this anytime."

"We've been summoned for breakfast." Dare grabbed a bar of soap and began lathering his hands as water beat down on both of them. "We don't have time for what I'd *really* like to do right now."

"Too bad," Lyra said with a moan as he soaped her breasts and tweaked her nipples.

"But we have just enough time that I can touch you." Dare set aside the soap. He continued lathering her breasts with one hand while he slipped his other between her thighs and slid his fingers into her folds.

Lyra gasped, her whole body trembling at the feel of his fingers on her clit. She grabbed his shoulders to steady herself. After their wild bout of sex last night, her clit was ultra sensitive and it barely took a few strokes of his fingers to bring her to climax.

The sensations stormed through her, shaking her from head to toe, and she practically fell into him. Her breasts met his water-slicked chest and his hard cock pressed against her belly. "I don't think I can take another orgasm," she mumbled as she tried to catch her breath.

He chuckled and pressed his lips to her wet hair. "I'll give you time to rest up for tonight."

• • •

Afer a filling breakfast of eggs with Mexican chorizo, along with flour tortillas, Dare and Nick headed downstairs to Nick's high-tech hidden room.

"I need to make some calls," Lyra said as they reached the bedroom where she'd left her pack. There was no way she could go into that surveillance room again. "I've got to check on Mrs. Y and get some things taken care of."

Dare caught her hand. "Don't let anyone know where you are."

"As if I could." Lyra snorted. "*I* don't even know where I am."

Nick gave her a look that said he remembered her "weird, paranoid neat freak" comment and she bit the inside of her cheek. He gestured to the cordless phone on a nightstand beside the bed. "Use one of my secure lines."

When they left, Lyra unplugged her charger from the wall and stuffed it in her pack. She intended to use Nick's line to make any calls, but she turned the cell phone on to see if it gave her a message-waiting notice. In a few moments the phone chirped and displayed a note that she did have a message.

When she dialed the number from Nick's line to check her messages, she found out the call was from Becca. "Everything okay?" Becca asked in the message, her voice filled with concern. "On my answering machine you sounded like something was wrong. Call me ASAP."

Lyra deleted the message, then hurried to return

Becca's call. Relief flowed through her when Becca answered, "Bisbee Market."

"It's me. Linda," Lyra said.

Tinkling bells sounded in the background, and Lyra knew someone must be coming in or leaving Becca's small hometown marketplace. "How are you?" Becca asked Lyra.

"I'm fine." Lyra gripped the phone tight. "I need you to do me a favor. Mrs. Yosko—you know, the elderly lady I live with?—needs someone to check in on her and buy her groceries. I won't be able to . . . for a while."

Becca paused. "Sure, no problem."

"Thanks." Lyra let out a big sigh of relief. "You know pretty much what I buy at the market for her, and she always pays for her groceries. I can even give you some money for helping her out for me."

Becca gave a snort. "I can't believe you'd think I'd charge you for assisting that poor old lady." A rustling sound and Becca sounded distant as she said, "Salsa's on aisle two." Her voice was clear again when she returned. "I'll check on her when I close up shop, and take some groceries while I'm at it."

"Thank you so much." The sense of relief uncoiled some of the tension in Lyra's muscles. "I know you need to get back to work."

"Where are you?" The sound of Becca's voice returned to concerned.

Lyra clenched the phone tighter. "I'm at a friend's house."

"Yes, Mrs. Parker, I'll be right with you," Becca said,

sounding distant again until she replied to Lyra, "Gotta go, sweetie. Don't worry about Mrs. Yosko."

"Thank you." Lyra relaxed her hold on the phone. "Bye."

When she punched the off button, Lyra closed her eyes for a moment. Thank goodness Becca could check in on Mrs. Y.

Lyra sat on the edge of the bed and stared into space for a moment. She should be there. She should be the one taking care of Mrs. Yosko. She'd come to care for the older lady so much.

Lyra's life in Bisbee had been so comfortable, and she'd even grown happy there. Now that was gone. Forever gone.

Damn Neal. Damn him, damn him, damn him!

She buried her face in her hands. She was so tired. So tired of being on the run. So tired of always wondering if The People were going to find her.

It was never going to end. No matter what she did, Neal would be there, somewhere. Even if she escaped this time, she would continue to live her life looking over her shoulder. She didn't know if she'd ever find any kind of peace, especially with Neal forming satellite compounds all over the United States.

Lyra startled when her cell phone played its musical tune.

She eased off the bed and went to it. When she checked the caller ID, it simply said, "Unknown." Not unusual—that's what it usually said when her landlord called her. But Nick had said to use his secure line, so she let the call go to voice mail. A good minute later the display said she had a message, so she dialed her voicemail box again.

The moment she heard the voice in the message she felt blood drain away from her face to her toes. Her legs trembled so badly she had to sit on the bed to keep from falling.

"Lyra," came Neal's voice. "It's time to come back to the fold." His tone had an almost hypnotic effect on some people. So smooth, calming, and masculine.

But it had the opposite effect on Lyra. It caused her stomach to clench so hard it hurt.

"Come home and meet your destiny, Lyra." His voice grew more intense. "Come and save your mother."

A strangled sound came from Lyra's throat. Save her mother?

Neal added, "You will call me, too, if you want to see the old lady again." He clearly enunciated a phone number as Lyra's body went ice-cold.

Old lady? He couldn't be talking about her mother. She was only forty-five.

"Not long now. Soon my semen will be in your body and you'll conceive our special child."

Lyra slapped her hand over her mouth. The phone bounced off the bed and clattered on the floor when she dropped it. She bolted into the bathroom.

She fell to her knees in front of the toilet and threw up. *OhGodohGodohGod.*

Her head spun as the taste of acid filled her mouth. She couldn't get his words or the sound of his voice out of her head and she heaved until nothing else would come up.

◆ ◆ ◆

The sound of sobbing tore at Dare's heart when he started to pass by the bedroom Lyra was using.

He strode through the doorway. In one sweep of his gaze he saw the phone receiver lying on the hardwood floor, but he ignored it. Lyra's sobs came from the bathroom and he hurried to her.

Dare found her on her knees with her hands braced on the toilet seat. Her arms trembled and her body shook with the force of her tears.

"Lyra. Honey." He went to her and saw she'd lost her breakfast in the toilet. He gently took her by the shoulders and she jerked as if startled by his touch.

"No," she said as he drew her to her feet. She kept her gaze off of him. "I don't want you to see me like this."

When she was standing, he guided her to the sink. "I'm here for you and I'm not leaving."

Her shoulders continued to tremble as he turned on the cold water that would be bracing and help her regain some control. He wrapped his arm around her shoulders as she cupped her hands beneath the running water and splashed her face with it.

"Give me a minute." Lyra couldn't keep the shakiness or embarrassment out of her voice. "Just wait for me in the bedroom."

"Are you sure?" He sounded so concerned she cried a little harder.

"Yes. Go. Please."

Dare gave her shoulders another squeeze, released her, and walked out of the bathroom. She raised her head and shut the door behind him. Why did he have to find her like this, so out of control, and having puked her guts up?

She rinsed out her mouth, splashed more water on her face, and flushed the toilet, trying not to look at the contents. The acidic smell was still strong, and she had a few more dry heaves before she calmed down long enough to wash her hands and face and rinse her mouth out again. It was all she could do to force thoughts of Neal and his voice from her mind, to keep from bursting into more tears, and to focus on the important parts of the message.

Her mother. He'd made threats against her mother. But what did he mean by "old lady"?

Mrs. Yosko. Oh, God. He couldn't have.

When Lyra could finally raise her head, she looked into the mirror. Her face was white, but her eyelids and the skin around her eyes were red and swollen. After a few more splashes of cold water on her cheeks and eyelids, she dried off with a hand towel, took a deep breath, and pushed her short hair behind her ears.

Her movements were slow and deliberate. She needed a few more moments before facing Dare and what Neal had said, along with the fact that she had to call him. She'd left her toiletry items in the bathroom, so she brushed her teeth, the mint paste taking away the acidic taste that had been in her mouth.

When she was ready, she took a deep breath, straightened her spine, and pushed the bathroom door open.

Dare was sitting on the bed, the phone receiver gripped tightly in one fist. His look of fury would have scared her to death if she didn't know him, and if she thought it was directed toward her.

Slowly he lifted his gaze and met hers. "He called you," Dare stated.

Lyra took a deep breath and slowly exhaled. "You listened to the message."

He nodded.

She shoved her hand into her hair and clenched it in her fist so tightly it hurt. Welcome pain.

The lines around his mouth softened and she could tell he was attempting to calm himself for her benefit. She bit her lower lip and tried to take a step forward but couldn't.

He got to his feet in a lithe, smooth movement. When he reached her, he wrapped his arms around her and drew her close so that her cheek rested against his chest. She slid her own arms around his waist and held on as tightly as she could. His embrace and his masculine scent were so comforting that she couldn't help but relax and sink into him, never wanting to let him go.

For a long time Dare simply held her and rocked her. "It'll be all right," he said against her hair. "I'll make sure it is."

"How can you?" she whispered. "He threatened my mother. And I think he has Mrs. Yosko."

Dare did his best to control his emotions as he held Lyra. He breathed deeply and forced himself to calm down the best he could. That bastard had left a message that had Dare boiling with rage. "We'll figure something out, honey."

She raised her head and looked at him. Her voice

sounded rusty and unused as she said, "I've got to call Neal now."

"I don't want to ever see you hurting so badly again." Dare gently stroked her hair that sifted through his fingers like strands of silk. "I'll kill that sonofabitch before he ever gets near you."

Lyra gave a long, shuddering breath. "You're not going to kill him." Her expression hardened. "I am."

Dare couldn't help a brief smile. "That's my girl." She was so complex. Vulnerable yet strong. She'd been through so much. She was a survivor. He continued to stroke her hair. "Although I'm not going to give you the chance."

"This is my fight, Dare." She narrowed her eyes. "I'm so tired of running. So tired of looking over my shoulder. Somehow this has got to end. I just don't know how." A flicker of wry humor twisted her mouth. "I could always cut Neal's dick off."

Dare winced but gave a soft laugh. "I'll provide the knife."

Her face paled. "I need to get this over with. I need to call him back."

The musical ring tone of Lyra's cell phone caused her to startle in his arms, and Dare's muscles tensed. He let Lyra slide from his lap until both of them were standing. He picked up the phone and saw "Becca Cell" on the caller ID.

Lyra took the phone from him. "It's my friend."

"Let it go to voice mail," Dare said.

She took a deep breath and nodded. A few moments later when she checked her message from Nick's line, her heart stuttered at the panic in Becca's voice. "Call me on my cell! Right away!"

Heart pounding, Lyra phoned Becca. She started to speak and words tumbled from her mouth. "Mrs. Yosko—she's not here. Her door was open and I went in to make sure she was okay. I've searched the whole house. She's not here, Linda. Anywhere."

Lyra's knees went weak and she sat on the edge of the bed. She glanced at Dare and he had a hard look on his face. *Oh, God. Neal really has her.*

"Call nine-one-one," Lyra said, her voice trembling. "She sometimes takes walks. Maybe she got lost."

"I'll do it now," Becca said. "She couldn't have gotten far, could she?"

Guilt washed over Lyra in a hot wave. "I haven't been there for three days. I don't know."

Becca went silent. So quiet that the hair at the nape of Lyra's neck prickled.

"I just spotted a note on the countertop, beside Mrs. Yosko's address book. The book is open to where your name and cell phone number are," Becca said slowly. "The note says, 'Let Lyra Collins know the old lady is safe in the compound.'" Becca paused as Lyra's spine went ramrod straight. "Who's Lyra?" Becca asked. "What does it mean by 'compound'?"

"Lyra's a-a friend of Mrs. Yosko." Lyra pressed her fingertips to her forehead. "The compound is—is a sort of retirement center. I'll go visit her."

"So, everything's okay?" Becca asked. "I don't need to call the police?"

Police? Should they call the police? Could they do

anything? She needed to talk to Dare first. He'd know what to do.

"Yeah, she's fine," Lyra said, pressing her fingertips harder against her skull. "I'll call you."

Becca said after a moment's hesitation, "All right. Talk with you later." She disconnected her cell phone.

When Lyra pushed the off button on Nick's phone, she looked up at Dare, who was now standing beside her, and a tear rolled from one of her eyes. "The People do have Mrs. Yosko. They left a note saying she's at the compound. I don't know which one. The People could have taken her to Oregon for all I know."

He shoved his hand through his hair, and that dark fury was on his features again. "Shit."

"Should we call the police?" She stood and moved toward him. "I'm afraid he'll hurt my mother. I'm afraid he'll hurt Mrs. Yosko if we do. But we've got to get her." Lyra clenched the phone. "Mrs. Y—she has meds that she takes every day."

Lyra started dialing her voice mail, sick to her stomach that she'd have to listen to Neal's voice and his threats against her mother and her friend.

"I wrote down the phone number while you were in the bathroom." Dare picked up a notepad—trust Nick to have a pen and paper in the room. Dare reached for the receiver she was holding. "Let me call the sonofabitch."

"No." She drew away and stepped back. "It's time I dealt with this."

Even as his features darkened, she dialed the number she saw on the pad.

When Neal answered, she couldn't open her mouth to say anything.

"Lyra," came Neal's smooth voice. "I know you're there. I can hear you breathing."

She swallowed and forced herself to speak. Even though she knew her words wouldn't make a difference, she still said, "Have Adam and Mark bring her back, Neal. Mrs. Yosko's dependent on medications. She could die if you don't take her home."

"Come back to The People," Neal said in his deep, hypnotic voice. "Bring the cowboy. He can take the old lady. But you . . . your place is beside me."

Bitter tears stung Lyra's eyes, but she refused to let them fall. "The Prophecy is bull and you know it. Stop chasing me and let Mrs. Yosko go."

"It's a simple exchange," he said, and she closed her eyes as he spoke, fighting to slow her breathing. "You belong in the fold, serving the Light."

OhGodohGodohGod.

The sick feeling in her belly warred with fury that burned through her like wildfire. She opened her eyes. Vaguely she was aware of Dare stirring beside her, but she couldn't look at him.

"Let Mrs. Yosko go," she said in a voice so calm it surprised her.

"It looks like I'll have to teach you your place when you return," Neal said with a hard edge to his normally serene voice. "I'll take it out on your mother for now."

"No!" Lyra shouted. "Don't touch her!"

"Then be at the Huachuca compound gate at ten tonight. The old lady will be waiting for the cowboy, and your mother won't be harmed. Mark and Adam will be ready for you, and they'll bring you to me."

"You bast—" Lyra started to scream, but the connection went dead.

She jammed her finger against the off button and almost flung the receiver across the room. Instead she took a deep breath and looked up at Dare. "Mark and Adam will trade Mrs. Yosko for me. Ten tonight. Huachuca compound gate."

"Like hell." Dare took Lyra by the shoulders. "I'm not making any kind of Goddamn trade. We're going to get Mrs. Yosko out and keep you away from those S.O.B.'s."

"If I don't go," she said, her voice shaking, "he'll hurt my mother. And Mrs. Yosko could die without her meds."

"Nick and I will take care of Mrs. Yosko," Dare said. "Then we'll figure out a way to get your mother out of the Oregon compound while exposing the bastard for weapons, drugs, rape, child molestation. We *will* figure out a way to get him."

"I'm the only way." Lyra's face was sheet-white. "Neal wants me so badly to fulfill that stupid Prophecy that I really don't have a choice."

Dare could barely keep himself from taking her by the shoulders and shaking some sense into her. *"No,"* he said, almost in a shout. "That's not going to happen."

Lyra clenched her fists at her sides. "If I choose to help, that's my right."

He braced one hand on the bedpost and ran his hand over his face, trying to control his emotions. All he wanted to do was protect her, hold her, and never let her go.

Dare did his best to keep his voice calm and controlled. "I don't give a damn what you think your rights are. The discussion ends now. You *will not* go near that compound."

Lyra's complexion went from pale to scarlet. She opened her mouth. Shut it. Whirled away from him and marched out of the room.

When he could no longer see her, he sat heavily on the bed and scrubbed his hand over his face. "Goddamn. Fuck. Shit."

CHAPTER *FIFTEEN*

They're well protected, but we can come up with a plan and rescue the old lady," Dare said, his fury like a hot blast to his skin.

They were in the surveillance room. Dare braced his hands on a portion of the wide polished wood that ran the length of the room, curved, and extended from another wall. A few padded chairs were positioned in front of monitors. Nick sat in one of the chairs, his fingers tapping on a keyboard as he and Dare both stared at a screen. A grid moved in various angles across the screen.

Dare pointed to a spot on the digital map. "There. We could take out the guards and cut through the fence."

"The guards are armed better than the Mexican Mafia." Nick tapped the keyboard and this time a clearer picture of the compound came up. He zoomed in close enough that he saw guards bearing weaponry so powerful it was illegal in civilian hands. "AK-47s and M249s."

Nick pointed to the screen. "Two ten-foot-high chain-link fences," he said, and Dare ground his teeth at the sight of the double fencing surrounding the compound.

Nick continued, "Looks like five-foot-wide rolls of razor wire from the inside to the outside fence."

Dare's shoulders vibrated with the force of his anger.

Nick clicked more keys on the keyboard and the view drew back as he said, "Guards stationed every twenty feet around the perimeter inside and out. We'll have to take out anyone who gets in our way."

"Now that we know what we're going to do with the guards," Dare said, "tell me what you've got for explosives."

After donning his Kevlar vest, Dare shoved daggers into the outside sheath of each boot while he stood in Nick's great room. He tried to shake off the fury that had gripped him since Neal Barker had first left the message for Lyra.

To prepare for the attack, Dare had dressed all in black from the pants he had stuffed into the rubber-soled boots specially designed for recon to the black cap he was wearing. He'd slung a utility belt around his waist with more ammunition and a couple of Nick's IEDs—Improvised Explosive Devices. His Glock was tucked into the back of his pants and his SIG-Sauer 226 in the utility belt. His shirt was long-sleeved to protect his arms.

Nick was decked out and armed much the same.

Lyra came upstairs, through the archway. She wore a black T-shirt with her blue jeans and jogging shoes. "You're not leaving me," she said when she reached them. "I'm going with you."

"Hell, no." Dare shoved another knife into his utility

belt and glared at Lyra. Just the thought of putting her in any kind of danger made his gut tighten.

She glared right back. "This is my fight, too. As a matter of fact, this whole thing is because of me. None of this would have happened if it wasn't for the fact that Neal is so obsessed with me and his freaking Prophecy."

"You're staying here." Dare brushed past Lyra toward the back door that led to the garage. The soles of his boots didn't make a sound as he moved. "End of discussion."

Lyra wanted to scream at the stubborn man and stomp her feet like a child. How ironic that the one place she didn't want to be was the one place she had to go. She'd been running for years. But she was tired of running and now it was time to turn and face Neal, to walk into the lion's den to save her friend, the woman who had been like a grandmother to her, and to save her own mother. With her hands on her hips, she said, "You can't make me stay."

He stopped long enough to cast a look over his shoulder. "You're not going with us."

"Oooooh!" Lyra clenched her hands into fists as Nick strode by her and followed Dare through the kitchen. "Listen, you S.O.B.," she said as she followed them.

They shut the door in her face. A couple of high-pitched beeps and the sound of door locks slamming home caused her to stumble back.

They didn't. They hadn't just locked her inside the house. No way.

Beyond pissed, Lyra jerked on the handle, but it didn't budge. Heat kicked in and she banged her fist against the door. "Let me out!" She hit it so hard her hand hurt. The door was so solid the only sound was the thump of her fist against the wood.

She lowered her hands. For a moment she gripped them tightly, then dropped her head forward in defeat, her forehead against the wood. "That S.O.B." Her limbs began to tremble with the force of her anger, and she raised her chin again.

There had to be some way out of this house. She went to the front door. Locked. The glass arcadia doors that led to a lush green backyard, just as frozen shut. It was like Nick had some kind of lockdown on the place.

"Dammit." She plopped down in one of the cushioned chairs in the great room and stared into space. A tingle crept up the back of her neck. What if something happened to Dare or Nick? She bit her lower lip hard, but the pain was welcome. She couldn't bear it if Dare was hurt . . . or worse. Not to mention Nick and Mrs. Yosko.

And what about her mother? Lyra had never forgiven her mother all these years for taking them into the cult. But Lyra didn't want to see Sara abused—or worse—because of her.

And because Dare hadn't taken Lyra, now her mother was in jeopardy, as well as Mrs. Y.

Lyra ground her teeth. Damn him.

Now all she could do was sit and wait.

Nick drove the Jeep toward the foot of the Huachuca Mountains, the vehicle's headlights slicing a path through the darkness. During the drive neither man spoke. The only sounds were the hum of wheels over asphalt, the infrequent whoosh of a car passing by, and the occasional sound of Nick changing gears.

Both men knew the base of the Huachucas fairly well, and the compound was in an area that Dare was more than familiar with. The compound was laid out in a large empty stretch surrounded by thick vegetation.

Instead of heading directly up to the front gate, Nick drove the specially equipped four-wheeler along a back trail. Pine and oak, as well as piñon trees and century plants, grew thick along the rocky dirt road they were traveling on. He shut off the lights and they both donned night-vision goggles.

When they came as close to the compound as they dared, Nick shut the Jeep down. For a moment there was only silence, with the exception of the slight tick of the vehicle from the heat of the engine. Nick and Dare both climbed out, and Dare silently shut his door to walk to the driver's side. He and Nick gave each other a quick nod before Nick slipped into the shadows and became one with the darkness.

Dare swung himself up and into the Jeep's driver's seat and started the vehicle. Dirt and rocks crunched beneath the Jeep's tires as he slowly drove back the way they came. When he reached the highway, he pulled onto it, flicked on his headlights, ripped off his night-vision goggles, buzzed up the windows, and headed for the compound's front gate.

It didn't take long to reach the well-lit compound. Dare glanced at the Jeep's illuminated clock. Twenty-two hundred hours—10:00 P.M.—on the dot.

Two guards wearing fatigues were stationed to either

side of the gate, their gazes focused on the Jeep. Both held AK-47s. Dare rolled the Jeep slowly to the gate and shut the vehicle down.

He turned off the headlights.

Despite the brightly lit compound, Dare couldn't tell if one of the people in the compound was the old lady.

He held on to the thread of hope that the dark-tinted windows of the Jeep would make it impossible for anyone to tell how many people sat inside.

The twin front gates slowly swung open.

Nick had better be in position.

Dare jammed the keys in his pocket, took a deep breath, and climbed out of the vehicle. He started toward the guards. Blood rushed through his veins as he neared the compound.

Just as he reached the first two guards, the heavens exploded.

The guards' attention whipped toward the wall of flames shooting up into the night sky.

In that moment of distraction, Dare drew out his Glock and slammed the butt of his weapon against one of the guard's temples, dropping him.

In a fluid movement, Dare jammed his boot into the other guard's midsection and took him out with one shot.

More screams and shouts along with another explosion reamed the night. People ran from one direction and the next.

Amidst all the chaos, Dare bolted for the next guard inside the front gate, who'd also swung his attention toward the explosion. The man turned and drew his gun. The compound was lit up brightly enough that

Dare could pick off the man and two other guards before they knew what hit them.

A quick scan and Dare's gaze landed on an old lady. She looked at the men surrounding her, then straight at Dare.

Four men stood around her, including Mark and Adam. Mark called out to more guards around the compound to bring Dare down.

Explosion after explosion rocked the night.

The armed men posted beside Mrs. Yosko didn't move until they saw Dare running toward them. Both guards looked like they wanted to run but raised their weapons. Dare dropped and rolled. Two shots and both collapsed to the ground.

As soon as her guards were taken out, Mrs. Yosko started hauling ass toward the gate. Pretty fast for an old lady.

Mark had been shouting directions but stopped when Dare reached him. As far as Dare could tell, Mark was unarmed, but he wasn't taking any chances. Dare held his Glock in his left hand when he reached the bastard. In the next moment Dare's right fist headed straight for the cult member's nose.

Mark countered with an upswing of his own, a powerful sweep that blocked Dare's punch. Dare caught his balance, ducked to the left.

Mark swung his fist toward Dare's jaw and shouted, "Where's Lyra?"

"You'll never get your Goddamn hands on her," Dare snarled.

From his side vision, Dare saw three men in fatigues running toward them.

With every ounce of strength he had, Dare slammed his fist into Mark's jaw—the same jaw he'd hit the other day.

The man's head snapped back.

He stumbled. Tripped and fell on his ass.

Dare didn't have time for the feeling of satisfaction that hit had given him. He'd needed the physical contact with the man who'd been chasing and threatening Lyra.

With a powerful kick to his midsection, Dare took Adam down next. The unarmed man flew back and struck his head on the rocky ground.

Dare's heart pounded full throttle. Now he had three more men bearing down on him at once. He blew away the first. Before he could fire again, Nick was behind the men. He was a blur as he took down the two still standing, using blows to their necks, backs, and knees. They weren't going anywhere.

"Now!" Nick shouted as he bolted to the old lady. As soon as he reached her, he scooped Mrs. Yosko into his arms and ran for the gate. Mrs. Y clung to Nick and looked over his shoulder at Dare.

Two guards wearing terrified expressions came at them as they reached the compound gates.

Even holding the old lady, Nick took one man down with a single shot. Dare nailed the second with two.

Nick and Dare ran for the Jeep with Dare guarding Nick's back.

Shots pelted the ground. One whizzed by Dare's ear. *Fuck. That was close.*

Nick deposited Mrs. Y in the back, then swung himself into the passenger seat while slamming the door behind him.

Dare was already in the driver's seat. He jammed the keys into the ignition, started the Jeep, and put it into gear.

He kept the headlights off as he spun the vehicle away from the compound. Nick handed him a pair of night-vision goggles, and he jerked them on as the Jeep tore down the road in the darkness.

Pings against metal. The bulletproof back window took several drummings.

Dare floored it. When they reached the desolate highway, the Jeep skidded onto the asphalt. It fishtailed and then evened out as he pushed the vehicle to its limit.

"Clear." Nick's sigh of relief was audible. "You sure know how to throw a party."

Dare ripped off his goggles at the same time he flooded the highway with the Jeep's headlights. He cast a glance over his shoulder at Mrs. Yosko, whose hair was wild about her face, but she had a lucid, determined look to her expression.

Just as he turned back to the road, the old lady said in an irritated voice, "They didn't let me bring my cat."

L yra died a thousand deaths as she paced in her bedroom. She rubbed her arms, feeling cold and hot all at once. How were Dare and Nick? Mrs. Yosko? Would any of them be hurt . . . or killed?

Lyra paced and paced. She couldn't sit still for long. She needed to do *something*.

The door to the bedroom jerked open.

Dare.

When she saw it was him, she ran to him and flung

her arms around his neck. He smelled of smoke, dirt, and blood. The scratches she'd given him on his cheek when they'd met seemed fainter, but maybe that was because he had a nasty bruise developing around one eye. The bruise around his other eye from that first escape from her home was yellowing.

She pulled away. "What about Nick and Mrs. Y?"

"Here and barely a scratch." Dare rubbed his forehead with dirty fingers.

"What about you?" Lyra asked.

He settled his hands on her waist. "I'm fine, honey."

"Well, good," she said just before she drew back and slammed her fist into his belly.

Dare gave a grunt of surprise and bent slightly before straightening, a confused look on his face.

"You bastard!" Lyra wiped angry tears from her eyes. His abs were so hard her hand ached. "Don't you ever do that to me again. Don't you leave me behind. And don't put yourself in danger like that ever again!"

He smiled. The jerk smiled. Just as she drew her hand back for another punch, he pulled her into his embrace, trapping her arms at her sides.

She squirmed, trying to get away from him, and even kicked his shins like she had the first time he'd held her when trying to save her from The People. "Let me go!"

Dare lowered his head so fast she didn't have time to catch her breath before his mouth claimed hers. He kissed her hard and fierce and gripped her so tightly she felt like he was going to crush her.

She fought against his kiss, against his touch, against his demands . . . and then found herself just melting into him, as if she was a part of him. She gave in. Completely. Totally.

She was his.

He tasted and smelled so untamed, so masculine, and kissed her with more intensity than he ever had before. Something was different, as if adrenaline was still pumping through him and he needed to release it.

She knew it was still thrumming through her, and it made her want him in ways she never had before.

His erection was just as hard and as fierce against her belly as his kiss was to her mouth. Lyra couldn't help it. She couldn't stay mad. At least not now. She wanted him with a power so intense she could barely breathe from it.

She'd read in a book once how warriors or soldiers had so much adrenaline pumping through them after a battle that they needed release, through some kind of physical activity, especially sex.

Dare was most definitely a warrior, and she felt that same need from her worry and her anger.

When he drew back, the desire in his gaze was as marked as the feelings surging within her. It was a look filled with intensity, fire, passion. Her lips felt bruised from his kisses, her face raw from his stubble. "Now," he said in a growl.

She nodded and hurried to remove her shoes and jeans. Dare just laid his utility belt on a chair, shoved his pants down far enough to free his erection, and took her to the floor. She gave a cry of surprise, but he was gentle despite the ferocity of his expression.

Immediately he was between her thighs. He braced

his arms to either side of her chest. His jaw tensed and he thrust his cock straight into her core.

Lyra cried out at the sudden invasion and pleasure. He was so big, so passionate, so powerful. She couldn't take her eyes from his as he drove in and out, pounding so hard he was hurting her at the same time he was pleasuring her. The feel of his pants scraping the insides of her thighs somehow heightened her pleasure. She gripped his biceps that flexed with every thrust and dug her nails into his skin. Sweat dripped down his forehead and the sides of his head, and dirt smudged his cheeks and jaws.

The feelings. So many feelings. Anger, fear, worry, desire, all wound up inside her. She felt herself spiraling, spinning, heading for territory she'd never been to before.

Darkness clouded her vision. Stars sparked in the darkness that almost kept her from seeing Dare's eyes. Her mind spun. Her body spiraled. Her orgasm exploded through her.

Her body bucked and his every thrust made her cry out.

Dare tensed. "Damn," he growled. "No condom."

He pounded in and out a few more times, then jerked his cock out of her core. His semen spilled onto her T-shirt. He continued to move against her, his eyes closed, his come spurting out in hot, wet streaks on her cloth-covered belly. When he stopped, he held himself above her, his eyes still closed, his biceps tense, the line of his neck taut.

The scent of his semen and her woman's musk mixed

with the strong smells of smoke and dirt. His breathing was deep and hard, and she swore she could hear the pounding of both of their hearts.

When he finally opened his eyes, he looked at her just before taking her mouth again in a rough kiss. His cock was growing hard against her belly, and she knew that with the power of their joined feelings on this night, they could keep going and going.

He raised his head and studied her with a look still filled with intensity, fire, passion. Her lips felt bruised from his kisses, her thighs and sex bruised from his thrusts, her back and tailbone bruised from the floor.

In all her life, she'd never felt so alive.

CHAPTER *SIXTEEN*

L yra took off the now-sticky T-shirt and Dare removed his shirt as well. The heat between them
was incredible, and she trembled from the force
of their joining and the power of their need.

Her hand ached from when she'd punched him,
but he didn't even sport a red mark where her fist
had landed against his firm abs. She went to him and
wrapped her arms around his waist and hugged him.
He engulfed her in his strong embrace and rested his
chin on top of her head. He was so tense she felt it in
the rigidity of his body against hers.

Dare still felt pumped from the small war they'd
waged, but he had lessened it by using Lyra's body. At
that thought he sobered. "Did I hurt you?"

She moved her soft lips to his chest and kissed him,
flicking her tongue out and sending a rod of desire
straight to his cock. "I'm fine."

Despite the fact that he wanted to take her again,
Dare and Lyra took quick showers, then dressed. They
started to leave the room to check on Nick and Mrs.
Yosko.

Lyra's cell phone rang.

She came to a complete stop. Dropped her hands to her sides, her eyes locked with Dare's.

Her stomach churned.

Who was calling this late?

Neal?

Dare's expression was grim as he pushed past her and picked up the cell. He glanced at the display. "It says 'Becca home.'"

A whoosh of relief went through Lyra. "That means she's calling me from her home number." She looked at Dare. "I know. Call her back from Nick's secure line."

He nodded. When her cell phone stopped ringing she went to the phone beside the bed and picked up the portable receiver. She dialed Becca's number and her friend picked up on the third ring.

"Hello?" Becca's voice sounded tentative.

"It's me," Lyra said. "You just called and I missed it."

"Oh." Becca sounded both relieved and stressed at the same time. "I was calling to tell you that I picked up Mrs. Yosko's prescription medications for you. I, um, noticed them on the countertop when I found the note. Her cat seemed hungry, so I took her, too."

"Oh, good." Lyra breathed out a long sigh. "Mrs. Y is here and she does need the meds right away. I know it's late." She glanced at the clock and saw it was after midnight. "But would you mind if I pick the meds and Dixie up in about thirty minutes?"

"Not at all." Becca's voice perked up. "You know me. I like to stay up late."

"Wait." Dare placed his hand over the mouthpiece. "Tell her to meet us in the middle of Bisbee High

School's parking lot. Dead center, where there's plenty of light."

Lyra frowned but nodded. "Hey, Becca. Can you do me a favor? Meet me at BHS's parking lot, in the middle, under one of the lights."

"Well, um, why?" Becca's confusion came across loud and clear.

"Humor me?" Lyra said, and tried to give a casual laugh.

"Er, sure," Becca said. "Thirty minutes at the high school lot."

"Thanks," Lyra said. "I'll see you in a few."

Becca clicked off. It was great that she'd had the foresight to get Mrs. Y's cat and meds.

Dare ran his fingers through his wet hair. "I don't like this one bit."

"She needs her meds, and *soon*." Lyra gave him a little shove so that she could walk past him. "Besides, Becca's been one of my closest friends for a couple years now."

Lyra went upstairs and was relieved to see the elderly lady reclining on the easy chair in Nick's great room. She looked a little tired but none the worse for wear. Lyra knelt beside Mrs. Y and brushed the woman's cottony white hair from her face.

"Are you all right, Mrs. Yosko?" Lyra said softly while her gaze swept over her, checking the woman for any visible signs of mistreatment.

"Fine, girl. How are you holding up?" the elderly lady said with a frown.

Lyra smiled, but it was a tired smile. "I'm okay."

Mrs. Y's watery brown eyes were fixed on Lyra. "Dixie's probably hungry."

"Of course." Lyra took her friend's hand and squeezed it. "We'll get her and your meds for you right away." She stood and let the woman's hand slide from hers. "You need to stay the night. We've got to find someplace safe for you to go before you can leave. With those bad men around, you're not safe."

"Sonsofbitches," Mrs. Y grumbled, and Lyra smiled. The elderly lady still had her spirit, that was for sure. Mrs. Y met Lyra's gaze. "Like I told you. You've got to stop running. Face them head-on and take them out," Mrs. Y said before Lyra could respond. "You were always looking over your shoulder, dear." The woman's expression softened. "Knew you were on the run from something. Could see it in your eyes."

Lyra hugged Mrs. Yosko's thin frame, her heart filled with love for the woman. The woman who had won Lyra's trust and her friendship, something that had been so hard to give.

As Lyra held her, Mrs. Y still had that comforting scent about her, but it mixed with smoke from what had happened tonight. What had she been through because of Lyra?

"I'm sorry," Lyra whispered. "If it wasn't for me, if I'd faced them head-on to begin with, none of this would have happened."

Mrs. Yosko drew away and gave Lyra a look of reprimand. "Girl, it's not your fault and you know it. Get over it. Now get the sonsofbitches."

Lyra's lips trembled as she smiled. "That's exactly

what we're going to do. Find some way to end this once and for all."

Drugs. Underage sex. Polygamy. Dare said those were all things that could put Neal Barker away if they could prove it. But how could they? And even if he was sentenced, would Neal come after her with more vengeance when he got out?

She turned her attention to Mrs. Yosko and her heart thundered. The woman had leaned back in her chair and closed her eyes. She looked weak and as if she might faint.

Lyra whipped around to face Dare, who had come up behind her. "We've got to get her meds. *Now.*"

Dare took a deep breath. Would the cult members have reacted this fast?

Hell, yeah.

Dare raked his hand through his hair. "I don't want to take any chances with you, honey. You shouldn't go."

"Give me a break." Lyra headed for the front door. "Besides, Dixie—Mrs. Y's cat—doesn't usually take to strangers." She glared back at him. "This time you are *not* leaving me."

Dare pulled on his black cap. His weapons belt hung from his waist, his Glock at his back. He was prepared for just about anything.

He sure as hell hoped so.

Dare's muscles remained tense as he guided his sports car through the Mule Pass Tunnel and then onto the street that would lead them to the main drag in Historic Bisbee, then on to the road that ran by BHS. It was close to 1:00 A.M. Exhaustion blurred his eyesight before it cleared again.

When they reached the lot, Dare instantly took in everything in sight. The green Buick that had seen *much* better days. A dark-haired woman stood next to the car holding a calico cat.

Dare frowned. Some of the parking-lot lights were out. The lighting was not optimal. His gaze roved the surrounding area. Where Becca had parked was in the middle of the lot, as Lyra had asked her, and no other vehicles were in sight. Bushes across the street on the east were a football field length's away, and the school itself was a good hundred yards away on the west and south. Nothing but a soccer and baseball field to the north.

He rolled his sports car to a stop beside the sedan.

In a quick sweep, he saw the woman looking beyond nervous as she stood by the driver's side door holding the cat. The cat squirmed, trying to get out of Becca's arms.

And then he saw it. The trunk wasn't closed properly.

Before he could stop her, Lyra opened the passenger door and climbed out with speed that surprised him. "Becca," she said. "Thanks so much."

"Lyra!" he shouted. "Back in the car!"

She ignored him. Dare had his Glock in his hand when he opened his own door and rushed out.

Dixie bounded from the woman's arms to the ground and arched her back. Gave a loud yowl and a hiss.

The calico cat's actions startled Lyra so badly she held her hand to her heart. Dixie rarely made any sounds, and Lyra had never heard her yowl like that.

Hair prickled at the nape of Lyra's neck as Dare grabbed her arm. "In the car. Now!"

The trunk of the sedan sprang open. Before he could get a fix on the shadowy forms, something pierced his clothing and buried itself in his thigh.

Fuck.

He aimed toward the trunk even as dizziness started to overcome him. He tried to get off a couple of shots, but Becca and Lyra were in the way.

Dare stumbled. His legs gave out and he collapsed. Slammed his head against the asphalt.

For a moment he heard voices as his head spun. "Sorry. Money. Oregon."

Then there was nothing but blackness.

L yra's heart lurched, harder, faster.

"Dare!" She screamed as he crumpled onto the parking lot. He had some kind of dart sticking out of his thigh.

Her gaze shot up to see Mark with a satisfied smirk on his bruised face and a gun in his hands. Adam was climbing out of the trunk behind him.

"You bastard!" she shouted as she charged him. She had her fist out, ready to slam it into Mark's face, when Adam caught her upper arms from behind and jerked her backward. She stumbled, her feet almost flying out from under her before she regained her footing.

Mark's smirk only increased as she screamed and fought against Adam's hold.

She threw a look at her friend. "Becca! Use your cell phone and call the police!"

Becca wrung her hands and looked apologetic. "I needed the money, Linda. I'm sorry."

"What?" Lyra went still and Adam tightened his grip on her. A slow buzzing started in her head. "Money?"

"The store is going under." Becca's voice trembled. "When they came to me and explained everything, I knew it was the right thing to do."

Lyra just stared at Becca, feeling like the world was caving in. "You—you were my friend."

Becca licked her lips. "Like I said, they explained how you belong in Oregon with your family—and all about your mental illness. You'll be okay."

Lyra couldn't think of a thing to say. She'd grown to trust Becca. Now that trust was gone. Gone. Gone.

"It's time to take you home," came Adam's voice behind her just before his hand covered her mouth and nose and she felt a sharp poke as he buried something in her right hip.

Drugs! A dart like what they'd done to Dare.

Goddamn it! What had they put into her body?

She struggled against Adam's grip, fighting with everything she had.

An odd feeling overcame her. She felt paralyzed. Floppy. Suddenly she had to focus all of her energy on breathing.

"I'm sorry." Becca's voice sounded distant, hollow.

Adam gripped Lyra under her arms. Mark picked up her useless legs.

As if she were a rag doll they carried her to the trunk of the car.

The stars above blurred.

Darkness swept her away.

Jackhammers pounded inside Dare's skull. He tried to open his eyes, but a bright light shot more pain through his head and he shut them tight again. "What the hell?" Every word pounded inside his head.

It all came back in a flood of memories. He and Lyra had been meeting a woman named Becca. Lyra had jumped out of the car and he had gone after her. The car trunk of the sedan had opened and pain had slammed into his thigh.

This time he did get his eyes open despite the pain and the bright light somewhere overhead. His head felt like cotton was wrapped around his brain and he had to shake the feeling off.

He was lying underneath one of the high school's parking-lot lights. His head ached like a motherfucker. Slowly—because the pounding in his head wouldn't let him turn much faster—he pushed himself up. His car was still running.

A cat's loud yowl screamed through his head. The calico cat walked back and forth in front of Dare's face, her tail twitching. On the ground where the sedan had been was a large clear baggie filled with what looked like bottles of prescription drugs.

He blinked. Tried to focus better. The cat meowed again.

He pushed himself to his feet. His thigh burned and he looked down to see a dart poking out of his leg. He yanked it out. It was a thin cylinder, about six inches long. A syringe. He brought it a few inches from his face. Veterinary. No doubt stolen. No doubt something to disable him while they carted Lyra away.

He spotted another syringe on the ground. His head spun as he leaned down, but he managed to grab it. Same thing.

Lyra was gone. The bastards had her and had used the same method to disable her. And she was helpless. If the assholes got the dose wrong, she might even be dying—or dead.

His mind still reeling, he stumbled to his car. His balance was off from the concussion he'd suffered from hitting his head on the asphalt when he went down. He had to hang on to the open car door until his head stopped spinning.

Dare braced both hands on top of the car. Pain and rage seared him so completely he couldn't see. Guilt lay like a heavy weight in his gut.

She couldn't be dead. No. They wouldn't take a chance like that. Their stupid Prophecy—that scum Neal would want her alive, just not able to fight back.

Dare clenched his fists. He had lost Lyra, but he was damn sure going to get her back.

He pushed himself away from the car, his head clearing with his determination. He almost fell over when he picked up the baggie of meds. When he opened the car door he tossed the bag onto the passenger seat.

Then he wrapped his hands around the cat's middle. She meowed again as he settled her into the passenger seat, next to the baggie. She looked both indignant and irritated—or something. He slid into the driver's seat to find the keys dangling from the column. Of course. The car was still running.

A vein in his forehead began to pulse in time with the pounding in his head. He ground his teeth. His whole body shook with fury as the full realization hit him.

He hadn't protected Lyra like he'd promised her.

Dare put the car in gear and started to head toward Nick's. His feet were so leaden as he pushed in the clutch and changed gears, he wished he'd bought a car with an automatic transmission.

The cat screamed and dug her claws into the leather upholstery. The scent of piss was strong as the scared cat clung to the car seat.

By the time he reached Nick's place Dare was ready to tear Neal Barker apart, piece by fucking piece.

After Nick opened the front door, Dare let the cat jump to the floor before he slammed the door shut behind him. His body was shaking almost uncontrollably.

"Lyra?" Nick said in a too-calm voice.

Dare swung around to face him, hands clenched into fists. Goddamn, but he needed to hit someone, something, anything.

"They got her." Dare's words came out like a roar. "I didn't protect her. They got her."

Nick scrubbed his hand over his face. "I figured."

The cat yowled.

Dare told Nick the full story. "Before I passed out I think I heard them say 'Oregon.' I think they're taking her there."

Nick's face darkened and when his gaze met Dare's, his eyes were cold, calculating.

Nick went to the wet bar, took out a bottle of scotch, and poured a shot. He strode back to Dare, carrying the scotch, and handed the shot glass to him.

Dare took it without question and slammed it back. The scotch was expensive and smooth, but it still burned the back of his throat as it went down. Nick took the empty glass from Dare's hand, refilled it, and gave it back to him. He downed it, welcoming the slow burn. It cleared the fog from his mind and took the edge off his rage.

"It's almost oh four hundred." Nick filled the glass again. "You're not going to be worth shit if you don't get some rest, even if it's only an hour or two," he said as Dare swallowed a third shot.

Everything within Dare shouted at him to go to the Oregon compound now and get Lyra out. But he recognized the fact that this time they would have to have reinforcements. Neal would be more than prepared for an attack.

Dare wiped his mouth with the back of his hand. Despite himself, the tenseness in his muscles eased due to the scotch. "All right." He handed the glass back to Nick, who filled it for a fourth time. After Dare slammed it back he could feel the alcohol starting to take effect. He rarely drank more than a beer or two, and this scotch was going to knock him on his ass.

This time he placed the shot glass upside down on the top of the bottle of scotch, then dug into his pockets for the baggie with Mrs. Y's meds. His sight was already blurring as he took the meds to the wet bar and set the bag on the granite surface. "Directions probably on the bottles. You know what to do."

His whole body was on fire from the scotch and his muscles were relaxing to the point where he knew he wouldn't be able to stand much longer. Not to mention he was still reeling from the blow to his head. He stumbled to the couch and fell flat on his back.

"An hour," he mumbled as his sight started to darken. "Wake me up in an hour."

D are woke with a start from his recurring nightmare—the bullet hole in his partner's head wouldn't leave his mind. Dare's throat closed as he thought of how he'd let down his partner.

And now Lyra.

Dim light from the skylights told Dare it was early morning. Damn, he'd only planned on sleeping an hour at the most. He didn't need sleep. He needed to get to Lyra.

Dare slid his hand over his face. It came away slick with sweat. He swung his legs over the side of the couch and pushed himself to a sitting position. His head spun from the movement and he had to grip the couch cushions until his knuckles ached in order to steady himself. He was pretty sure it was mostly from the drugs and concussion rather than the scotch.

But neither dulled the stark fact. Dare buried his face in his hands.

He'd lost Lyra.

And he'd fallen in love with the woman who was now back in her own personal hell.

CHAPTER *SEVENTEEN*

She was dreaming. No, it was a nightmare. Lyra kept her eyes shut tight and refused to open them. It wasn't possible she was back in the hands of The People. It wasn't.

Coarse cloth covered her body, and it chafed her bare nipples. She was naked beneath a robe, its sash tight around her waist. The feel of the handwoven cloth on her body was too familiar for this to be a dream.

As were the ties at her wrists and ankles. She was flat on her back on some kind of thin mattress, bound, and spread-eagled. Her bindings were made of thick twine and didn't give a fraction when she tugged against them. Her wrists and ankles ached, her head pounded.

Tears threatened to spill from behind her closed eyelids, but Lyra forced herself to concentrate on her anger instead.

Damn Neal. Damn him!

And someone she'd trusted had betrayed her. Becca had taken money in trade for Lyra's freedom.

Her eyes burned even more. It had been so hard to trust anyone, and once again she'd been screwed over.

She'd trusted Dare to protect her, and here she was.

No, it wasn't his fault. She'd known from the beginning that she was responsible for her destiny. She should have insisted on running again until he finally let her go. Even as the thought crossed her mind, she knew that would never have happened. He had considered it his duty to protect her.

Lyra bit her lower lip. No more thoughts of that or anything else. She had to focus on the present.

She needed to open her eyes. She had to face reality eventually. And the sooner she came to terms with her predicament, the sooner she could start making plans on how to get out of it.

Slowly she lifted her eyelids. Blinked. Her mind spun, and she shut her eyes. When she finally blinked again, some of the fuzziness slipped away. Her surroundings gradually came into focus. She felt soreness in her hip where the men had plunged the needle.

She was someplace dim, and canvas slanted from poles. A tent, of course. The People lived in tents—except for Neal. He had always lived in the Temple itself.

At the thought of him, her stomach churned. Every time she had thought of him over the past five years she would get sick to her stomach. Now it was worse.

This was a much larger tent than she ever remembered any of The People living in. None of The People were allowed to have anything larger than a small tent, or to own anything save their clothing. Everything else was shared and made by The People themselves. They made their own clothing, blankets, soaps, shampoos, candles, and so on.

There was a light hanging from above, though. A real incandescent light. Probably lit from a generator. The People had to use candles in their tents, and only as long as necessary.

She tilted her head to see more. She was lying on a thin mattress on the floor and she was tied to metal stakes that had been driven through the canvas floor and into the ground. When her gaze traveled the space, she felt woozy and had to close her eyes for a moment. She opened them and saw that the only other things were an altar, a burning red candle, and a strange object beside it.

The flicker of the red candlelight through the glass jar was almost mesmerizing. She pulled her gaze from it and saw that the object beside the bar was a bong— she recognized it from being around Neal so much and from the heavy marijuana smell hanging in the air.

A sudden thought knifed through her and she felt as if she'd been stabbed. She was naked beneath the robe . . .

Had she been raped?

She took deep gulps of air and tried to control her breathing. Of course not. She would have been able to tell the moment she woke up.

A cold chill iced her heart. If Neal was successful and "married" her, she knew what he would force on her. The thought made her so nauseous that bile rose up in her throat and she felt like throwing up again. She shoved the thought back and steeled herself.

Would Neal take advantage of her while she was tied up?

The Prophecy.

A huge sigh of relief eased through her, and her

muscles relaxed some. Part of the Prophecy was that no one, including Neal, was to have sex with her until they were married. Only then would he consummate their joining.

Consummate.

Oh, God.

She closed her eyes for a moment until she was calm enough to open them again. She turned her thoughts to Dare, and a myriad of emotions welled within her. This time she almost did cry. She needed him. To hold her, to love her.

Her heart ached and she bit her lower lip when a new realization hit her. She'd fallen in love with Dare, with everything about him.

She loved Dare's protectiveness, his determination to rescue those he cared about, even a woman and an old lady he didn't know. His sense of humor, his easy camaraderie with his friend. His sexy grin. The way he kissed her, made love to her, and made her feel whole.

No matter that she'd been taken, he had her trust . . . and her love.

But she just might never see him again if she didn't find some way out of this mess. Hope flickered within her. Dare and Nick had saved Mrs. Yosko. Could they save her in time, too? What about her mother?

Lyra frowned. Was she in Arizona, or had they brought her to Oregon? She took a deep breath and her heart sank. There could be no mistaking the clean Oregon air and the strong scents of cedar and Douglas fir.

The canvas flap opened and more of the clean, humid mountain air flowed into the tent. For a moment she couldn't make out the large, dark form ducking into the tent. But when the flap settled closed again and her eyes readjusted to the dimness of the tent, her body went cold.

Neal.

He hadn't changed much in five years. He was still a good-looking man with his high cheekbones, blue eyes, and long black hair that passed his shoulders. He still had that same charismatic smile.

A smile that made her stomach curdle.

"Lyra." Neal's smile broadened as he lowered himself on one knee beside her. He brushed her hair from her face and she flinched and tried to move her head away. As if she'd had no reaction to his touch, he continued to stroke her hair. "It's good to have you back."

Lyra didn't respond. She was afraid to. Too often she had witnessed new inductees being drugged until they settled into The People's way of life. She needed her wits sharp and clear.

Neal settled his hand on her belly and she recoiled—only her bonds kept her from moving more than a fraction. He smelled of marijuana.

"Soon the new Messiah will be growing in your womb," he said as he pressed his hand against her. "You're ready now."

Lyra swallowed the acid rising up in her throat. She broke out in a sweat. Her stomach heaved. Her eyes watered.

She turned her head to the side, facing Neal—and puked.

"Fuck!" His shout as he scrambled away from her barely registered. "Too much juice in that tranquilizer," he growled.

She didn't have much in her stomach, and dry heaves continued to wrack her body. Moisture ran from the corner of her mouth and she shuddered. She saw the swirl of his robe and felt the rush of air over her face as he stormed out of the tent.

Lyra took deep breaths and turned her head to face the tent's peak. A bitter laugh lodged in her throat. Yeah, right. A tranq didn't have anything to do with it.

In moments, a blond woman ducked into the tent and Lyra turned to look at her. Shock registered on her face, probably from seeing Lyra tied down. The woman carried several coarse cloths, two cups, and a cloth bag. She composed her features and knelt on the floor beside the mattress.

"I'm Carrie." The woman lifted the back of Lyra's head and brought the cup to Lyra's lips. "Take a drink of water, swish, and spit into this empty cup."

Water dribbled down her chin as she obeyed, but she was relieved to get most of the taste out of her mouth after a few swishes.

When she finished, the woman named Carrie set the cups aside and she dabbed a wet cloth down the side of Lyra's face. Carrie was pretty, with green eyes, a small nose, and her long blond hair tucked behind her ears. "I'm not even going to ask where you came from or how you ended up like this," Carrie murmured. "I just hope he unties you soon."

"Sorry you have to clean this up." Lyra looked back at the ceiling of the tent. She couldn't watch Carrie or she'd end up with more dry heaves.

The mattress dipped where Carrie wiped up the mess, and Lyra heard the sound of cloth scrubbing cloth. "Hope you feel better," Carrie said, and Lyra turned to look at her. She stuffed the wet cloths into the bag, then picked it up along with the cups. The woman gave Lyra one last sad look and slipped out of the tent.

Lyra gave a deep shuddering sigh as she stared up again. She still tasted and smelled acid, but it wasn't as bad. Would she throw up every time Neal touched her?

Again canvas rustled and Neal entered the tent. His face appeared above hers and he scowled. She bit the inside of her cheek to keep from spewing venom. That would definitely earn her a pill of some kind or another.

"Don't you have anything to say, Lyra?" Neal raised one eyebrow.

"Please untie me." She glanced up at one of her wrists and back to Neal. "They hurt."

He looked thoughtful for a moment. "My flock needs to see you with me before our joining tonight."

Tonight?

"They need to see the woman who'll be the new First Wife." He reached into a pocket of his robe and brought out a pocketknife. "As long as you behave like a Prophet's wife should, then I'll allow you to remain free." His eyes turned cold and his smile vanished. "But if you so much as look at the gates, I'll have you bound until our joining ceremony. Do you understand?"

Lyra nodded in quick, jerky movements. "Yes."

He raised his eyebrow again, giving her an imperious look. "Yes, what?"

She blinked. Tried to think what he meant. *Oh.* "Yes, Prophet."

This time his smile was one of satisfaction. He flicked the blade of the pocketknife open. "After tonight, you'll refer to me as Husband."

The shock of actually seeing him, and the revulsion at his touch earlier were quickly being replaced by a hot wave of anger. She fought to keep her expression placid. "Yes, Prophet."

He cut the bond from the wrist closest to him, then leaned across her to get to her other wrist. His smell of sweat and marijuana was nearly suffocating as his robe pressed against her face. When he moved away and both wrists were free, she rubbed them, getting the circulation going.

When he had cut all her bindings and had tossed them aside, he drew her up. The canvas floor was rough beneath her feet. Her legs wobbled. Her knees buckled and she nearly dropped, but Neal caught her. He wrapped his arms around her waist and drew her tight against him until she felt his erection press her belly.

Another dry heave caused her gut to clench and her throat to close. If she could get hold of his knife she'd cut his dick right off.

She avoided his gaze, but he brushed his lips across her forehead. "Tonight, Lyra."

She just barely kept herself from screaming and slamming her fist into his nose. She trembled from the force of her anger and tried to breathe deeply to calm herself. Fighting him would do no good. He'd just drug her and have her tied up again and she'd have no chance to escape.

And her mother—his threats against her. Had he already carried them out?

When he finally drew away, he gripped Lyra's chin in one of his hands and raised her face so that her gaze met his. "I've missed you."

He scowled as he moved his hand to her head and grasped several strands of her hair. "I'm not happy about what you've done to your hair." He clenched it tighter and pulled so hard her eyes watered. "Tonight that's one thing I'll have to punish you for. Make sure you don't give me any other reasons."

Lyra swallowed. He was going to whip her for changing her hair color? No way. She'd never give him the chance.

When she didn't answer, he said, "For every request you refuse, your mother will be whipped. You can watch."

Pinpricks moved beneath her skin at the threat.

"Keep your head lowered when in my presence, as a wife of the Prophet should." Neal released her hair, then palmed the back of her head and forced her into the submissive posture.

It was all Lyra could do to control herself. She wanted to scream and punch Neal. She wanted to ram her knee into his balls so bad her body ached with it.

No matter the feelings tangled up inside of her all these years, she would never want to see her mother whipped or beaten—anything that Neal was capable of.

A wild mixture of emotions raged through Lyra like a thunderstorm. Anger at Neal. Anger at her mother. Fear for her mother. And love. Yes, she still loved her mother, she just couldn't let go of the fact that Sara had brought them willingly into the cult.

"Stay a few steps behind me." He raised the tent flap. "Keep your gaze lowered."

Lyra ground her teeth and followed him out of the tent and into the compound.

Despite Neal's instructions, she couldn't help but raise her head and look at everything around her.

Oregon. She was really back in the compound beneath the towering Mount Hood. Mixed feelings flooded her about her surroundings. Before she knew the Temple of Light existed, she'd been to the nearby beautiful town of Sandy and to Mount Hood with her father and mother. Those had been good memories.

They had spotted Roosevelt elk, blacktail deer, bighorn sheep, and once, from their car, a black bear. All the memories came to her sharp and vivid as she stared at Mount Hood through the trees. And what about that time they'd seen a bald eagle soaring through the sky? It had been an amazing sight.

Now it was the last place on earth she wanted to be. A knot formed in her throat. The memories of the cult overshadowed all that had once been good and special.

She had no idea how Neal had managed it, but she was here.

"I flew you in my private plane," Neal said, startling her enough that she jerked her head from the view of Mount Hood to look at his satisfied smile.

How does he have a private airplane? But even as she asked herself the question, she knew. Like he had been when she escaped, Neal had to be running drugs and who knew what else. Not to mention, he took everyone's money and personal belongings when they entered the cult, "in the name of the Light."

Lyra pushed her attention back to her immediate surroundings. It was as if she'd never left. The People quietly went about their business, performing their tasks. Always working. Nothing less would be tolerated.

Along with the scents of Douglas fir and cedar, her nose caught the smells of farm animals, alfalfa hay, and rich soil. One cow gave a low *moo,* sheep and goats made their *baaaa* and *naaaa* sounds, and chickens clucked.

An oncoming storm brought the scent of rain and clouds just close enough to block the sunlight but not the view of the mountain. It was July, but quickly cooling. Used to Arizona weather, she rubbed her arms to warm herself from the light chill.

She'd forgotten all about Oregon's scents and sounds and the weather.

But the sights—the nightmares of being trapped with The People again—had never let her go.

At least a hundred tents, if not more, spread across the huge compound. Neal had his People arranged in groups, tents circled around large areas where The People in that particular group performed their duties.

Another wooden temple was being constructed in the background. Men and teenage boys climbed around the temple structure, working on it, and the pounding of hammer against nail and wood rose over the other sounds. The structure was still being framed out, in the early phases of construction.

Children gathered kindling, the bigger kids grabbing larger pieces of wood. Teenage girls watched the toddlers, giving them small tasks to do. Lyra knew that all children were "educated" by their parents, more or less a version of being homeschooled.

And brainwashed.

Women performed chores "befitting them." Her heart tugged when she recognized women she had once co-existed with. Two of the girls she'd been more or less friends with during her three years in the cult were now, of course, adults. Both of the women had been married to older men when they were around fifteen. The pair chatted, but they never stopped moving their hands in whatever work they performed, whether it was sewing, knitting, or a variety of other tasks.

One woman shucked Indian corn while another stirred a pot of pinto beans, and still another plucked feathers from a boiled headless chicken. Circles of rocks confined cook fires, and a lot of cooking was going on.

"For the feast tonight," Neal said as if reading her mind again. He smiled despite the fact that she wasn't looking down. "After our joining."

A beautiful woman with a slender figure, long dark hair, and big brown eyes caught Lyra's attention. She was like an automaton as she washed clothing, scrubbing a robe using an old-fashioned tub and washboard. Lyra's heart hurt. The woman was definitely drugged, someone who hadn't wanted to be here.

"Unfortunately," Neal said as he noticed where she was looking, "Gloria has been confused about her place with The People. She'll soon realize this is her new home." He smiled and reached for Lyra's hand and gave it a squeeze. "Just as you were confused. But you're home now, where you belong."

A man around Lyra's age approached and Neal's face broke into a pleased and obviously proud smile. Immediately she recognized the young man. Jason had been seventeen when she was taken into the cult. He'd always treated her okay even though he was considered superior to her by being a male and Neal's eldest son.

By the hard glint in Jason's blue eyes, something had changed. Gone was the amicable look he'd given her in the past. She nearly recoiled from the hatred in his gaze.

When he looked at his father, that glint was gone, to be replaced by a pleasant expression.

Neal clapped the young man on his shoulder as he looked at Lyra. "You remember Jason, I'm sure."

She swallowed. "Of course."

"Head down in the presence of the Prophet," Jason ordered her with an imperious look.

Lyra's cheeks burned and she bit back the venom she wanted to spew at him. "Yes, Jason," she said in a bitter, angry tone as she lowered her head.

"Jason is of course my first in command," Neal said with that same pride in his voice.

From her position of submission Lyra managed to see Jason's expression of fury before a mask of serenity crossed his face when his father looked at him.

Neal slapped his hand on his son's back again. "I think the Temple workers need a fire lit under their asses."

Jason nodded. "I'll be happy to light that fire."

"The pride of my life," Neal said as she raised her head to look at him. He was staring after his son with fatherly love while he watched Jason's back as he left.

The lines on Neal's face had softened. "Only our child can match or surpass the pride I feel for Jason."

Lyra blinked. If Jason knew that, it was no surprise he'd looked at her with such hate. As far as she knew, very few people had known about the Prophecy when she'd been brought into the Temple of Light, or of the so-called "new Messiah."

Lyra glanced beyond Neal and thoughts of Jason vanished. "Momma?" she said as she looked at the woman who had brought her into the cult.

Seeing her mother—actually *seeing* her—was like a punch to Lyra's gut.

Sara Collins had aged considerably in the last five years. She'd been a beautiful woman, but now she looked tired and . . . old. She'd gone from a healthy, full figure to being slender, almost frail. Lyra had inherited her green eyes from Sara, but those eyes were no longer bright and filled with life. They were dull and sad.

"Once you left, Sara could no longer cope," Neal said close to Lyra's ear.

A heavy weight slammed into Lyra's chest. Had she caused this change in her mother? Or had living with the cult done this to her? Had Neal mistreated her because Lyra left?

Despite the feeling of anger that had followed her since her mother and Neal had brought them to the compound, Lyra felt something more that she'd pushed aside long ago. The love she'd had for her mother *before*. Trust, no, but love . . .

Ignoring Neal and not bothering to keep her head down in the pretense she was obeying him, she skirted women, children, and cook fires as she ran to the far side of the circle of tents. Small rocks dug into her bare feet and dark soil coated her toes as she hurried. A low murmur followed in her wake as she walked past people she'd known and those she hadn't.

When she reached her mother's side, Lyra stared down at her. Sara was crocheting what looked like a pair of baby booties.

Lyra sat on a large pine log beside Sara. They were next to a fire, and Lyra's face was immediately warmed. A cast-iron pot hung from the cooking frame within the rock-encircled fire.

The skin around one of Sara's eyes was black, and her lower lip had a healing cut. Were those from punishment dealt out from Neal because of Lyra?

"Momma?" Lyra said as she stared at her mother.

She slowly raised her head and looked at Lyra. Confusion, followed by shock, flashed across Sara's battered face. "You're not supposed to be here." She reached out and grasped Lyra's wrist, hard. "You're not supposed to be here!"

Lyra reeled. Words wouldn't come to her mouth.

"This is Lyra's place, as I've told you many times, Sara." Neal squatted and placed his hand on her shoulder. "You've known this since you brought her into the fold." Neal's knuckles whitened and his fingers dug into Sara's shoulder. "Isn't that right?"

"I—" Something flashed in Sara's eyes then she looked away, her gaze downcast. "Yes, Prophet."

Things were not computing in Lyra's mind. Her mother had brought her to The People. Sara was the reason this whole thing had happened, right? Lyra had not lived with her mother long in the cult, as Lyra had been forced to live in the Temple, but never once did Sara show any signs that she disagreed with "the Prophecy."

Neal released Sara's shoulder, and the pained tension in her face eased. He tried to take Lyra's hand, but she jerked away and drew her mother into a hug. It took a moment before Sara's arms wrapped around Lyra. She felt her mother's tears against her skin at the neck opening of the robe. "I'm sorry, baby," Sara whispered. "So sorry."

Before Lyra could respond, Neal grabbed her by her upper arm and jerked her to her feet. She stumbled and almost fell. Her gaze was still on her mother, who bent over her task of crocheting the booties, her graying hair hiding her face and her tears.

Lyra whirled on Neal. "What did you do to her?"

His jaw tensed and his eyes grew dark. "Do you want to be tied up again?" he said in a tone so low that no one else should have been able to hear him. "Perhaps convinced in other ways?"

For one long moment, perhaps too long, she glared at him. But she came to her senses and dropped her gaze so that she was looking at her dirty toes. "I'm sorry, Prophet." *Bastard.*

As they walked away from Sara, Lyra's stomach churned more at the thought that her mother was probably knitting baby booties for Lyra and Neal's child. Apparently her mother hadn't wanted Lyra here after all, and now was being forced to make clothing for the grandchild that shouldn't be.

"You need rest," Neal said as he strode ahead of

Lyra. "Tonight's an important night and you'll want to be refreshed when we come together as man and wife."

Lyra's body shook as heat rose in her chest. Her cheeks flushed and she had to force herself to keep from balling her hands into fists. She kept her head down as she followed Neal back to the tent. All these years . . . Had he kept her mother here against her will, too?

Lyra's thoughts turned back to the early days when they had arrived at the Temple of Light. Had her mother been perhaps too serene? Too at peace with life among The People? Had she been drugged all that time?

Lyra and Neal reached the tent and he didn't bother to hold the flap open for her. As a good little submissive woman, she was to follow in his wake and not expect anything from him, even small courtesies.

When she was in the tent and her eyes had adjusted to the dimness, she saw fire in Neal's gaze as he stared at her. His hand twitched at his side. She didn't lower her eyes and she held her chin up.

Neal slapped Lyra so hard she dropped. She fell onto her side, hit her head on the floor, and cried out. Stars sparked in her head, and she tried to push herself to a sitting position.

"You seem to have forgotten your lessons." He knelt on one knee beside her, his voice hideously dark when he said, "Never make a sound when I punish you. From tonight on that includes every time I fuck you in the name of the Light." With that he swung his hand and slapped her hard enough to make her fall back again.

Tears stung at Lyra's eyes from the pain, but she

didn't cry out, and she didn't bring her hand to her throbbing cheek. Instead she lowered her gaze.

She'd get even with him. One way or another, she'd get even.

He grasped her face in his hand tight enough to make her eyes water and forced her to look at him. "Because you haven't lived among The People for a while, and have forgotten our ways, I'll forgive you for your behavior in front of my People and your attitude toward me. But I won't put up with it anymore. Got that?"

Lyra nodded the best she could with his hand on her chin. "Yes," she said.

Neal raised his free hand again. "Yes, *what*?"

She lowered her gaze. "Yes, Prophet."

"Now," he said as he released her chin, "you'll rest for the ceremony. I'll send a couple of my other wives to prepare you for our joining." He caressed her face, almost tenderly. "And then I'll fuck you so many times you'll beg for mercy."

A chill crept down Lyra's spine.

His tone changed, he lowered his voice, and it came out in a deadly growl. "You'd better be a virgin, or I'll make you wish you were dead. You'll carry the new Messiah, but you'll be punished." He scratched his nails down her cheek. "Are you still a virgin, Lyra?"

She slowly nodded. What else could she do?

"You'd better be telling the truth." His eyes were dark and deadly looking. He grabbed her hand and jerked her to her feet, but she managed to keep from stumbling this time. "Lie on the mattress," he said. "Guards will be posted outside the tent to *protect* you while you rest."

Neal gave her a small push and she tripped toward the mattress. She shuddered at the sight of the stakes at each corner of the bed.

"So much as peek your head outside the tent, and I'll have you bound and drugged until your preparation for the ceremony." He narrowed his brows. "And Sara will receive her first whipping."

Lyra swallowed and lowered her gaze. "Yes, Prophet." She knelt beside the mattress that was damp in one spot and still had an acidic smell. She settled herself on top of the dry part of the mattress, on her side. She kept her eyes averted from his.

She saw only the hem of his robe as he whirled away from her and marched out of the tent and into the sunlight. Only when he was out of sight did she bring her hand to her stinging cheek. It burned against her palm.

Lyra had never felt so hopeless in her life. Before, there had always been some kind of hope. She'd been on the run, but she'd escaped The People, kept away from them, always prepared to flee if she needed to.

"What about Dare?" she whispered to herself. "Will he come for me? In time? Or will I figure out some way to escape?"

With my mother, too?

Lyra curled up and hugged her knees. Yes, no matter what, there was always hope.

CHAPTER *EIGHTEEN*

D are continued to sit on the couch cushions, staring at the floor, until the spinning in his head slowed and his vision cleared. He'd failed Lyra. A stinging sensation pinched at the back of his eyes and he ground his teeth.

He wasn't going to let her down again. He'd get that Neal Barker and he'd get to Lyra, no matter what it took.

When he could look up, he ignored the churning in his gut and saw Nick standing in the doorway of the kitchen.

" 'Bout time you woke up." Nick raised a cup with steam wafting from it. The smell of coffee filtered through his senses. "Got a fresh batch brewing."

Dare pushed himself up from the couch and onto his unsteady feet. He was still wearing the same clothing he'd worn last night when they'd gone to Becca's home. The little bitch who had betrayed Lyra.

Lyra. Dare flexed his hands at his sides. He couldn't get the thought out of his head. He'd let her down. Goddamnit, he'd let her down.

Nick headed back through the archway and Dare followed, his legs growing less unsteady as he moved.

When he reached the kitchen he blinked at the bright light and put his hand over his eyes for a moment before dragging his hand down his face. His stubble chafed his palm.

He took the steaming mug of black coffee from Nick and inhaled as he brought it up to his mouth. Just the rich aroma helped to clear his head. The coffee burned his tongue as he took a long draught.

"What time is it?" Dare growled after another hit of the strong brew. "Why didn't you wake me, Donovan?"

"Six A.M." Nick lowered his mug. "You needed the rest and so did I."

"Well, good morning to you," came Mrs. Yosko's voice from the kitchen nook.

Dare turned and saw the old lady sitting at the table, petting the calico cat perched in her lap. He hadn't noticed Mrs. Y was in the room.

"Got some cereal for you." Nick put a box of cornflakes, a quart of milk, a bowl and spoon, and a sugar jar in front of the elderly woman. "A can of tuna for Dixie, too. I'd fix you something a little more appetizing, but Dare and I need to get our plans made and get out of here."

"Hmph," she said, but by the gleam in her eye, Dare figured the lady enjoyed putting on a crotchety façade.

"Morning, Mrs. Yosko." Dare raised his cup for another quick draught.

She poured her cereal into her bowl as she looked directly at Dare. "You lost her."

The woman's words hit him like a hammer to his chest.

"It's time this ended once and for all," she said without

pause, her brown eyes focused on his, and she seemed amazingly sharp. "That girl has been on the run for too long. She needs to be able to live a free life and not be looking over her shoulder all the time."

Dare ground his teeth. "I'll take care of it."

Mrs. Y gave a single sharp nod. "I know you will, son." She turned her attention to her cereal and poured milk on it. "Now there's the matter of getting me out of your way."

Nick leaned against the counter, his arms folded across his chest. "You can stay until we get back. Make yourself at home."

Dare gripped the handle of his mug tighter. "We've got to keep you safe."

"Thank you," she said as she poured a teaspoon of sugar on her cornflakes and milk.

She waved her frail hand as if brushing him off. "I can't do for myself anymore, so it's time I went to the retirement home. I've been putting it off, keeping an eye on Lyra. But now she has you."

Dare raised an eyebrow. "You've been keeping an eye on her?"

After eating a bit of her cereal, she jabbed her spoon in the air toward Dare. "Who do you think let Manny know those S.O.B.'s were trying to find your place? I've kept tabs all over Bisbee.

"Lyra doesn't know this, and you'd better not tell her," the lady said with narrowed eyes, "but I'm the landlord of the house we live in and I let her pay rent at a dirt-cheap rate. That girl deserved a break. Knew it the minute I saw her. By the look in her eyes, I knew she was on the run. I have agents handle the property—

all my properties—so she doesn't know," Mrs. Yosko said, "and I expect she never will."

"Won't hear it from me," Dare said with a whole new appreciation for the woman.

When she looked at Nick, he held up his hands. "Landlord of what?"

"That's my boys." She gave a smile, all gums and teeth. "I'll stay here as you do what you have to do to get Lyra back and finish this mess once and for all."

She had *that* right.

"Can't bring in law enforcement, can you?" Mrs. Y stated with a firm expression.

"That's what we figured." Dare nodded. "Last thing we want is a standoff with the cult members, and the feds tying our hands. We need to get Lyra out safely *now,* and not wait for the officials to get a valid warrant. We'll get her out and let the local PD and SWAT come in. They'll call in the ATF and DEA to help clean up the mess."

"Good thinking," Mrs. Yosko said.

After things were settled with Mrs. Y, Dare and Nick got down to business.

Nick had wrangled a friend into flying him and Dare in a small jet to the Sandy River Airport outside Sandy, Oregon. His contact had been able to check the logs and found that another jet had set course for the same airport early that morning.

Despite his increasing desire to fly to the commune this minute and go charging into the compound like a maniac, Dare listened to his partner. Nick had called in some old favors, and several combat-experienced men would be meeting them outside a town close to the compound. A couple of the men lived within driving distance, and the others would fly in.

They'd give that sonofabitch Neal Barker something to remember.

"When will your men arrive?" Dare asked Nick as they packed their gear.

"About the same time as us, early evening. They'll meet us at a cabin they're going to rent, not too far from the town of Sandy. Manning lives in Portland and is taking care of the details."

"The cult won't expect us to follow them to their compound so fast."

"That, or they'll be even more prepared."

By the time they'd arrived at the secluded cabin outside of Sandy, the small town close to the compound, it was 6:00 P.M., eighteen hundred hours. The sky darkened not long after they arrived, and the air smelled of rain. Looked like they might just have a storm brewing. All the better cover for tonight.

The four men looked dead serious when Nick and Dare caught up with them at the cabin. With the addition of Dare and Nick, the six of them were large enough that they barely fit into the small front room. After they all arrived, there were a few quick grins and signs of camaraderie as they slapped one another on the back and shook hands all around. Nick made the introductions to his old military buddies.

Mike Freeman was as big and muscular as a tank, with a blond crew-cut and a barbed-wire tattoo around the biceps of one arm. Eric Harrison, also a powerfully built man, sported a long brown ponytail and gold earring. Aaron Lloyd stood shorter than the other men at maybe five-eleven, was dark-haired, and had amber eyes that reminded Dare of a hawk, and the man was just as muscularly built as the rest of them. Black-haired Tiger Manning had a tattoo of a Bengal tiger on his forearm, and was perhaps the fiercest-looking of the bunch, with black eyes that held no doubt he was ready to kick some major ass.

After their greetings, it was all business. Dare had already noted huge bags of various shapes and sizes lying around the cabin's front room. No doubt there were some serious firearms and other surprises in their equipment.

Fat drops of rain started to plop against the windows. Two of the men dragged a table from the kitchenette to the center of the front room, and Nick spread the map out on it. Dare took the lead in explaining the layout of the compound as they crowded around the table.

"According to the satellite maps, it looks like they have guards stationed every ten feet, inside and out," Dare said as he pointed to the perimeter of the compound. "If it's anything like the smaller compound in the Huachucas, it'll have double chain-link fences five feet apart with rolls of razor wire running along the top." He also showed the locations of the main gate and a smaller one in the back.

"No doubt they have cameras at all angles, too," Nick added.

"From the satellite pictures taken when it's dark," Dare said, "they keep that place lit up like a Christmas tree at night."

"What kind of weaponry are we looking at?" Freeman said in his deep southern drawl as he shoved his fingers through his blond crew-cut.

"From what we saw at the other compound," Nick said as he looked around the table at the men, "the guards are armed with M249s and AK-47s."

"If what I suspect is correct, they're into running drugs, so trading arms might be how they're getting their supplies," Dare said. "These bastards are into a slew of crap that could put them away for a long time, and that would be icing on the cake."

Dare discussed the obvious lack of experience of the guards in the Arizona compound. "I think we'll be looking at a different ball game here. This compound is larger and has been here a good long time. Long enough for them to develop some solid security systems."

The men outlined several strategies and came up with a plan A and a plan B. Dare was satisfied and certain they wouldn't have to use plan B. With this team, he had no doubts execution would be perfect and they'd get it right the first time.

When they were ready to roll, it was nearing dusk and rain poured on the windows in a steady thrum.

"Sonsofbitches are in for one hell of a surprise," Lloyd said.

Harrison's gold earring glinted in the room's dim lighting as the corner of his mouth turned up in an almost vicious grin. "Bring it on, baby."

"Fuckers won't know what hit them," Tiger Manning growled as he narrowed his dark eyes.

Dare sucked in a deep breath and let it out in a slow exhale. Neal Barker was going down.

CHAPTER *NINETEEN*

D espite Neal's orders that she rest, Lyra got to her feet as soon as he left. She jammed her hands into the pockets of her robe and began pacing the length of the tent. Her face and head ached from his slaps, and just the thought of them pissed her off even more.

For now she had to concentrate on figuring out some kind of plan. The tent was high enough that Neal's head hadn't even brushed the top and long enough to give her a lot of pacing room.

What could she do with the threats against herself and her mother? Lyra wouldn't be of use to anyone if she was drugged, and she couldn't let her mother be whipped. She brushed her sweaty palms on her robe. The scrapes on her hands barely hurt any longer, the scrapes she'd had from the time she'd slipped down those concrete stairs what seemed like ages ago.

Her thoughts turned toward her memories of the Temple and Neal's riches. He had a room a hundred times larger than any of the tents The People lived in. She hadn't been allowed to speak about it, of course. Neal had rationalized it all as necessary means to communicate with the original Prophet Jericho. How was it that The People seemed so blind to the fact that Neal didn't practice what he preached?

The man had his own private jet, for cripes sake.

She slipped her hands out of the pockets of her robe and picked up the bong. The sickly sweet scent of marijuana was strong.

Lyra tensed, her arms shook, and she almost flung the hunk of ceramic across the tent.

She steadied her hand, lowered the bong, and set it back beside the altar. To have something to do with her hands, she clasped them together and continued her pacing.

What could she do? The fact that not as much light was coming through the canvas told her it was getting darker. Was it that late into the afternoon? Her heart beat faster. She had to do something before Neal forced the wedding on her.

But what?

A plopping sound came from above her head and then another. She looked up at the tent's peak, wondering what it was as another plop hit followed by multiple ones. *It's raining,* she thought with satisfaction. Maybe Neal would be forced to hold off on the "marriage" until at least tomorrow. The People would have to bring all that food back into their tents, and the cook fires would be extinguished.

Drops fell harder until they were pounding on the canvas. The clean smell of rain and pine slipped in through a small gap in the tent flap. Her hope grew as the rain came down in torrents, splashing outside the tent, louder and louder yet.

She paused in her pacing and picked up the bong. Her thoughts turned to her mother. Had she been too harsh in judging Sara? Had Neal kept her drugged, threatened her, or done any number of things?

The rustling of the tent flap startled Lyra into dropping the bong. When it hit the floor the ceramic bond broke into several pieces at her feet.

Lyra slowly looked up into Neal's face that was reddened with anger and his eyes filled with fury. Rainwater dripped down his face, and his robe was soaked and clung to his body. "I ordered you to rest," he growled. "And instead I find you breaking tools of the Light that you have no business touching."

"I—I'm sorry, Prophet." Lyra lowered her eyes. "I—"

His backhand came so fast she didn't see it coming. Pain slammed into her cheekbone and eye, and she fell onto her back. Her head struck one of the iron stakes at the foot of the mattress and she screamed.

God, the pain!

Through the fuzz in her head she saw that Neal had his hand raised, ready to strike her again. Instinctively she rolled onto her belly to protect her face. She braced herself for the blow, but instead Neal's robe brushed her and when she opened her eyes she saw his knees at her side.

Fingers prodded her scalp and she cried out again. It hurt so bad she couldn't help the tears pouring from her eyes like rain was pouring on the roof of the tent. She felt stickiness at the back of her head as he touched her, and she realized it was blood. The thick fluid started to creep down her neck.

"Bitch," he said in a low, threatening voice. "First I

have to punish you for not remembering your place. But this—now your hair will have to be cleaned and the bleeding stopped."

He shoved her as he stood and she bit her cheek to hold back a groan. It hurt so bad she couldn't stop the tears. She was so pissed at Neal she could claw his eyeballs out, but right now she didn't have the strength to stand, much less attack him.

His wet robe whirled and brushed her face as he stood. She heard the clank of ceramic and she was sure he'd picked up the broken bong. The slap of his sandals was loud as he crossed the tent, and the rain was louder when he lifted the flap. It was muffled again when it closed.

Lyra lay where she was, pain spreading across her scalp from the wound, and her face from where he'd backhanded her. More blood dribbled down her nape, and it trickled around her neck to her throat. How badly was she injured? She knew she'd hit the stake hard enough to damn near crack her skull. Head wounds tended to be bloodier than other types of injuries, from what she remembered.

She tried to relax and force the dizziness in her head to stop. Was Neal going to leave her there? Maybe he'd have to call off the "wedding." At least that thought gave her some comfort.

The tent flap opened behind her, sweeping in the smell of rain and a sudden chill that caused her to shiver.

"Lyra," a voice said, and she recognized her mother at once. Lyra tensed, then relaxed at Sara's presence as she knelt beside her. "Oh, sweetheart, I'm so very sorry," Sara said as a soft cloth pressed against the wound.

"Momma." Lyra gave a shuddering sob but didn't try to turn to look at her mother. And then the anger Lyra had held so tightly in her chest started to slip away. "I missed you," she whispered. And with those words she knew it was true. She had blamed her mom, hated her even, but Lyra still loved her.

"God knows I missed you," Sara said as she lifted Lyra's short hair and dabbed another cloth around her neck, wiping away more of the blood. Lyra noticed her mother said "God" and not "the Light." Sara continued to wipe away the blood. "I was so happy when you escaped. Your fate isn't to be Neal's wife. I've always believed that."

"Then why didn't you tell me?" Lyra hiccupped, then swallowed. "I thought you believed him."

Sara gave a loud sigh. "Not once he claimed you. Then I knew everything was all wrong. I tried to tell him that, but the next thing I knew I was walking around seeing lights and stars and mindlessly doing everything I was told. I couldn't think straight. I couldn't even go to the bathroom without help."

"He drugged you, right?" Lyra said, then sniffed. "All this time I thought you supported him and that you believed in the stupid Prophecy."

There was a rustling sound behind Lyra before a cool cloth was pressed to the side of her face where Neal had backhanded her. It gave her the tiniest bit of relief, and she blew out her breath in a hard rush.

"I regretted bringing you into the Temple of Light

nearly since we arrived. At first being with The People helped me. It gave me a feeling of belonging and comfort, and being surrounded by friends as I grieved for your father."

"I miss him so much." Lyra hiccupped again. "And leaving you . . . I've always felt a sense of loss beyond Daddy's death. It was you. I missed you."

"I don't know what to do now." Tears were in Sara's voice as she removed the pad from the back of Lyra's head and replaced it with another. "I don't know how to save you from Neal."

Lyra couldn't answer as she gritted her teeth against the pain when her mother started to wash the blood from her hair.

"You're twenty-three now." Sara's voice had a smile to it. "I've thought of you every day. Every year on your birthday I've had my own private celebration. A celebration that you were free."

Lyra blinked back a new rush of tears. "Not anymore."

Sara leaned over and kissed the wetness on Lyra's cheek. "I'm sorry, baby," she whispered.

Lyra's head hurt so bad she could hardly sit up. When she finally rose, her head felt woozy, but she turned so that she faced her mother. They studied each other for a long time before Lyra flung her arms around Sara's frail frame. "Momma," Lyra sobbed, "I'm so sorry about everything."

"Shhh, baby." Sara embraced Lyra and slowly rocked her. "None of this was your fault. It was mine. I was so lost without your father, and Neal was so . . . attentive. He appealed to that part of me that was always needy."

"I know." Lyra sniffled again. "But don't blame yourself. There's just something about Neal that makes people believe in him."

Her mother squeezed tighter, then pulled away. Tears glistened on her cheeks, and Lyra's anger grew at the sight of her mother's battered face.

Sara reached up and wiped Lyra's tears from her eyes with her fingers. "Something deep in my gut tells me you'll be free again."

"What about you, Momma?" Lyra took her mother's hands in her own. "Do you want to be free, too?"

With a smile Sara said, "I'd kill to use a real bathroom and take a hot shower."

Lyra couldn't help a sniffly laugh and wiped more tears away with the back of her hand. "Then you'll leave with me."

Her mother sighed. "Sweetheart, I don't think that's in the cards for me."

Lyra touched her mom's graying hair and looked into her green eyes. "We'll make it happen." Lyra dropped her hand to her side and looked around the tent. "Since we're together now, we could figure something out to escape."

Her gaze landed on one of the slender iron stakes buried in the earth beside the mattress. Despite the spinning feeling in her head, she crawled over to the spike and clasped her hands around the smooth metal. The thing didn't budge. She gritted her teeth and pulled again. This time it gave a little. She scooted away just far enough so that she could ram her bare heel against the middle of the stake. It moved several inches sideways and Lyra smiled. When she got back on her knees and jerked on the stake, it came out easily.

Lyra held the partially dirty stake tightly in one fist and examined it. Like she'd hoped, the end of the stake was pointed—sharp enough to make an excellent weapon.

She brushed off the dirt and saw Sara kicking one of the other stakes like Lyra had. She tucked her own into a pocket of her robe and went to her mother. Lyra wrapped her fingers below Sara's and together they yanked the second stake free.

Lyra's heart beat faster. "Hide it, Momma," she said, and Sara's stake disappeared into her robe. "We'll wait for the right time and then—"

A breeze blew into the tent as the flap opened.

CHAPTER *TWENTY*

In the room filled with high-tech equipment, Neal studied multiple monitors that showed almost every space along the perimeter of the compound. The rain made the view in each monitor a little fuzzier, but it was all clear enough that during daylight hours they would be able to see anyone who approached. He'd had the guard increased when Lyra had been brought into the compound. No one would be able to penetrate his fortress and endanger his fold.

"Is every one of the floodlights functioning?" Neal asked.

"It'll be bright as day." Larry leaned back in his chair and smiled. "No way will anyone get by our men like they did under Mark and Adam's watch."

Neal scowled and felt a slow burn in his gut. "Mark and Adam let down The People last night in the Arizona compound. That had better not happen here."

"I've studied and restudied the tapes from that attack." The techie's smile faded. "Only two men, but they knew exactly where to hit, where it was darkest, and where the camera's blind spots were.

"Here the floodlights will keep a surprise attack impossible if they do come after her," he continued.

Neal steepled his hands. "In the name of the Light, I expect you to do your duty and keep them out." Just before he turned away he said, "If not, you'll find yourself on the cross of the Light."

A flash of fear crossed Larry's face. *Good.* The Prophet Jericho hadn't been pleased, having said as much to Neal when he'd meditated in his room while Lyra had been sleeping after her return to the fold. It'd been all Neal could do not to take her before the ceremony, but the Prophecy had been clear.

Neal scowled as he walked out of the dry Temple and into the pouring rain. He was instantly drenched again, his robe soaked, his long hair clinging to his neck, and raindrops rolling down his cheeks. His sandals slapped the wet ground, and mud splashed onto his toes.

When the first scent of the oncoming storm had greeted him, he'd ordered several of The People to put together the "gathering shelter." Upon occasion they'd had to use the canvas shelter to hold one of Neal's many sermons for his fold. Today it would be used for his joining with Lyra.

Just the thought of taking Lyra made his dick hard, and when he glanced down he saw that it was outlined by the wet robe clinging to his body. He pulled the cloth away and forced himself to control his reactions to the thought of finally having Lyra after all these years. Too bad he'd had to wait until she was over eighteen.

However, the Light had spoken.

Neal reached the gathering shelter and moved out of the rain. Satisfaction seeped into his veins. Not much longer and Lyra would be his.

The shelter was an enormous spread of canvas fastened to many metal poles, with ropes staked at the ground, keeping it taut all around. At the far end of the shelter was a platform where he would perform the ceremony that would make Lyra his thirteenth wife and the additional steps to move her into the position of First Wife.

Carrie and Julia should be preparing Lyra now for the ceremony. They would make sure no remnants of blood from the wound at the back of Lyra's head would show, nor the growing bruises on her face.

Stupid bitch.

As he watched several of The People preparing the shelter, Neal took a deep breath, let it out slowly, and calmed his thoughts. Rain pounded on the tented ceiling and dripped off the edges in loud splashes.

When Neal had backhanded her, he'd simply been teaching Lyra her place. That her head had struck the stake was another way Jericho was punishing her for leaving the fold and for her irreverence for the Light.

Gradually all tension released from Neal's body and he absorbed the power of the Light. He took another deep inhale and smiled. Soon he'd have Lyra, and everything would be as it should.

CHAPTER *TWENTY-ONE*

T wo women holding various items entered the tent. The flap shut behind them. One of the women was the blond, Carrie.

Lyra tensed. Had she and her mother been seen pocketing the stakes?

Sara looked at the two women and cleared her throat. "Carrie, Julia. Have you come to help me with Lyra's wounds?"

"No," the brunette, who must be Julia, said. "We've come to prepare the new First Wife for the joining ceremony."

"Prepare me for the ceremony?" It was as if a freezing wind chilled Lyra's face. Ice sliced through her veins, and she shook from the cold that overtook her body. "What about the rain?" It was all she could think of to say.

Carrie placed bottles, a hairbrush, and a circlet of white silk flowers on the floor. "The Prophet has had the gathering shelter set up for your joining."

"I'm Julia, the Prophet's tenth wife." The dark-haired woman set a paper-and-twine-wrapped bundle next to the supplies Carrie had placed on the floor. She turned to Sara. "The Prophet wants to see you, Sister."

Sara and Lyra exchanged a quick hug, and when Sara kissed Lyra's cheek she whispered, "Don't give up hope, Angel." Lyra almost started to cry again as her mother released her and stood. Sara gave a slow nod to each of the wives, then slipped out of the tent and into the rain.

Lyra felt the heavy weight of exhaustion to her core and sat on her haunches. Carrie knelt in front of Lyra, and Julia moved behind her.

"He hurt you." Carrie slid her shaking fingers gently over the side of Lyra's face. Lyra flinched and Carrie dropped her hand away.

Julia said, "Shush!" from behind Lyra.

"That was courtesy of Neal." Lyra managed a wry smile. "In the name of the Light, of course."

Carrie's mouth curved into a sad smile. "Of course."

Lyra felt in that moment a sort of kinship with these ladies. No doubt Neal had abused them all in some fashion or another, in "the name of the Light."

In the next moment Lyra cried out as Julia started brushing her hair. Lyra's eyes watered from the pain of her head wound.

"I'm so sorry, Sister," Julia said from behind her with a definite sound of apology in her tone. "I should have been more careful."

After her hair had been cleansed, Julia gently began sweeping Lyra's short hair up and fastening it above her wound. It took a few clips to do it since her hair wasn't long anymore.

Carrie opened a short, fat bottle and began to dab a beige substance on Lyra's face. Makeup to cover her bruises, of course. Neal probably had all kinds of things stashed away that The People weren't allowed to use, with the exception of the "favored" and himself. Not that she thought he'd use makeup.

Lyra had to bite her lip to hold back more cries as the women worked on her face and her hair. Her face hurt where Carrie dabbed on the makeup, and Lyra didn't think her headache was likely to go away for days.

Carrie smoothed the makeup all over Lyra's face. "You were with The People before?"

"Shhh," Julia said again.

Lyra sighed. "I ran away when I was eighteen. That was five years ago."

"And he's been looking for you?" Carrie leaned back, tilted her head, and examined Lyra's face. "The bruises are pretty well covered now, but your face is a little swollen."

"Yeah, he has." Lyra ground her teeth. "I'd thought that maybe I was safe from him. So much for that."

Carrie took a small brush and dabbed it in a pale pink powder from a compact before lightly applying it to Lyra's cheekbones. The People didn't wear any kind of makeup, so it surprised Lyra that more than foundation to cover the bruises was being put on her. "So you really don't want this?" Carrie asked.

Lyra gave a sigh of exasperation. *Duh.* "I've been running away from it all these years. I just want out of here before this ceremony."

Carrie took the silk flower wreath and set it on Lyra's head. "Looks like it's a little late for that."

"Don't remind me," Lyra said. "I keep hoping I'll wake up from this nightmare."

Carrie leaned forward and her lips met Lyra's ear. "Me, too," Carrie whispered before drawing back and busying herself by opening the big paper-covered bundle.

"The two of you had better start showing respect for the Prophet," Julia said, and moved around so that she was standing in front of Lyra, a frown on her pretty face. "You need to get up."

Damn. No finding any kinship with Julia. "Why do I need to get up?" Lyra asked, a little more leery of the woman.

"To get dressed," the blond said.

Lyra placed her hand against her pocket that held the stake. It hadn't occurred to her she'd have to change.

"My head's still woozy." Lyra placed her palm to her forehead. "I might need some help."

Each wife took one of Lyra's hands and helped her to her feet. They steadied Lyra as she wobbled a bit, and her head hurt even worse.

When she was standing on her own, she took a deep breath. But it caught in her throat when Julia said, "You need to take off your robe."

Heat rose to Lyra's cheeks. "Not in front of the two of you."

"It's part of the preparation." Carrie held up a beautiful white robe with shining white flowers and leaves embroidered along the hem. The design was so subtly sophisticated and the material so rich it surprised Lyra.

"This is what each wife wears for the ceremony?" Lyra asked as she ran her fingers over the incredibly soft material.

Carrie laughed. "Are you kidding? Nope. Neal said something about you being 'the Chosen.'"

Lyra jerked her hand back. This was real. Wayyyy too real.

Her anger at Neal doubled. Tripled. No, it was more than that. If it weren't for his threat against her mother, Lyra would refuse everything these women were doing to her. No, she couldn't see Sara whipped. Or killed.

Lyra tried to refuse getting undressed in front of the women, but finally she had to give in. Apparently she didn't have a choice in a whole lot of things.

Her cheeks were so hot she must have been bright red when she dropped the robe from her shoulders to the floor of the tent and was completely naked. The stake in the robe's pocket made a soft thudding sound when it hit the tent floor, but Carrie and Julia didn't seem to notice.

Instead of putting the new robe on Lyra, they opened a couple of vials and poured oil onto their palms. Immediately the smell of jasmine filled the tent.

Lyra's heart started. They wouldn't.

They would.

"No way—," Lyra said as the two women rubbed the oil between their palms, then began applying it to Lyra's body. She trembled as they rubbed it up and down her legs, her ass, her back, and even her breasts.

"Sorry," Carrie said. "His orders."

Lyra groaned and clenched her fists. She remained rigid the entire time the women prepared her.

When they were finished, her body gleamed in the light and she smelled so strongly of jasmine that she knew she'd hate that scent for the rest of her life. Next,

Carrie and Julia helped her into the ceremonial robe. It felt soft against her skin as it slid over the body oil.

Instead of needing a belt, her robe fastened at the sides, making it hang straight in the front and back, and giving her voluminous sleeves.

No pockets. Lyra's heart plunged. She had no way to carry her "weapon."

Unless . . .

When Carrie and Julia finished fussing with Lyra, and Carrie had applied some clear gloss to Lyra's lips, the two women handed her a small mirror.

Lyra's eyes widened and she looked at herself from side to side to see that her red hair had been swept up with clips in a way that hid her wound. The crown of white silk flowers encircled her head, and she felt like a flower child of the sixties. The robe was beautiful on her. She couldn't tell where the red marks were, and her cheekbones looked higher from the light coating of blush that looked almost natural. Her lips were moist and soft. She looked pretty.

"Stunning," Carrie said, and in the mirror's reflection Lyra saw Julia looking at her thoughtfully.

Lyra sucked in her breath and closed her eyes. It was Dare she wanted to see her like this. Not Neal. *Not Neal.*

When she opened her eyes again, Lyra wanted to rip off the flowers, shred the robe, scrub off the makeup, and take down her hair. Instead she trembled with a combination of fury and fear.

Rain continued to drum on top of the tent, and it fit Lyra's mood perfectly. "I don't know why you all had to go through the trouble of getting me ready," Lyra said. "I'm just going to get drenched when we go outside."

Carrie picked up a folded piece of canvas that had been under the white robe. "It's our job to hold this over your head and make sure you don't get wet."

"How much longer?" Lyra glanced to the tent flap.

Carrie shrugged and looked at Julia. "Would you say about an hour?"

Julia frowned. "Whenever the Prophet summons, then we'll know."

Lyra vibrated with the need to carry through with the part of her plan that included the stake. From the way Julia had been acting, she'd be heading straight for Neal to tell him.

Think, think, think!

Lyra reached up and touched the back of her pinned-up short hair and jerked loose a clump while trying to make it look like she was just checking it. "Carrie," she said, and slightly turned so that the woman could see the back of her head. "Some of my hair is falling down."

"I'll take care of it," Carrie said, and immediately brought her hands up to Lyra's head.

"Um, Julia?" Lyra asked in her most apologetic tone, then coughed. "My throat is so dry. I really need a drink of water."

The dark-haired woman looked to the tent flap and back to Lyra. "It's still raining hard."

"Please?" Lyra asked, keeping her voice low enough that she hoped it sounded scratchy. "I don't think I'll be able to talk when it comes to it."

Julia whirled and ducked out of the tent without another word.

Lyra pulled away from Carrie before the woman had finished pinning her hair.

"I have one more thing to add to my 'costume.'" Lyra went to her dirty tan robe, dug out the stake, and picked up the sash. She raised the white robe, exposing her thigh, and tied the sash around it until it was wrapped triple around her leg. She took a deep breath, picked up the stake, and slid it into the bindings.

When she looked up, Carrie's eyes were wide and her mouth was open.

"I'm not going down without a fight." Lyra glanced at her leg to make sure the stake wasn't outlined by the robe. Thank God the folds were thick enough it couldn't be seen. She glanced up at Carrie. "You won't say anything, will you?"

"Not a chance," Carrie said.

CHAPTER *TWENTY-TWO*

Dare was satisfied with what he'd seen so far of Nick's men, and his confidence grew that they would rescue Lyra. He just hoped to hell it was in time.

All six men prepared quickly and efficiently. Each man dressed in waterproof black combat gear and smudged his face with black. They armed themselves to the teeth, each man with his own choice of weaponry that he specialized in or preferred to carry. H&K, M4, MP5, and M16 rifles, and even a Rocket Propelled Grenade (RPG) launcher. Tiger Manning was an explosive specialist, and Dare wasn't sure he wanted to ask what some of the items were in his belt and pockets.

Dare had some of his own firepower in addition to his weapons, including one of the IEDs Nick had developed. Adrenaline pumped through Dare's body, leaving him feeling like he could run a marathon in fifteen minutes.

He braced his hands on the table with the map and looked to each man as he spoke. "You know what needs to be done," Dare said. "We've made our plans and you don't need me telling you your job. Let's just do it."

"You got it, bro," Lloyd said.

"Those fuckers are as good as dead," Manning growled.

"Watch out for civilians." Nick slapped Manning on the back.

"Anyone with a gun is fair game, though," Dare added. "If we can find anything on them like a drug stash, and can get and keep the gates open," Dare said, "we'll contact local law enforcement and let them have at it. By then we'll be long gone with Lyra."

"Don't worry about the gates." A confident grin slid across Freeman's face. "They're as good as gone."

The men laughed some of the tension off and high-fived all around the room. When they checked the clock and it was time, they sobered as they left the cabin, out into the rainy night.

L yra trembled so badly she had to sit on the mattress that still had the acidic smell. The stake rested against her thigh and the tie was almost too tight. At least it should stay up.

I can do this. He'll never expect it. Only problem was, she'd have to do it after they were "married." She couldn't take any chances with any of the other idiots around.

Only one plan sounded plausible. She'd act like the docile new wife. When they were alone, the first opportunity she had, she'd knee him in the groin so hard he'd go down . . . Then she'd have to kill him.

The thought of killing another person caused her to break out into a sweat.

He deserves it. What he's done to all these people, to me . . . he deserves it. Damn him. Damn him, damn him, damn him!

Still, could she drive the stake into his throat and then his heart when the moment came? She clenched her fist in her lap and hardened her determination. What other choice did she have?

If she just injured him and ran for it, he'd be able to call out to his guards and they'd get her. And then she wouldn't be able to get her mother out. Neal might even kill Sara because of Lyra's actions.

If she did get away with her mother, Lyra would still be on the run from him for the rest of her life. Unless he was dead.

Lyra buried her face in her hands, not caring if she smeared the makeup. Not caring if she messed up her hair. Her head ached more than just from the pain of her wounds. She'd had the mother of all headaches since she'd had the up-close-and-personal contact with the stake. But it also ached from the magnitude of her thoughts and the choices she'd have to make.

Carrie and Julia both sat quietly on the floor. None of them seemed to know what to say. Julia was even more soaked from the rain after having retrieved a cup of water for Lyra. The water only made her want to pee, but she forced herself to take several swallows. Damn, she needed a bathroom.

All of Lyra's senses seemed heightened as she waited. It was so quiet she could hear the sound of Carrie's and

Julia's breathing and the ever-present drumming of rain on the canvas over their heads. The tent had chilled and she was not only trembling but shivering, too. The tent still smelled like marijuana, rain, and earth.

When the flap finally opened, Lyra startled so badly she almost fell off the edge of the mattress. Pain shot through her head as she jerked her face from where she had buried it in her hands, and she opened her eyes.

Mark ducked in through the opening and his braid swung over his shoulder. Rain soaked his tan shirt, his jeans, and his hair. His jaw was purple where Dare had punched him in that bus stop parking lot.

He gave Lyra a smile filled with such complete hatred that she nearly recoiled at first, and then the feeling was followed by the desire to take him out. Where was her baseball bat when she needed it?

"What do you want?" she asked, her jaw so tense she could barely speak.

"It's time to fulfill the *Prophecy,*" Mark said with an expression that told her he felt exactly what he'd said at the bus stop—he didn't care if she lived or if she died. More like he wanted her to die. She didn't get it. Why would one of Neal's highest followers act this way?

"Come on." Carrie stood, took one of Lyra's hands, and squeezed it. "It'll be okay," she added softly.

"No," Lyra said clearly as she looked at Mark's face. "It will never be okay."

At that he smirked and ducked out of the tent. After Mark left, Carrie and Julia unfolded the large piece of canvas they were going to hold over their heads. Carrie picked up a pair of white slippers.

Lyra swallowed hard, then swallowed again. She'd

thought she'd been shaking before, but that was nothing compared to right now.

It was all so surreal, like a nightmare come to life.

It *was* a nightmare come to life.

Five years she'd been running away from this. *Five years.*

And now it was too late. She had no options left until after the ceremony, and even then it wasn't much of an option. She didn't think she'd ever get over it if she failed and Neal raped her. Which was exactly what it would be. Rape. The mere thought of it left her feeling unclean, and she wanted to scrub herself inside and out.

And yet if she struggled and refused, they'd drug her. She wouldn't even be awake to defend herself. If she ran now, Neal would hurt her mother.

Rage bubbled in Lyra's veins.

Trapped.

Trapped like a cow in a barn, waiting for the stud bull.

Well, this bull was going to end up castrated.

Mark returned and held the tent flap aside while Carrie and Julia raised the canvas over Lyra's head and their own. She paused at the threshold, between the canvas floor and mud, and prayed lightning would strike or something so that she would never have to go with Neal into the Temple.

She was tempted to let her robe drag in the mud, but she played the part of the good little wifey-to-be and gripped the cloth in her fists, raising her hem just high enough that only her ankles showed. Mud squished between her toes.

As they made a small procession through the compound, her thoughts turned to Dare and she wanted to cry. She'd never forget the way he embraced her, or the wonder of his kiss, or the incredible ways he made love to her.

Many of The People lined up along Lyra's path toward a great shelter. Lights, no doubt provided by a generator, made everything as clear and bright as daylight. The place was already filled with lots of people, but a pathway had been kept clear for her to walk to the platform she saw at the far end of the shelter.

She bit her lower lip as they got closer and closer. Everything became more and more surreal.

When they finally reached the shelter, water was pouring from its edges, falling hard on the canvas over her head until they were in the mostly dry shelter. The ground in here was slightly damp, so they must have begun erecting it before the rain got so hard. Lyra kept her gaze averted from everyone staring at her.

Carrie and Julia removed the tarp and handed it to Mark. The women led Lyra to a flat, deep bowl of clear water. Lyra stepped into it and smelled more jasmine as the water clouded with mud from her feet. The women dried off one of her feet at a time, helping Lyra to balance and sliding one slipper on before allowing that foot to touch the ground, then doing the same with the other.

She let her robe drop, and the hem barely brushed the top of her slipper-clad feet. The shoes were white and embroidered with flowers that matched her robe. The whole outfit would have been beautiful if she didn't hate it so much.

When Lyra looked up, her gaze met Jason's. The hatred in his eyes was so intense it caused another chill to race up her spine. She couldn't look away until her companions started to escort her through the walkway in the midst of the gathering.

Lyra's vision blurred so that she couldn't see any of the faces watching her. The silence inside the shelter was deafening. All she could hear was the pounding, pounding, pounding rain.

Each slow step she took was another step toward a fate she'd never truly thought would happen.

One step. Another. Another.

She reached the left side of the dais. She would have to walk up two steps before standing on the platform, then take a few more steps to stand in the middle.

Lyra looked from her feet, and her gaze met Neal's across the platform. A smile of sheer pleasure and satisfaction was on his handsome face. He'd changed his clothing. His hair was long and loose about his shoulders and his head held high.

He looked like the devil.

Neal took a step up the platform.

Carrie and Julia urged Lyra to take hers.

He stepped up again, and the two women had to force Lyra on.

When both Neal and Lyra stood at either end of the platform, he began walking toward the center. Lyra didn't want to move, but her ever-present companions guided her forward.

Blood rushed in Lyra's ears. Hatred and anger burned her gut. How could this be happening? How could this be real?

Her eyes met Neal's blue ones and she couldn't look away. She filled her gaze with as much venom as she could, but he simply gave her a satisfied smile.

When Lyra finally reached the center of the platform, Julia and Carrie slipped away, leaving her alone, face-to-face with Neal.

His smile broadened and he reached out and took one of her trembling hands in his.

CHAPTER *TWENTY-THREE*

Dare and the other men climbed out of the Hummer and the Range Rover that two of the men had driven to Sandy. Since Manning lived in Portland, he was only a forty-five-minute drive away. Freeman was stationed in Seattle, so he and Manning both had been within driving distance. Lloyd had flown in from L.A. while Harrison had taken a jumper from Vegas.

The six men were silent. Dressed all in black with black smudged on their faces, the men were barely visible once the headlights were turned off. They each had their assault rifles slung over their shoulders and other serious weaponry. They checked to make sure their micro ear transmitters were working.

It was a fair hike through the forest of Douglas fir, cedar, and maple trees and around rock outcroppings to the compound. They needed to be parked far enough away that they wouldn't be noticed, yet close enough for a quick escape.

Smells of exhaust from the vehicles quickly faded, to be replaced by scents of earth, loam, and a rain-washed breeze. Rain drummed through the forest, landing on them in a solid beat.

"Time." Dare smudged water droplets off the face of his watch with his gloved hand. It was eleven minutes after eight. "Twenty eleven hours," he said in military time. The other men checked their watches and each gave a quick nod.

"Let's do it," Dare said.

Without a word Nick's men pulled down their night-vision goggles and melted into the darkness, silent and swift. Not a twig snapped or the sound of clothing brushing vegetation could be heard as they moved away. Nick slapped Dare on the back, then vanished just as silently into the night.

Dare's heart pounded and he set his plan into motion. He now had sixteen minutes to get into position and wait. He'd holstered his Glock at his side, his Beretta at his back, and, slung over one shoulder, the AK-470A3 rifle he'd borrowed from one of Nick's war buddies.

Earlier Dare had sheathed knives in each boot, and his weapons belt was more than well equipped. His combat gear was loose enough for ease of movement, yet protected him from most of the rain. Despite the fact that his clothing was waterproof, some wetness crept in through his collar. Water ran in rivulets down his face but rolled off his clothing.

Drenched leaves and sticks made no noise beneath his feet. His boots sank slightly into the wet ground as he progressed. Wet branches slapped his face.

When he reached the compound he raised his goggles and let them rest on top of his head. The place was lit up bright as day. When he reached his post, he was careful to remain hidden behind an enormous fir tree, then peeked around it, confident he wouldn't be seen.

He caught sight of a pair of large unusually colorful bats flapping around one of the floodlights. Probably hoary bats dining on insects. The guards standing beneath the light were obviously professionals and didn't even look up at the swooping and hovering mammals.

Most of the guards stood with feet and shoulders squared, rifles in their hands, their gazes sweeping the night. *Shit, yeah,* these men looked far more experienced than the clowns at the Arizona compound.

Through the chain-link fence Dare saw the countless dirty white tents. There was one much larger canvas-covered structure that he didn't remember seeing on the satellite map. People huddled in the rain outside the covering, but many stood beneath the canvas— what he could see from his side view. Some kind of gathering. Dare and his men would have to be extra careful. He didn't want any bystanders to get hurt during the raid.

His gut told him the structure was the first place he needed to head once inside the compound.

He moved so that his back was to the tree, facing away from the compound. He checked his watch.

Three minutes.

Dare forced himself to take deep breaths. Clear head, keep emotions at bay. It wouldn't do him, Lyra, or the other men any good to charge in like a madman. Everything had to go according to plan, perfect execution.

The stakes were high. Lyra could be taken away by Neal Barker. If he escaped with Lyra during the raid,

Dare might never be able to find her. Goddamn it, but the bastard better not have raped her. The mere thought had Dare's head aching and his arms trembling from the need to get to her.

Two minutes.

Adrenaline surged through his veins as he readied his grip on his sniper rifle. Seconds dragged by. Dare fought with himself to keep Lyra's smile out of his thoughts. *Concentrate on the job.*

One minute.

Blood pounded in his head. He took another deep breath.

He slid around the side of the tree, keeping close to it and in the darkness. He raised his rifle. Sights set on his first target. Glanced at his watch.

More seconds dragged by. The pounding in his head increased with the flash of every second on his watch.

"*Now!*" came Manning's voice over the transmitter.

Two seconds and an explosion rocked the compound. Flames shot up into the sky.

Every light along the perimeter of the fence went out. Darkness outside and inside the compound. With one shot, Manning had done his job and had taken out the main generator with the RPG.

Screams came from the compound.

Guards shouted and looked at the forest, trying to see their hidden, silent, and deadly enemies. They were easy targets and they knew it. Some shot a steady stream of bullets blindly into the forest.

A few lights came back on in the compound, dim this time. Backup generators, no doubt.

Dare moved so that his back was to the tree again.

Deep breath. Keeping low, Dare swung around the tree so that he braced himself on one knee and the rifle against his shoulder. Using the weapon's night-vision scope, he started picking off the guards one by one.

When all the guards were down in the immediate vicinity, Dare slung his rifle over his shoulder. He'd be in close quarters for search mode and would need to use his handgun. There was enough light coming from the compound that he didn't need his night-vision goggles. Yet.

He unholstered his Glock and aimed it at the closest guard who moved. One shot and he dropped.

That caught the attention of another injured guard, but Dare took him out with a single shot. The man's shout before he fell was merely background noise, like the sounds of other shots and small explosions.

Without stopping for a breath, Dare jerked one of Nick's special IEDs from his weapons belt. He yanked the pin, lobbed the bomb over the razor wire between the double fence.

He bolted away from the fence, dived onto the muddy ground. The bomb's explosion ripped through the night. The force of it rocked Dare, but he kept his face turned away.

More explosions went off around the compound. More screams from people inside.

Dare kept low as he got to his feet and assessed the situation. The IED had done its job and had blown holes through both fences. Nick had created the bombs so that the IED would only spread in a five-foot radius, just enough to get Dare through.

The guards along the perimeter were mostly down or frantically trying to locate their foes. Gunshots pierced the night from both the remaining guards and Dare's team. He took out two more men before he headed for the fence opening.

Keeping down, Dare bolted for the hole in the fence. He rolled through the first hole and had to flatten himself. With his belly to the ground and both hands on his Glock, he shot two more guards.

He rose up and dived through the second hole. In seconds he slipped into the maze of tents, heading for the large canvas structure he'd noticed earlier.

When the power went out and the first shots rang through the night, Neal clenched Lyra's hand and swung around, as if someone might be at his back. He started shouting orders to his men while people began to scream and shout, mostly women.

Some lights came on, but they were dim.

"Men, secure the compound!" Neal shouted as he held on to Lyra. "Women and children, to your tents. *Now!*"

Lyra's heart pounded as he ignored her and directed his people. The men obeyed his orders at once, as if trained for a day like this. The women were another story. They looked beyond shocked and confused, and the mass pushed out of the tent. Lyra prayed no one would be trampled.

What was happening had to be Dare and Nick. It *had* to be! Shots and explosions came from all directions. It was obvious whoever was out there had reinforcements.

The platform bucked and Lyra stumbled. Only Neal's hold on her kept her from falling.

The flood of people screaming and running from the shelter seemed like it would never end.

Hope filled Lyra and she yanked her hand from Neal's. She whirled and ran from him. She made it to the bottom of the stairs when he caught her by the hair and jerked her up against his chest.

Pain screamed through her head. Despite the agony, she kicked back, her heels connecting with his shins, and she struggled with all her might.

"Bitch!" Neal shouted as he yanked her hair so hard it drove her to her knees on the damp ground, grinding dirt into the white robe. Tears poured from her eyes from the pain, but she tried to block it out. "Mark, get Sara!"

No!

Neal pulled Lyra up by her hair to her feet, so hard and so fast that stars flooded her vision and her legs wouldn't support her.

Despite the continual pain, immediate relief flowed through Lyra as he released her hair. He caught her underneath her arms and kept her back to his chest.

Even though she was wobbly, she began to fight him again. She struggled, kicked back, tried to pry his hands from her body—

Until Neal put a knife to her throat. She felt the bite of metal against her flesh and she stilled at once.

"Prophecy or no, I *will* kill you, Lyra, before I let another man have you." Neal paused before continuing, "But I don't think that will happen—Sara will die unless you follow my instructions. *Do you understand?*"

"Yes," Lyra mumbled as Mark dragged her mother closer, also with a knife to her throat.

Neal pressed the knife harder against her, his voice rising. *"Yes, what?"*

Lyra winced from the feel of the blade. He was even more insane than she'd thought. "Yes, Prophet!"

An explosion blasted the compound, followed by another and another, and the ground seemed to tilt. When Neal stumbled backward, the dagger sliced into Lyra's flesh, bringing a fresh bout of pain. Blood trickled down her neck. Just a little more pressure and he'd have slit her throat.

Neal steadied himself and moved the blade away from Lyra's neck and spun her around to face him. "Stupid bitch!" Blue eyes wild with fury, he grabbed her by the shoulder with one hand and backhanded her on the other side of her face so hard she fell again. Vaguely she was aware of the wreath of flowers tumbling off her head.

Pain burst through her skull yet another time and she saw white sparks against a gray background. She tasted blood in her mouth from where her cheek had slammed up against her teeth. The beatings were making her dizzy and weak, and the tears from the pain wouldn't stop flowing. Only the adrenaline rushing through her kept her from passing out, and the press of the stake against her thigh gave her hope.

He was going to pay. And he was going to pay big.

Neal grabbed her arm and jerked her to her feet, brought her around so that the knife was again at her throat, her back to his chest. He dragged her backward, heading out of the tent.

As Neal started to drag her from the shelter, the lights went out again.

The entire compound was dark.

More bombs went off, illuminating small parts of the compound at a time.

Flames shot up into the air.

People shouted and screamed—the sounds came from everywhere.

When Neal jerked her backward even harder, Lyra cried out.

"Shut. Up. Bitch!" From her side vision she saw that her mother was being taken in the same direction and, like her, had a knife at her throat. "Fight me and I start slicing up Mommy."

A combination of deflation and hope clenched Lyra's chest. But hope rose above all. This attack had to be Dare with reinforcements.

Lyra let Neal drag her into the pouring rain. Instantly she was drenched. She had to work to keep her footing on the slick, muddy ground.

A flare from an explosion lit up the night. In that second of light, her gaze landed on Jason, who stood beneath the shelter.

He smiled. A cold, cruel, and calculating smile.

W hen the lights went out again, Dare jerked down his night-vision goggles.

It was pure pandemonium in the compound with all the shrieking, shots being fired, and more explosions that helped serve as diversions as he searched for Lyra.

He reached the canvas shelter and slipped around the back wall. Dare dodged cables and stepped over spikes holding the shelter up. He held his Glock in his right hand.

When he made it around the back side of the tent, he saw two women being dragged away from the shelter by three men.

Through the green glow of the goggles it was difficult to see their faces, but he knew in his gut that one of the women was Lyra.

The pain from the slice at Lyra's throat burned like fire, and her head spun from being slapped so much, not to mention her other wounds. She might as well have been in a car crash. Everything was starting to catch up with her, and she had to fight the dizziness away as Neal dragged her toward the Temple that was illuminated by an occasional explosion.

Smells of smoke and something sharp and acrid filled the air despite the heavy fall of rain. Cold, wet night air chilled Lyra, and goose bumps rose on her flesh.

The men dragged Lyra and Sara up the steps leading into the Temple. Two armed men stood at either side of the doorway, their guns aimed at the five people approaching them.

"Stop pointing the fucking guns at me," Neal growled.

The men lowered their weapons.

The door burst open. Lyra saw a fat man run through the doorway, illuminated by a fiery glow in the background.

"Where the hell do you think you're going, Larry?" Neal shouted as the man rushed past him.

The man didn't pause as he ran down the Temple steps. "I'm out of here!"

Neal turned his gaze on one of the guards. "Kill him."

The guard raised his rifle and shot the man called Larry in his back. The fat man dropped without a sound, and Lyra's belly churned.

"Just get out of the way and let me into the Temple!" Neal shouted. He paused and looked at both guards. "Shoot anyone that comes near."

"Yes, sir!" both men said.

Mark backed up so that Neal could enter first with Lyra. When Adam opened the Temple door, Lyra blinked from the low lighting coming through the doorway. Additional generators, no doubt.

Lyra couldn't see Neal's face from the position in which he held her, but she was able to see Mark's. He glanced at Lyra's mother, who stood placidly beside him. "She's not going anywhere," Mark said with a smirk. "She's so drugged, she doesn't even know what's going on. After all these years, this time she took them without a fight."

Lyra stared at Sara. They'd drugged her mother?

Neal moved Lyra forward through the foyer and to a door. Adam jerked it open. Neal removed the knife from Lyra's throat and shoved her. She fell through the doorway into a room lit only by flickering candles. She landed on her hands and knees, jarring her teeth.

The Temple's main Prayer Room, a place she'd been too many times before she escaped. The immediate scents of burning candles and an all too familiar sickly sweet smell met her nose, along with the odor of polish from the wooden floor. The only thing in the room was yet again one of Neal's altars with his "tools of the Light." This altar was bigger, though, extending from one side of the room to the other.

Neal jerked her up by her hair again. Blackness started to close in on her until all she saw was a pin-prick of light. This time it was much harder to keep from blacking out. She took a deep breath to get oxy-gen into her system. Her vision blurred, then slowly cleared.

A measure of relief flowed through her when Neal released her so hard she landed on her ass. At least the knife was away from her neck and he wasn't pulling her hair.

She rested her head against the wall she was next to and tried to slow her breathing and her heart rate. She watched her mother being forced into the room onto the floor. Sara didn't even make a cry when she was thrown into a corner and kicked in the side by Mark.

Neal first. Lyra would kill Mark next.

Adam shot a bolt in the door, locking it. In the glow of the candlelight, Lyra watched Neal, his eyes wild and his long, wet hair sticking to his face and neck. De-spite all he'd done to her since she'd been kidnapped and brought back to The People, she'd never seen him look so furious. So furious that his face was red and he was shaking with rage.

"I should kill you and be done with it," Neal said to Lyra.

From the corner of her eye she saw Mark's and Adam's expressions. Mark appeared pleased, where Adam looked shocked.

"However, you are the Chosen," Neal continued, "and you *will* face your destiny once we get through this." He stepped closer, his dagger still in his fist. "But the Prophet Jericho said nothing about not beating you daily once the baby is born."

Lyra swallowed and shrank against the wall. Neal had an insane light to his eyes and looked like he was barely holding himself back from beating her now. She didn't know how much more she could take before passing out and being unable to help her and Sara make an escape.

The press of the stake against Lyra's thigh was constantly in her thoughts. How was she going to use it to get herself and her mother out of here?

Dare. Please, God. Dare.

"Weapons," Neal said to Adam and Mark without looking at them.

Each man grabbed a rifle from a cabinet Adam opened. It was filled with what looked like sophisticated weaponry. With a series of clicking noises, they loaded their rifles. Mark handed his to Neal and snatched another, loading it with the same efficiency he had used with Neal's rifle.

Neal grasped the dagger he'd held to Lyra's throat in one hand, the rifle in the other. He slid his knife into a pocket of his robe yet still watched Lyra. Adam and Mark did the same, putting their knives away in the pockets of their jeans in favor of keeping both hands on their rifles.

Lyra's heart thumped as she looked from Neal, to Mark, to Adam. All three were prepared to use their guns. All three were prepared to murder anyone who tried to rescue her and her mother. Lyra and Sara were hostages. Truly hostages. And Neal was a madman.

"Through the tunnel." Neal grabbed Lyra's hand and jerked her to her feet as he looked at Adam and Mark. "If anyone follows us, shoot to kill."

Neal's gaze met Lyra's and she went cold. "You promise *now* to fully cooperate or your mother's dead."

CHAPTER *TWENTY-FOUR*

After the men shoved the women into the Temple and the door closed behind them, Dare slipped through the darkness toward the building. He analyzed the situation, taking in the pandemonium around him as well as what he had to get through to make it to the Temple and in the door.

To either side of the entryway stood a guard who searched the night with his rifle, ready to take out any unwelcome guests.

Dare holstered his Glock and jerked his rifle from over his shoulder. At this distance he'd need it.

He pushed his goggles up, raised the rifle, and looked through the night-vision scope just in time to see one of the guards aiming directly at him.

Shit.

Dare dropped and rolled, continuing to move at the same time bullets whizzed past him. He didn't hesitate, and as he turned he popped off a round of shots, taking out the shooter and the man next to him.

When Dare was certain the men were both down, he pushed himself to his feet, checking around him to make sure there were no more guards. He slung the rifle over his shoulder again. He'd lost his goggles when he rolled, and he had to scoop them up and slip them back on.

Even as he made his way through the mud puddles and pouring rain, more explosions continued around the compound. Sounded like the boys were having a good time with those diversions.

Dare drew his Glock and Beretta, each one aimed at one of the guards' bodies. He crept up to the huge building and cast glances over his shoulder to make sure no one else was in sight. When he was certain both men were dead, he holstered the Beretta.

His earpiece crackled.

"Where are you, Lancaster?" came Nick's voice.

"Temple, main door." Dare wrapped his hand around the door handle.

"Two seconds," Nick said. "I'm right behind you."

Dare cast another glance over his shoulder. In moments a shadowy figure approached. Dare crouched and held his gun steady. Through the green view of his goggles he couldn't tell if it was Nick, and he wasn't taking any chances.

"It's me, buddy," Nick said as he got closer and Dare made positive identification.

"Watch my back." Dare glanced at each felled guard. He'd never let down his awareness of them. "I'm going in."

"I've got you," Nick said, this time without the transmitter, as he reached Dare.

Dare nodded and opened the door. He held his Glock in the ready position as he peered inside. Not a sound. He rounded the door frame and found himself in a foyer. A door directly in front of him, hallways leading to the left and the right. At the end of one hallway a blue glow spilled out of a doorway. From his position it looked like there were cameras and monitors—some kind of surveillance room.

It was dark in the opposite direction. With his goggles on, Dare saw they were in the clear.

Nick closed the door behind them and they both paused. Dare clenched his fist tighter around the butt of his Glock as he listened. Still not a sound. He looked at his feet and saw smeared footprints leading into the door directly in front of them.

He tried to open the door. Locked. He glanced at Nick, who was looking in the direction of the room with the blue glow.

"Freeman, Harrison," Dare said over the transmitter. "Temple, front and center. Manning, Lloyd. Take the back."

All four men acknowledged Dare's orders, and he turned to Nick. "I'll head through here," Dare said as he removed a silencer from his belt and screwed it onto the end of his Glock. "You check out that room."

Nick gave a quick nod and headed down the hallway. Dare pointed his weapon at the door handle. Two shots and the bolt was history.

Hinges creaked as he pushed the door open to reveal a room lit only by candles. He held his gun ready and moved it from side to side. The room was empty, as he'd suspected. No exit in sight—but muddy tracks were smeared on the wooden floor along with water puddles from the rain.

Dare closed the door behind him—he didn't want any

unwelcome surprises creeping up without some kind of noise. The creaky hinges would take care of that.

The room smelled of candle wax, wood, and something else. Dare sniffed. Definitely marijuana. Not much in the room. An altar, candles, a few supplies. To the right an open cabinet with a few choice weapons, and empty slots where others must have been.

Through the green glow of his goggles, he followed the muddy trail of smeared footprints to a wall. The seams blended so well with the rest of the wall, he almost couldn't make them out.

He didn't have time to figure out how to open it. He drew one of Nick's IEDs from his weapons belt. This one was special. It was designed to make little noise while it more or less burned a hole through whatever it was attached to.

It already had an adhesive strip. Dare pulled off the plastic covering the adhesive—it would give him ten seconds to get away from the wall.

Just in case, Dare went as far back as the door and ducked down. In seconds, the IED flared with a crack and burned a hole through the thin plasterboard.

Flames still burned around the edges of the opening as Dare reached it and stepped through into a dimly lit area. He pushed up his goggles. He was on a landing, and a set of stairs led down to a hard-packed dirt floor and dim lights were strung overhead. They probably used the tunnel for illegal activities, not to mention it made a great escape route.

It had been too long since the men and women had entered the tunnel. He needed to get going and get going fast.

"I see you, Lancaster," came Nick's voice over the transmitter, and Dare looked up to see a camera overhead. "This is a surveillance room. Can't see our targets—yet. There's a well-monitored exit. Has to be their destination."

"Harrison, Freeman?" Dare said into his transmitter as he hurried down the tunnel, following the tracks and drops of water smudging the dirt.

"Just reaching the Temple," came Freeman's voice.

"Check out the rooms to either side of the one dead center," Dare said as he made his way down the tunnel. "Then follow me."

"One minute and I'll be covering your—" Nick's voice crackled just before Dare's transmitter went dead.

As she was forced down the tunnel, Lyra felt the press of the stake against her thigh. A lot of good it was going to do her against three big men with guns.

The five of them were drenched and Lyra's teeth chattered. The mud that had been beneath her feet had been replaced by hard-packed earth.

Neal gripped his rifle with both hands and glanced at Lyra. "As soon as we get out of here, I'll take you where you'll never be found, where you can never escape again. If you ever try, I'll kill your mother."

Lyra found it hard to breathe. Just the thought of what Neal could do made her chest seize.

They reached a sort of garage and came to a stop. Boxes were stacked on boxes around the circumference of the area. But in the middle were two black Hummers.

Neal pointed his gun directly at Lyra. "Don't move." He glanced at Sara, who had been shoved down the tunnel and looked like an automaton. "I have to thank your mother for bringing you to me." Neal smirked. "As soon as I met you I knew you were the Chosen. I made sure you had nothing to keep you from being brought to the Temple of Light."

Everything started to blur around the edges of her sight. "What do you mean?" she said slowly as her skin began to tingle and the hair at her nape rose.

Neal's wicked smile moved from Lyra to her mother and back. "I set your father up. Called in the report about the bank robbery. Had a sniper ready to take your father out."

With every word, Lyra's heart sank, her head spun, her legs wobbled. "You had my dad killed?"

Neal shrugged. "I needed you and that couldn't happen while he was around." He glanced at Sara. "With your spineless mother, I knew I'd have you both once the cop was out of the way."

Fury chased away every ache, every pain, and for the first time since Lyra arrived in this place she could think clearly. "You bastard." Her voice rose in strength. "No matter what happens right now, or in the future, you'll pay. One way or another, you'll pay."

Neal narrowed his eyes. He aimed his rifle at Sara's head.

A shot echoed through the room.

Adam dropped to the floor. Red stained his shirt over his heart.

Lyra looked up in time to see Dare around the corner

of the tunnel. At the same time she shoved up her robe and jerked out the stake.

A loud boom from Neal's gun.

Sara screamed and grabbed her left shoulder. Blood blossomed on the tan of her robe as she fell and landed on her back.

Lyra screamed, too. She tightened her grip on the stake.

Mark swung his rifle toward the tunnel and started shooting at the same time he backed around one of the Hummers. His weapon was an automatic, and every bullet kicked up dirt from the tunnel walls.

Despite being shot, a suddenly very alert Sara dug her hand into her robe.

She pulled out the stake she had taken in Lyra's tent.

Sara launched herself at Mark and buried the stake in his thigh.

"Fuck!" Mark shouted, and fell behind the Hummer, his rifle clattering beneath him. His legs disappeared as he started crawling out of sight.

Neal grabbed Lyra's arm and started to pull her around one of the Hummers.

With all the fury piled up inside her, Lyra twisted away from Neal's grip.

She raised the stake high as he turned back to her.

Lyra drove the point of the stake straight into Neal's groin.

Neal screamed, a high-pitched sound. He dropped the rifle and fell to his knees. He yanked the stake from his groin and doubled over, still shrieking. Blood poured over the dirt floor. The stake rolled away.

Neal's whole body jerked and shook. He grabbed his rifle and pointed it at Lyra.

Dare rounded the vehicle. Rage filled him and he didn't have to stop to think. One shot in the center of his forehead and Barker was gone.

"Momma!" Lyra yelled, and started to run to her mother, but Dare held her back with one arm.

"Get down!" he ordered, his voice coming out harsh with his command. "Stay behind the wheel of that Hummer. Mark is still around."

Lyra hesitated as she gave another look at her mother, who lay on her side, looking at Lyra. "Listen to him," her mother got out in a croak.

Lyra nodded, then obeyed and sat with her back against the vehicle's giant wheel. Dare's keen gaze had taken in her appearance the moment he spotted her with Barker. Her face was bloodied and bruised, and blood dried in a thin line across her throat.

If it weren't for another man with a gun out to kill them, Dare would have taken even greater satisfaction at finally ridding the world of Neal Barker.

Instead Dare kept low, both hands on his Glock. Nick was in the room now, and Dare motioned with his head in the direction Mark had crawled, then pointed at the opposite end of the Hummer for his partner to take that angle.

Dare slowly peeked around the Hummer. No sign of Mark, but a blood smear marred the dirt floor. The man was injured from the stake. An injured man was even more deadly.

Freeman peered around the tunnel, searching the

room with his gun. "Secured, Lancaster?" Freeman asked.

"One man. Armed," Dare said. "On the other side of the second Hummer."

"Let's give him some company," Harrison said, and Dare looked over his shoulder just in time to see the man punch a button on the wall and a large garage door rise up with loud creaks and groans, a door wide and big enough for both vehicles to drive out of.

Freeman, Harrison, and Nick all took places around the Hummers and aimed their assault rifles toward the opening.

"Yo!" Dare jerked his head toward Manning's voice but didn't see him in the darkness. "We've taken down every fucker up here. Gotta get on out. Cops are close."

Screams of distant sirens met Dare's ears. "One more asshole to get rid of," he said, and moved around the Hummer, only to see Nick at the opposite end.

They made it to the second vehicle and, as one, swung around only to face each other again. No Mark. Only a bloody stake on the floor.

Dare quickly took in the smeared footprints, the spots of blood, and the fact that the door of the Hummer was slightly ajar. He jerked his thumb toward the door and Nick gave a sharp nod.

The engine roared to life.

"Shit!" Dare barely rolled out of the way before the vehicle backed up the ramp—then Mark sped forward and rammed the Hummer into the other one, where Lyra was hiding.

Lyra cried out.

Dare saw red.

He fired off a round at the driver's side of the Hummer but only made pockmarks in the bulletproof glass. His men were doing a job on the vehicle, too, but the bullets couldn't pass through the metal or the glass.

This time the Hummer roared up the ramp.

"Clear!" Manning shouted.

Dare and the other men dropped to the ground. A thump-pop sound.

An explosion beneath the Hummer.

The vehicle raised up from its hind end. Flipped onto its back. Skidded into the garage and rammed the other Hummer.

Manning, Lloyd, and Freeman guarded the entrance to the garage as flames roared on the Hummer's underside.

Nick and Harrison aimed their guns at the driver's side door of the vehicle as the door popped open and Mark tumbled out. He was weaponless, and blood smeared his forehead.

"To your feet," Nick shouted. As much as they all probably wanted to, they couldn't shoot an unarmed man.

Dare went to Lyra, grabbed her hand, and drew her to her feet.

"I knew the bitch would ruin everything." Mark had his hands behind his head and leaned a bit to spit blood even as he glared at Lyra. "Should have killed her when I had the chance. Neal was too fucking obsessed with her and the fucking Prophecy."

"Tie up the bastard," Dare said, and he knew murder was in his expression. "Leave him in the tunnel for law enforcement to put him behind bars." He glanced at the still-burning Hummer. "We've got to get the hell out of here."

"Bitch!" Mark shouted as Nick searched him and tossed out a knife he found in the man's boot, beneath his jeans.

Freeman slung a rope to Nick and he made short work of tying the man up, hands and ankles, and dragging him into the tunnel.

"Fucking bitch!" Mark screamed. "You killed him. You ruined everything."

Dare's thoughts of murder were interrupted when Freeman said, "We found a serious shitload of drugs and military weapons. These guys are going down."

Lyra had run to the woman lying on the floor on the other side of the Hummer. She rolled her mother so that she could cradle Sara in her lap. Sara took shallow breaths. Blood soaked her robe at her shoulder and chest. Her head tilted back, her eyes closed.

Only her low moan told Dare she was still alive. Lyra turned to him as she held her mother. Tears flooded Lyra's battered features. "Help me. Please!" she cried.

Dare holstered his Glock and hurried to Lyra and her mother, confident that Nick and the other men would watch his back in case anyone else came at them.

Dare bent to check Sara's wound, hoping it wasn't fatal. When he pushed aside the opening of her robe the tightness in his gut eased. It looked like a clean shot through her upper arm. Just as Dare was about to pull out his dagger to cut strips of cloth from the woman's robe to bind the wound, Nick handed him a bundle.

"Figured Barker would be good for something," Nick said.

Dare grabbed the cloths and folded one into a thick pad to press against the wound, then quickly bound it.

Siren screams were louder now. The cavalry had arrived. They had to get the hell out of there.

Lyra found herself being drawn out of the garage by Dare and into the pouring rain with four men—six including Dare and Nick. Nick carried her mother. Lyra ran behind Dare, who'd released her hand so that he could keep his grip on his gun.

It was so dark that she almost didn't see *him.*

Jason.

She came to a complete stop and screamed. He lunged for her. He grabbed her neck and squeezed hard as he took her to the ground.

A strangled sound came from her throat.

"Bitch," Jason shouted, his eyes wild. "You killed my father."

Jason was jerked away. His hands slipped from her neck.

Dare slammed his fist into Jason's face. He flew back and landed on his ass, but he quickly scrambled to his feet.

Jason whipped out a knife as he charged toward Lyra again. A shot echoed through the night and he crumpled onto the ground.

Lyra's gaze was hazy from the rain, but she saw one of the men still had his gun aimed at Jason's body—a hole was in the center of Jason's forehead. Lyra turned her face away. The sick feeling in her stomach multiplied.

The sound of sirens screamed in Lyra's head. Dare reached for her hand. He helped her to her feet, then swept her into his arms, startling her into letting out a small cry.

All six men tore through the forest. Dare seemed to carry her effortlessly as they ran, as Nick did with Sara. The sirens and lights flashed through the forest. Of course the men wouldn't want anyone to know they had anything to do with the attack on the compound, so they ran like hell. Lyra noticed they all had goggles that they pulled over their eyes as they ran, no doubt for night vision, so that they didn't run into anything.

It seemed like they ran forever, but before she knew it, they were at two large black vehicles. One was a Hummer like the two in the garage. The other she thought was a Range Rover. They piled into the vehicles. Lyra found herself on Dare's lap in the backseat of the Hummer while Nick cradled Sara next to her. One of the men Lyra didn't know still had on a pair of those strange-looking goggles.

Dare and Nick had ripped their goggles off their heads and tossed them in the back. The dark-haired man started the vehicle and tore out of the hideaway— with the lights off. Another man she didn't know was in the passenger seat.

Dare held her midsection tighter, obviously trying to keep her from falling off his lap. Lyra grasped the back of the passenger seat as the vehicle jolted them while they traveled down a rough dirt road.

Once they neared the paved highway, the man driving the Hummer pulled off the side of the road and into a thick grove of trees. She looked over her shoulder and saw the Rover pull up behind them. Lights of countless law enforcement vehicles and fire engines going to the commune flashed through the rainy night.

"Think the cops will see us?" Lyra whispered.

"We're hidden well enough, and the vehicles should blend with the night," Dare said.

"What about Momma?" Lyra trembled as she looked at her mother, who was still lying in Nick's arms.

"No blood spotting the pad." Nick glanced at Lyra. "Looks like she's not losing any blood. When I wrapped it, the wound looked clean. I think she'll be all right till we get to the cabin."

When the flood of lights waned on the road and concentrated on the compound, the driver of the Hummer pulled out and continued to drive off-road with his lights off and the goggles on.

What was going to happen to all The People? Would those who weren't guilty of any crimes be treated as the innocents they were?

When they reached an isolated cabin deep in the woods, Dare and Nick carried Lyra and her mother inside and took them to a room. Vaguely Lyra wondered whose cabin it was.

When they were in the bedroom, one of the big men brought in a first-aid kit. Nick settled Sara on one side of a large bed and started tending to her wound right away.

"She'll be all right," Nick said as he glanced up. "Clean shot, bullet went straight through the fleshy part of her arm."

Relief flooded Lyra.

Then she started shaking. Her skin turned to ice,

and her head spun. She felt all the blood drain from her face.

Dare scooped Lyra into his arms. "She's going into shock."

He took her to the other side of the bed and immediately wrapped her in blankets. Her whole body went numb.

This time when blackness closed in on her she didn't fight it.

CHAPTER *TWENTY-FIVE*

Red, orange, and blue flames illuminated Neal's features and were reflected in his eyes. His expression was crazed, insane. He stalked her, a dagger raised high. His mouth twisted in an evil smile. Red horns sprouted from his head, and his tail whipped around and lashed Lyra's face. Pain ripped through her and she stumbled back.

Neal raised the weapon higher. It turned into a pitchfork with three daggers for tines. He raised the pitchfork—

He exploded.

Flesh and blood splattered the room.

He was gone.

Gone.

Neal was forever gone.

She stood in the corner, shaking as blood drenched her robe.

Arms wrapped around her from behind.

A warm embrace that she melted into as she slipped into a safe and loving sleep.

• • •

L yra slowly opened her eyes. Her eyelids felt heavy and she blinked a few times.

Slivers of light peeked through blinds on a window. Her face burned, her throat burned, and her head and body ached. Her mind tried to sort out the dream from reality. This time instead of ending in terror, it had ended with her feeling that she was finally safe. Finally.

And the arms around her had made her feel secure ... and loved.

Memories were at the tip of her consciousness, but she couldn't quite grasp them. Her sleep-fuddled mind tried to puzzle them out. Slowly the memories came into focus. Neal. Being kidnapped. Being beaten. Hurting Neal with the stake. Neal being shot. Then all of them escaping.

The heavy arm draped over her waist and firm body pressed against her back made her feel very alive. *Dare.* She allowed herself to relax into the embrace. The feeling of being safe and loved filled her with a power that made all of her pains not matter.

Shock jolted her out of her dreamlike state. She sat up and pushed Dare's arm off. Fear rushed through her.

"Momma!" she said in a rusty croak.

"Shhh." Dare sat up beside her and wrapped one of his arms around her shoulders as she jerked her head up to look at him. He gave her a hint of a smile. "She'll be all right. She's in another bedroom."

Lyra sagged against Dare. He brought them both back to lie on the bed, and he turned her so that she was snuggled against him, one of his arms wrapped around her as she pressed her cheek against his chest. Her face stung from the contact, but she didn't care. She was in his arms again. And her mother was going to be all right.

Lyra gradually became aware of her surroundings. They were in a strange room. "Where are we?"

Dare pressed his lips to her temple that wasn't bruised. "My ranch."

"Where's Momma?" she asked.

"In one of the spare bedrooms." He pressed another kiss to her skin. "Resting."

Lyra breathed a deep sigh of relief until her thoughts returned to the nightmare at Neal's compound. "What about all of The People?"

"Law enforcement will sort things out," he said. "Only those leading the cult will be arrested. It'll take some time, but they'll separate those who are innocent from those who belong in jail." He lightly stroked her hair from her face, and she felt like he couldn't get enough of touching her. "There were so many drugs and so many weapons that those responsible will be put away for a long time."

"I don't understand how they'll do that—separate the innocent from those who deserve to be put away," she said.

"They have their methods." Dare offered her a smile. "Like I said, it'll take time."

Lyra was quiet for a moment. "I know some people were there against their will, but others truly believed in Neal and the Temple of Light. What do you think will happen to them?"

"Those who choose to leave the cult will hopefully be reacclimated to a normal life free of tyranny. The others . . ." Dare shook his head and sighed. "I guess we'll have to see how they pick up the pieces. They might go to one of the satellite compounds and follow the leadership of Neal's other commanders for all we know."

She rubbed her face against his chest despite the ache in her cheek. "I feel so bad for all of them." She hesitated. "Did—did anyone die? Other than Neal, Jason, and Adam?"

"Yes." Dare paused, his look serious. "But as far as I know, no civilians were killed. Only injuries, none fatal."

Lyra didn't know what to say as her gaze locked with his. People had died. Because of her?

Dare seemed to read her expression. "No, honey. You can't take responsibility for anyone who died. They were men who knew what they were doing and who were most likely involved in weapons trading and running drugs."

Then it occurred to her she'd forgotten one other person. "Mrs. Yosko. How is she?"

Dare grinned this time and touched his finger to her nose. "She decided she wanted to go into the retirement center. She called it 'the old farts' home.' "

"That sounds like something she would say." Lyra gave a soft laugh. "So she chose to go there? No one forced her?"

"She actually seemed pleased." Dare ran his finger along her cheekbone. "Although Nick's not so sure about it."

Lyra cocked an eyebrow. "And why's that?"

"Mrs. Y insisted that Nick keep Dixie."

Lyra choked with laughter. "I can just imagine how *that* went over."

Dare's grin broadened. "Let's just say that Mrs. Y won."

Lyra sniggered again.

One more thought came to her mind, but this one made her chest so heavy she could barely breathe, and all laughter and happiness left her. "It was Neal all this time." A ball of pain expanded in her throat and her eyes burned. "He had my dad killed. It was all because of me. All because of me. It was *my* fault."

Dare narrowed his eyes. "What do you mean, Neal had your father killed?"

She looked up at him through her watery gaze. "Neal set my dad up." She hiccupped. "He had a sniper shoot Dad so that Neal could take me into the Temple of Light."

Dare brought her closer to him. "I'm sorry, honey."

"So it's my fault," she whispered as she closed her eyes.

"Hey." Dare grasped her chin and forced her to open her eyes and look up at him. "You can't take the blame for any of this. Not one bit. I'm not going to let you. He was a crazy sonofabitch and absolutely none of this was any of your doing."

Lyra wasn't sure the heavy pain in her chest would ever go away.

Exhaustion finally overcame her as Dare held her close. Her body went limp, and she relaxed into a deep sleep.

D are stood behind Lyra as she paused to look in the mirror in his bedroom. Every time she looked at her bruised features and the scab on her throat she felt sick to her belly, yet relieved at the same time.

Neal Barker would never hurt her or anyone else again.

She couldn't feel sorry for him.

It had been six days since the "incident," and the swelling on her face had gone down and her bruises were yellowing around the edges. But her heart and soul—those would take a lot of time to heal.

Her eyes met Dare's in the mirror and she saw that he still felt anger at what she'd gone through, but his features softened every time he looked at her.

She pulled away from him and started down the hallway to the room Momma was staying in. Lyra's heart also ached for her mother. To have let everything go to Neal and be left with nothing.

"If my landlord will let me come back, my mom and I can live in the house in Bisbee," Lyra said to Dare as they entered Sara's room. "I make enough with my art that I can support both of us."

Dare cleared his throat. When she glanced at him her heart did a little flip-flop even though he wore a frown. "We'll discuss this later," he said.

She blinked. What was with him?

Lyra went to her mother and sat on the chair beside Sara's bed. Lyra brushed her lips over her mother's forehead, leaned back, and smiled. Despite her bullet wound and the beating, Sara was looking so much better already, younger even, now that she'd been taken away from the cult.

"How are you feeling today?" Lyra asked her mother.

"Just tired." Sara managed a weak smile. "I'll be up and around by tomorrow."

Sara was taking longer to heal than most people

with her type of injury, Dare had told Lyra. The healing process was longer for Sara because of the trauma she'd been through—and was still going through. She'd spent eight years in a cult. The pain of that experience wasn't going to heal for a long time.

Lyra and her mother had spent a lot of time talking over the past six days. They had so much to catch up on. During the times Sara had been awake, they'd shared tears at the sad things that had happened in their lives and smiled and laughed at happier memories.

Lyra had cried about feeling responsible for all that had happened, and her mother had wanted to take the blame for even introducing Lyra to Neal. But in the end they came to terms with the fact that it all came down to an insane man and now it was time to get on with their lives.

She'd even told her mother about the time she'd met Nick. She gave a wry smile at her description of him. A weird, paranoid neat freak. He might be a neat freak, but he definitely wasn't weird or paranoid. He was absolutely gorgeous and cautious rather than paranoid. There must be something in his past that made him wary of being easily located.

Kind of like herself, Lyra thought.

What she hadn't talked to her mother about was her growing feelings for Dare. Just thinking about him created that crazy sensation in her belly. Lyra was happy her mother genuinely seemed to like Dare.

Dare left the room and Lyra spent more time with Sara. When her mother's eyelids started to get droopy, Lyra stood. "Get some rest, Momma."

Sara smiled. "I know you have other things to attend

to." She looked at Dare, who walked into the room as she said that, and Lyra's cheeks heated.

Dare took her hand and led her from the bedroom, his grip warm and firm. It was surprising how much of a gentleman Dare was. He always helped her into the SUV or car before getting into the driver's side, escorted her places with his hand at her lower back, and opened doors, allowing her to go first. He seemed to know just when she needed a hug and when she needed a little distance.

Something that meant so much to Lyra was that Dare had gone to the home she had shared with Mrs. Yosko and retrieved all of the materials she used to create her artwork. He'd even given her one of his spare bedrooms to use as her place to retreat and work on projects while her mother recovered. It was therapeutic to create, and it helped bring Lyra to terms with her new life. It still hurt to think of the people who'd betrayed her in her life, like Becca, but Lyra could move on.

She'd never be on the run again.

Lyra had kept busy these past days during the times Dare left to tackle one of his PI cases or to work his ranch. She liked having a little breathing room. She'd always needed space at times, which was when she did her artwork. Besides, there was something special she'd been making for Dare.

While they walked from her mother's bed into the front room, Lyra studied his profile. He was so sexy with his slightly wavy short brown hair, his coffee brown eyes. He had the sleeves of his denim shirt rolled up to his elbows, and she liked to watch the play of muscles in his forearms, his long, strong fingers. He had a way of looking at her that made her feel like she was the most beautiful woman on earth.

Only problem was that he'd been treating her like a fragile piece of glass since he'd rescued her. She wanted more, so much more.

He'd been so attentive. They'd talked so much, shared stories of the past and more of their hopes and dreams, and he'd helped her through the trauma she'd experienced.

The one thing they hadn't discussed was the two of them.

Was there a "two of them"?

When they reached the great room, Dare glanced at her and her cheeks heated at being caught studying him. He gave her that sexy smile of his that just made her want to dissolve into a puddle of liquid heat. It sent those butterfly sensations straight to her abdomen.

Lyra drew in a deep inhale and slowly let out her breath.

Dare brought her around to face him. He traced his fingers over the bruises on her face so lightly it felt like a feather brushed her skin. "Are you feeling better?" he said in a husky voice.

She nodded and his hand slipped into her hair. "I'm fine. Especially when I'm with you."

"Me. Too." He cradled her cheeks and brushed his lips across hers. "I just can't get enough of you, Lyra Collins."

She sighed with happiness. The way he made her feel . . . she'd never felt so loved and cared for. Not since her father died.

This was different. So much more different.

But if Dare didn't make a move soon, she was going to jump him. "Hold on." She drew away from his light kiss. "There's something I want to give you."

He cocked a brow. "Lead the way."

Lyra took him by the hand and led him to the other side of the house and the spare room she'd been using for her artwork. On the table in the corner there were strips of metal and a few creations. But not what she'd hidden away just for him.

They walked toward the closet and she let his hand go. Dare paused at the table and picked up the small, flat tin that she'd created long ago. He smoothed his thumb over the well-worn metal. "You carry this everywhere, don't you." It was a statement.

Lyra gave a sad smile. "It's very precious to me." She moved beside him and took the tin, then carefully opened it. Inside the flat container, nestled in tissue paper, was a policeman's badge.

"Your father's," Dare said.

She lightly stroked the badge with her forefinger and took a deep breath. "Eight years and it still hurts." She closed the tin and Dare wrapped his hands around hers and together they held on to the box.

"I'm sorry, honey."

She reached up and kissed him lightly on his stubbled cheek. She tried to step back. Dare placed his forehead against hers, and she said, "I'm not sure I'll ever get over the feeling that it was my fault."

"It wasn't your fault," he said with his forehead still against hers. "Let it go."

She sighed, then drew back. "What about you? You blamed yourself for your partner's death. Have you let it go?"

Dare had given it a lot of thought during the week since they'd raided the compound and brought Lyra home. The memory of the day his partner died was still clear. But the guilt . . . There'd been nothing Dare could have done to save his partner. Just like Lyra wasn't responsible for her father's death, Dare hadn't been responsible for his partner's.

Dare met Lyra's gaze. "I'm working on it."

She cupped his jaw in her hand. "We'll work on it together."

They still held the tin within their clenched hands, his palms warm around hers when their lips met. He slipped his tongue into her mouth, and she danced with him, loving his masculine taste and his scent of desert wind and male.

When he pulled away and released her hands, he brushed his knuckles lightly over her cheek. "I can't stop thinking of what he did to you."

"I'm fine." She smiled. "You can stop treating me like I'm going to break."

"You're precious," he said, and brushed his lips over her forehead.

Lyra set the tin on what had become her worktable, next to a metal windmill created from slices of old soda cans.

He picked up the yellow teddy bear on her worktable. "Was this from your father?"

She shook her head. "From Momma." She took it from him and hugged it before setting it aside. "It was the one thing small enough I could take that she'd given me. I didn't realize just how much I missed her until I saw her again. I wanted to blame her for everything, but inside I knew it wasn't her fault."

Lyra gave a sad smile. "The bear and the tin with my dad's badge were in a small backpack I always wore when Neal took us to the commune. They're small enough that I was able to stuff them into the pockets of my robe before he took everything away from us."

Dare's features tensed, and she tried to brush it away with the back of her hand. "I have something just for you," she said.

She moved away from him and opened the closet door. She withdrew a bouquet-filled vase and turned back to him.

"Roses." Dare swallowed a lump that formed in his throat. "You stopped making them after your father died."

She handed the handmade vase and roses to him and gave him her sweet smile. "Now I'll make roses for you. I hope you like them."

For a moment Dare couldn't find the words to express what her gesture meant to him. Damn, even the backs of his eyes stung.

Some of the roses were buds, while others were in full bloom. They had been designed from all types of metal, each rose a different color—reds, yellows, blues, pinks. The vase was one of her hodgepodge designs that he loved.

Dare swallowed again and gripped the vase tight in his palms. "They're beautiful."

He set the bouquet on the table and brought her into his embrace. "Thank you," he whispered against her ear. He lightly kissed her from her earlobe to her mouth. For a long time he just held her. She felt so good in his arms, and he was never going to let her go.

Dare raised his head and looked at Lyra. Her face was flushed and her green eyes seemed darker than they usually did.

"*I* have something for *you*," he said, and she gave him a surprised look. He cradled the vase of roses in one arm and took her hand with his free one. He squeezed it, then led her out of the bedroom, down the hall, and into the master bedroom they had shared over the past few days. Where he'd just held her every night, wanting more than that but waiting until she was healed. Until she was ready.

He flicked on the light switch, and two lamps turned on, one on either side of the bed. After he released her hand, he set the vase of roses on top of the bureau and moved to the nightstand, which was the only place he could think to hide the box until he felt the time was right. This was definitely the right time.

With his back to her, he withdrew the black velvet jeweler's box and wrapped his palm around it, hiding it. He faced her again and she looked at him with a puzzled expression. When he strode back to her and they stood but inches apart, he opened the box and raised it so that she could see the ring.

Lyra caught her breath and her heart lurched. She brought her hand to her throat as she stared at the diamond, her eyes wide. It was beautiful. A simple square-cut diamond that must have been at least a carat was in a platinum setting and nestled in black velvet.

Slowly she raised her eyes to meet his. He was smiling and yet there was uncertainty in his eyes, too.

"Will you marry me, Lyra Collins?" His voice was low and husky.

No words would come out of her mouth. She felt dazed, as if it were all a dream.

"I think I fell in love with you the moment you shot me with that pepper spray." He grinned, then his face went serious again as he caught her left hand in his and raised it. "Say yes."

Lyra opened her mouth. Closed it. His brown eyes locked with hers, and she didn't ever want to look away. When she could finally speak, it came out in a low whisper. "Yes."

He grinned and took her mouth with a hard, possessive kiss. Her mind swirled. The whole room felt like it was whirling around them. Had Dare just proposed to her? And she'd accepted?

He drew away, smiling, and withdrew the ring from the box. Her heart pumped like mad as he set the box aside and slid the diamond and platinum ring over her ring finger. The diamond caught the light and sparkled. The band was a little loose, but she didn't care.

Dare had told her he loved her. He'd asked her to marry him. She flung her arms around his neck and pressed her cheek against his denim shirt. "I love you, Dare. I don't know when it happened, but it just felt right, like we were meant to be together."

"We are." He pressed his lips against her hair. "Always."

CHAPTER *TWENTY-SIX*

D are took Lyra's hand and led her to the bed. Her heart raced and her thoughts spun. She was going to marry Dare. It didn't seem real.

When they reached the side of the bed, he slipped his fingers into her short hair that had now turned a shade of strawberry blond as the dye had faded. He cupped her head, obviously taking care not to touch her wound. His brown eyes captivated her, drawing her in and making her feel as if she were a part of him. The marks on his face from when she'd scratched him were all but gone, and his bruises had faded.

He brought his mouth to hers and gently moved his lips as if taking his time to savor her, like they had all the time in the world. The slight brush of his mouth sent tingles radiating throughout her, even more than when he'd kissed her other times.

The pressure on her mouth increased. Dare gently bit her lower lip and she sighed. A sigh full of longing and love and the thought of a future together with him. To be with him always.

He slipped his tongue into her mouth. She loved the taste of him. Loved the way he explored her, lightly running his tongue along her teeth, then the inside of her cheeks. The texture of his tongue against hers added to the eroticism of the kiss. She'd never felt anything like this before.

She returned his kiss, exploring his mouth as he had explored hers. It was a delicious sensation as their lips and tongues moved together. Her breathing grew heavier and she felt the rise and fall of his chest against hers. With the softest touch that made her shiver, he slid his hands from her hair and moved his fingers down her shoulders, then forearms, up to where she had her arms wrapped around his neck.

He gently took her wrists and brought her hands down and linked his fingers with hers. The ring on her finger felt good as they squeezed their hands together. He placed his forehead to hers again and pressed their bodies closer. His erection was hard against her belly, and his belt buckle rubbed her skin through the light T-shirt she wore. He kissed her again, just the slightest of kisses.

Dare released Lyra's hands, his gut tightening as he looked down into her green eyes. She was so sweet, so full of life and surprises. Her gift had touched him so deeply that it magnified his feelings for her. He had never known what it was like to truly love a woman until he met Lyra. He thanked whatever divine powers there might be for bringing her into his life.

He brushed her hair out of her eyes. Her lips were moist and her expression one of need and love for him. "You are so beautiful," he murmured. "From that first moment, I knew you were special."

She gave a mischievous smile. "Even with the pepper spray, huh?"

"Especially with the pepper spray." He rubbed their noses together. "If it wasn't for the fact that deep in my gut I knew that you were the one for me, I would have been more nervous about asking you to marry me. But hell, I wouldn't have taken a no."

Lyra drew away just enough to kiss the end of his nose. "You didn't have to ask me twice."

He skimmed his fingers down her sides and felt her shiver beneath his touch. He gripped the ends of her T-shirt and drew it up and over her head, with her help. He rubbed his palms over her white cotton bra and squeezed, enjoying her soft moan and the puckering of her nipples.

Butterflies zinged through Lyra's belly. Dare lowered his head and caught one of her nipples through the bra with his teeth, then sucked the taut nub into his warm mouth. The wetness between her thighs grew, and if he didn't remove all her clothing soon, even her jeans would be damp.

She tilted her head back and she slipped her fingers into his hair as his mouth moved to her other nipple. The one he captured felt warm and filled her with such desire she didn't know how much more she was going to be able to take, and they'd only just begun. Her abandoned nipple was chilled by cool air on the white bra but was no less sensitive than the other nipple.

He reached around her and unclasped her bra, and she promised herself she was going to buy satin and sexy lingerie from now on. But like the times before, he didn't seem to care what she wore. He was more intent on unwrapping her piece by piece.

When he tossed her bra aside, he took both of her breasts in his hands and pressed them together so that he could flick his tongue across one to the other and back. Lyra couldn't hold back a whimper as she clenched her hands in his hair.

Dare released her breasts and raised his head. "I want to touch you everywhere."

Lyra let her expression show that she agreed by locking her gaze with his. His coffee-colored eyes looked more like a shade of espresso, they were so dark.

He knelt and took one of her shoes in his hands and she released his hair to brace her palms on his shoulders. After untying the laces, he slipped off the shoe and set it aside, before doing the same with the other. Her socks went next. As he took off each sock, he stroked her foot from the heel to the arch, making her shiver. He took them off in such a sexy way that it made her feel like her feet were major erogenous zones.

When he finished with her shoes and socks, he remained kneeling and slid his palms up her thighs to her waist. He hooked his index fingers in her waistband on either side of her, and his fingers caressed her belly as he brought them around to the button of her Levi's. He unhooked the button, then unzipped her jeans.

He was going so slowly, every movement so sensual, like he wanted to make this moment last forever. Something they would treasure throughout their lives.

Dare slipped her jeans over her hips, down her thighs, and she braced her hands on his shoulders as she stepped out of her Levi's. Still on his knees, he buried his face against her mound and she heard his deep inhale. More moisture wet her folds and her musk was so strong that even she could smell herself. His tongue darted out and she gasped with pleasure when she felt him through the cloth of her white cotton panties. She was definitely buying something sexy for the next time they made love.

Just the realization that they would be making love again and again throughout their lives had her heart thumping harder and heat flushing over her skin.

"I can't believe I'll have you forever," he murmured as if reading her thoughts. He slipped his hands inside her panties and began to draw them down. "To have you, to hold you, to be with you . . ."

"Always," Lyra said as he pulled her panties all the way down and she kicked them aside. "You're mine, cowboy."

He gripped her thighs and looked up at her. The corner of his mouth turned up in that sexy grin that made her knees weak.

Dare buried his face against the curls of her mound, this time without the barrier of her panties. She clenched her hands in his shirt at his shoulders and cried out when his tongue slipped into her folds. He lapped at them in soft, smooth strokes and her legs quivered. When he nipped at her clit, the only thing that kept her from falling was the fact that she had her hands braced on his shoulders.

He continued to taste her but moved one of his hands to her folds and slipped two fingers into her core. He gently pumped his fingers in and out of her channel as he continued to lick her folds and suck her clit. Wild sensations built within her, flowing from where he was touching and tasting her and moving down her legs, up to her belly, over her breasts, and straight to the roots of her hair. Her limbs quivered and she knew she was so close to climax that her thoughts began to spin. She could think of nothing but his tongue on her, his fingers inside her, and the burning heat building up within her.

One more swipe of his tongue and she lost it. Her knees buckled and not even her hands on his shoulders could hold her up. Sparks were shooting through her body and she'd never felt so much heat. She was on fire.

Lyra found herself on her knees facing Dare. He clasped her hips as she continued to tremble, and he kissed her. Just the gentleness of his kiss, the taste of herself mixed with his masculine flavor, and the feel of his hands on her hips made her orgasm continue until she finally stopped shaking.

"Dare." She collapsed against him, her head to his chest, his shirt abrading her nipples.

They were still kneeling as he rubbed his hands up and down her bare skin at her sides and her back. "You're even more beautiful when you climax. I wish you could see yourself."

"Mmmmm," was all Lyra could get out at that moment.

When her breathing and the pounding of her heart slowed, she looked up at Dare. "Your turn. I want your clothes off."

"So do I." He kissed her, then drew her up so that they were both standing.

She unsnapped his western shirt, forcing herself to

take it as slow as Dare had. It was so hard when what she really wanted to do was rip his clothes off and have him inside of her. She moved her hands up his solid chest and lightly traced the wound on his shoulder. He caught her hand and held it to the scar, and they looked at each other for a long moment.

She moved their hands away from the spot and pressed her lips along the scar. She began to trail her fingers over his chest, loving the feel of his skin beneath her fingertips.

Dare held his breath and his cock ached as the beautiful naked woman before him rubbed her palms over his chest, her hands exploring him. Her eyes were dark and smoky as she raised her head to push his shirt over her shoulders. It slid down his arms, and he let it drop to the floor.

Lyra's palms skimmed his biceps to his forearms and wrists, then back up again until her hands were flat at each of his sides, on his rib cage. She ran her fingers over his abs at the same time she leaned closer and licked his nipple. The sensation of her warm tongue on him went straight through his chest to his groin. She tasted each nipple, and the cool air made the tiny nubs harder when she moved her mouth and tongue away. He'd never realized his own flat nipples could be erogenous zones, but the way Lyra was flicking her tongue over them and sucking—it about made him come unglued.

She kissed her way from his chest, slowly trailing her tongue through the light sprinkling of hair. She licked and nipped at him from his abs to the waist of his Wranglers. She knelt and surprised him by reaching around him, grabbing his ass, and squeezing both cheeks.

"You have such a nice ass," she murmured, and he would have laughed if his erection weren't straining so hard against his jeans that it actually hurt.

Her focus was totally on her task as he watched her lick the skin around his navel. She dipped her tongue inside and he groaned. A rush of pleasure radiated from his navel straight to his cock.

Lyra slid her fingers around his waistband until she reached his belt buckle. She abandoned his navel to lean back just enough to unfasten the buckle and pull the belt from the loops of his Wranglers. She tossed it aside and it clunked on the wooden floor, then slid her palms down one pant leg to his boot.

"We've got to get these off," she said as she looked up at him and their eyes met.

She was so beautiful, especially with her hair tousled, her lips swollen from their kisses, and her body bare of any clothing. She had the prettiest breasts, with large nipples that made him even harder. The light brown curls of her pussy were moist, and he loved her scent of roses combined with her woman's musk.

"Hold on," he said, his voice husky with need for her.

He braced his hands on her shoulders as he toed off each boot, then kicked them aside. Lyra smiled and pushed up one pant leg and eased his sock down over his heel and then his toes. She tickled the bottom of his foot and grinned up at him when he said, "Lyra . . ." Damn, he hadn't even known he was ticklish. She teased him again as she drew off his other sock and threw it on top of the first.

When his boots and socks were off she reached for the button on his Wranglers and fought with it a bit before it came undone. He could breathe again as she unzipped his jeans and his erection was no longer bound by the stiff material.

"I love your thighs," she said as she pushed his pants down his legs to his calves and feet and he kicked them off.

When he was naked, he grasped Lyra by the shoulders and drew her up with him. "I can't get enough of you." He pressed his lips to her hair and held her by her waist as he brought her up with him to stand.

Lyra melted against him and sighed as she slipped her arms around his neck. She tilted her head up and he brushed his lips over hers.

"I'm ready for more, Dare," she said against his mouth. "I want this night to last forever."

He moved his lips from hers as he slid his fingers into her hair and cupped the back of her head. "We have all the time in the world."

Lyra eased one of her hands from his neck, to his abdomen, to his cock and wrapped her hand around it. To her satisfaction, he was so thick and hard.

"When it comes to you," he said as she trailed her fingers up and down his cock, "I can't get enough."

"A little less talk," she said as she flicked her tongue over his nipple again, "and a lot more action."

Dare laughed at her teasing, but it turned into a groan as she caught his nipple with her teeth. He brought his fingers from her hair, pinched her nipples, and she groaned in return.

He took her by the hand and led her to the bed. Lyra

eased onto the comforter on her back, her head on a downy soft pillow, her knees slightly bent. Dare gave her a look that made her feel beautiful and wanted . . . and loved. He climbed onto the bed and moved between her thighs, spreading them wide so that his big body would fit between them.

Crazy zinging sensations shot through her belly as he looked down at her. He leaned forward and braced his hands to either side of her arms and he bent so that he could suckle one of her nipples. Lyra wiggled beneath him, raising herself up to meet his hot mouth. He moved to her other nipple and she reached for his cock that was pressed tight against her folds. She wrapped her fingers around it and squeezed, and he gave a loud groan against her breasts.

"I want to be inside you so bad I can hardly stand it," he said as he raised his head and their eyes met.

"Do it." She guided his erection toward the entrance to her core.

"I want to feel you around my cock." He leaned down and gently kissed her lips. "We talked about children."

"Dare?" She released his erection, her belly going a little crazy. "You want—you want children. Now?"

"With you, more than anything." He stared down at her and smiled.

"Me, too." She returned his smile and brought his cock slightly into her core and arched her hips to try to take in more of him. "Make love to me. Just like this. Nothing between us."

Dare slid his thick erection into her, deep enough to make her cry out with pleasure as he immediately hit a sweet spot inside her. She wasn't even sore anymore.

He held himself for a moment, his eyes closed. "Sweet Jesus, but you feel like heaven wrapped around me."

Lyra remained still beneath him, enjoying the sensation of him filling her, stretching her, and being a part of her.

He opened his eyes and their gazes locked again. She couldn't get enough of those eyes, his strong features, and that stubble along his jawline. Everything about him was strong and virile, from the power of his muscular body to the way he took control and did whatever he could to protect her, to save her. Yet he made her feel strong, too.

Dare began a slow rhythm, moving in and out of her, never taking his eyes from hers. Lyra's body flushed with heat from head to toe as she felt every thrust, every movement of their bodies as they rocked together. He paused and leaned back enough that his cock almost slipped from her body. She couldn't help a small whimper and reached for him. He took her hands and laced his fingers with hers, pressing her engagement ring tight against her finger. He drew her arms high over her head before beginning that slow, steady rhythm within her core again.

It felt so good to have his hands linked with hers. The way he held her raised her breasts, and he dipped his head to take one of her nipples in his mouth. Lyra moaned as he gently suckled, then moved to her other nipple.

Sweat rolled down the side of his face and droplets splattered on her breasts. She inhaled as he drove in and out, the scent of his male musk and their sex beyond intoxicating. Her hair was matted with perspiration and their bodies were slick as they moved together.

"I could stay like this, wrapped up inside you." He raised his head and brushed his lips over hers. "I can't tell you how much I love you."

His words sent such a thrill through Lyra that it pushed her closer to a climax she knew she'd never forget. "I never thought I'd find somebody to love until you." She paused when he plunged in deeper and she gave a soft moan. "I still can't believe you're mine."

Dare gave her his sexy grin and ground his groin hard against hers. "You mean you're mine."

"Whatever," she said in a teasing voice, then grew more serious. "Just make love to me."

"I am." Dare began thrusting harder and faster and she moaned with every movement he made. Hotter, wetter, slicker.

Sparks of heat radiated throughout her body, igniting her beyond the heat in her body. Her skin tingled and she felt as if electricity was zipping from her navel to where they were joined at her core. A climax began to build within her. She felt it from her head to her toes and she began to tremble, she was so close, so very close to the edge. "I'm going to come, Dare."

"Do it, honey." He thrust so hard she cried out as it pushed her to that very peak that she was about to tumble over. "Let me see you come."

Lyra felt like she was one tingling mass of nerves. She shook so hard as her orgasm rocked her body that she clenched her thighs tight around Dare's hips, as if that would ground her. Because she was flying. Flying in a sky filled with stars and brilliant white light.

It never seemed to end, and she wasn't sure she wanted it to.

Dare looked down at Lyra, watched her body flush dark pink and her throat work as she shouted her release. Her body trembled beneath his, and their bodies bucked together as he thrust harder and harder inside her.

All sensation had gathered at his cock and balls, and he ground his teeth to keep from flying over the precipice so that he could watch Lyra as she came.

"Dare. Dare!" She shook but met his every thrust. "Come inside me. Now."

He plunged two, three, four times more, then shouted as his semen exploded out of his body and into Lyra's core. His cock throbbed as her channel continued to clench him, drawing out his orgasm. He squeezed their laced fingers as his body trembled. He thrust until he couldn't take one bit more.

Dare collapsed onto his side, drawing Lyra with him. He kept his cock inside her, not wanting to part with her in any way. They both were breathing hard and her breasts moved against her chest.

When his breathing slowed, he brushed his lips over hers and drew back.

"You found me," she said with a smile.

He squeezed her to him. "And I'm never going to let you go."

Read on
for a sneak peek at
Cheyenne McCray's new sexy paranormal romance

WICKED MAGIC

COMING FALL 2007

Rhiannon sat on a couch in the common room, her legs tucked up beside her, Spirit at her side. The cocoa-colored cat had stayed close to her ever since Rhiannon had been kidnapped just a few short months ago by the Fomorii. She'd been saved by Silver, Hawk, and Jake, and a few of his officers, but so many witches hadn't made it.

At this moment the room was filled with D'Danann, PSF officers, and witches, all discussing the next plan to get to Ceithlenn and the demons. They had all agreed that the goddess must be near the location where they had battled the Fomorii and the Basilisk.

The chattering around Rhiannon became nothing more than a low drone as she petted Spirit and pushed all thoughts from her mind. Especially thoughts of a certain D'Danann warrior who she'd almost had sex with in the basement.

Bless it! She didn't even know the man.

As she reached deep inside herself for some semblance of calm, she began to feel lightheaded. Her vision blurred, and her ears felt as if they were stuffed with cotton. Her hand stilled in Spirit's fur.

Everything went hazy, and she felt as if she were being transported out of her body, traveling, traveling. And then she stopped.

Rhiannon found herself in a large and sumptuous penthouse room. She looked at her hands, then ran them down her skirt and felt the brush of her palms against the soft material. Her sandals sank into plush carpeting, and she felt her chest rise and fall with every breath.

It smelled strange. Like burnt sugar and jasmine.

When Rhiannon raised her head, the vivid image of a woman filled her gaze. The woman paced back and forth before a window, but the wooden blinds were drawn so no view could be seen.

The woman was incredibly beautiful, with red hair that wasn't a natural shade but suited her. She had the most interesting eyes—they seemed to shift colors like a wavering mirage. She wore a rather revealing leather catsuit that barely covered her nipples or her crotch.

Just like the flame-haired being.

Rhiannon's heart beat faster.

She felt as if she were drifting, dreaming, yet still there, whole, in the room.

Ceithlenn. The name rolled through Rhiannon's mind, and her heart moved into her throat. The woman *was* Ceithlenn, the goddess, but in human form.

Something stirred in the corner of her vision, and Rhiannon gave a soft gasp of surprise. Darkwolf. She ground her teeth from thoughts of what the evil bastard had done. If it wasn't for him summoning the Fomorii, *none* of this would be happening.

Not far from him was Junga in her Elizabeth form.

The sight of the demon woman made Rhiannon want to throw up. It was that bitch who'd given Rhiannon the scars on her cheek.

She looked back to Darkwolf and saw him staring at Ceithlenn. His handsome features were blank as if he were intentionally keeping his expression unreadable so the goddess wouldn't know his thoughts. The stone eye Rhiannon remembered seeing when she'd been captured by the Fomorii was still resting on Darkwolf's chest, but it was cold and lifeless, not the throbbing red that it had often become.

Tension suddenly crackled in the air, and Rhiannon's attention snapped back to the beautiful woman. Ceithlenn was sniffing the air, her gaze slowly sweeping the room as if she were searching for someone.

Then her eyes focused directly on Rhiannon.

As if Ceithlenn could see her there, in the room.

Suddenly, a sensation like invisible fingers digging into her brain caused Rhiannon to gasp and drop to her knees.

Ceithlenn's power grasped at the Shadows deep inside Rhiannon, driving into the places no one should have been able to touch.

Rhiannon screamed from the pain and clasped her hands to the sides of her head.

Ceithlenn growled and extended her hand, palm facing Rhiannon.

Her heart felt lodged in her throat as she writhed on the floor.

The room seemed to billow. Expand.

A tremendous *boom* shattered Rhiannon's ears.

A great force slammed into her chest.

Excruciating pain filled her mind, her body.

Rhiannon screamed again before everything went dark.

Rhiannon's scream tore across the common room just as Keir walked through the doorway. His heart thundered. He reached her before anyone else and caught her in his embrace as she slumped forward on the couch.

Spirit jumped down onto the floor but staggered, as if affected by whatever was wrong with Rhiannon.

Keir's heart pounded as he felt the pulse in her neck. Relief surged through him to find it sure and strong. Her breaths were so shallow that he had not seen her chest move. He ignored everyone as he swept her up and stood while Rhiannon remained limp and pale.

"What's wrong with her?" Keir said to Silver just as she reached his side.

"She must have had some kind of vision." Silver swept a loose lock of Rhiannon's auburn hair away from her smooth cheek and placed the back of her hand to Rhiannon's pale skin. "I just happened to glance up from across the room and saw that she was in some kind of trance—I've seen that same expression many times." Silver's eyes met Keir's, a look of fear on her face for her friend. "But then she jerked back like something had slammed into her and she screamed. That's never happened during any of her visions before."

"Where is the healing witch?" Keir asked, then saw the half-Elvin witch, Cassia, pushing her way through the crowd.

"Up to her room." Cassia gestured toward the stairs to the upper-level apartments. "We'll get her to bed and then I'll take care of her."

Keir still could not explain why he felt the tremendous need to protect this woman, or why he wanted her so badly. But right now all he could think about was getting her safe and well.

Holding Rhiannon tightly in his arms, he followed the Elvin witch up the stairs to Rhiannon's apartment. When Cassia unlocked the door with her magic, it swung open and he caught the light citrus scent he had come to associate with Rhiannon. Cassia flicked on the lights, revealing a room as bright and colorful as Rhiannon herself. Splashes of reds, yellows, greens, blues, and purples greeted him from lamps to framed pictures to couches and chairs and to her kitchen canisters, towels, and potholders.

Cassia led the way to the bedroom and pulled back the sheets, and he laid Rhiannon on the bed. Even her sheets were a bright shade of yellow.

Keir took her small hand and gently stroked her fingers in his as Cassia held her palms over Rhiannon's chest.

Iridescent sparkles glittered over Rhiannon's body as Cassia moved her palms above the witch. She looked startled for a moment. "It's worse than I thought—some kind of blackness is inside her."

Cassia removed her hands and the sparks vanished. Her face had an expression of deep concern. "I need to get a few things. You leave and let Silver take care of her while I run to my place," she said as she hurried from the room.

"I will not leave," Keir growled as he gripped Rhiannon's hand tighter and leaned over to see her beautiful face.

"Out of the way, you big numbskull," Silver said as she tried to push past him.

Before he could respond or move, Rhiannon's eyelids fluttered open. For a moment her green eyes met his, her expression going from puzzled to pleased to very displeased.

Keir gripped her hand tighter. "You will be all right, little one," he said in Gaelic before he allowed Silver to gently push him out of the way.

He released Rhiannon's hand and backed up. He sat in a chair beside the doorway, arms folded over his chest and his legs crossed at his ankles. He did not know why it was so important to ensure that Rhiannon was all right, but it was, and he had no intention of leaving.